TANGLED WEB #2

OBSESSED

Book #2 of the TANGLED WEB trilogy

Aleatha Romig

New York Times, Wall Street Journal, and USA Today
bestselling author of the Consequences, Infidelity, and Web of
Sin series

COPYRIGHT AND LICENSE INFORMATION

2019 Edition License

OBSESSED

BLURB

Everything changed the night our eyes met across the room. His green gaze upon me prickled my skin with uncustomary warmth while my peek beneath his cuff—of a riot of color on his wrist—sparked my insatiable curiosity. Tall and mysterious, Kader was a man whose secrets I longed to know.

Little did I realize that the night we met was only the beginning—the beginning to the end of the existence I knew. With my life's work now stolen and being offered to the highest bidder and friends and colleagues scattered, the future was unclear.

I'd wanted to believe that Kader was my eye in the middle of the raging category 5 hurricane my life had become.

Nothing could be further from the truth.

What will happen as his assignment becomes our obsession?

From New York Times bestselling author Aleatha Romig comes a brand-new dark romance bringing us back to the same dangerous underworld as *SECRETS*. You do not need to read the *Web of Sin* trilogy to get caught in this new and intriguing saga, *Tangled Web*.

OBSESSED is book two of the *TANGLED WEB* trilogy that began with *TWISTED* and will conclude with *BOUND*.

Have you been Aleatha'd?

PROLOGUE

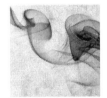

The end of Twisted, book #1 of the Tangled Web trilogy

Laurel

*A*s the echoes of my ecstasy began to fade, beneath my touch his muscles grew taut. No longer still, the concrete room filled with the same sound that had woken me the other day.

It had been a roar.

It hadn't been a lion.

The beast had a name.

Kader.

I wrapped my arms tighter around his neck as I buried my face in his shoulder.

This wasn't the time to cry, but that didn't stop my reaction.

"I didn't mean to hurt you," he said after a kiss to my forehead.

"It's not that."

Pushing up with his arms, he eased out of me. "I shouldn't—"

I lifted my finger to his lips. "It was..." I feigned a smile though he couldn't see me. "God, it was...mostly great."

"Mostly?"

Was there humor in his tone?

"I think I need practice."

The bed started to shift and I reached for his hand. "Don't leave. Please stay here."

With a sigh, he lifted the covers over me.

I waited for the door, for the indication he'd walked away. Instead, after a moment, the blankets moved. "You need to scoot over if you want me to stay."

"You'll stay?"

"I'm tired. The *door to the outside is locked.*"

Was that a yes?

Excitement sparked to life as I slid over toward the wall. The mattress moved as he lay down and pulled the covers over both of us.

Within the eye of the storm, I'd found a stranger to

protect me from dangers I didn't understand. As we settled in beside one another, I relished his warmth. When I turned on my side facing him, I realized that not only was he wearing a t-shirt, but his legs were covered in soft pants.

"I think this dress code is unfair," I said.

Kader rolled toward me as his large palm skirted over my skin; from my shoulder it went down over my breast, waist, and hip. It came to a stop as his fingers splayed over the soft flesh of my backside. "I don't know. It seems fair to me."

"I don't know how I became your job. I really know nothing about you or who hired you, but thank you for doing your job and keeping me safe."

For longer than I expected, silence settled over the room. It was as his hand on my backside flexed, pulling me closer to his warmth that he replied, "You're mistaken. That wasn't what I was hired to do."

"It wasn't?"

"No. I was hired to kill you."

MASON

Over seven years ago within a Chicago skyscraper

My nerves were on edge, every sound magnified, even the weight of my shirt seemed exaggerated. Running my hand over the back of my neck, the stubble from my short hair felt like bristles beneath my palm. Nothing helped. The sense of confinement worsened as I paced the concrete floor, watching large screens that wouldn't show me what I needed to know, where I needed to be.

I was a trapped animal.

A lion restrained to the zoo.

Bursting with ability, innate and primal, the king of the jungle should be on the African plains, not behind bars.

No, I wasn't in jail though at the moment it felt like it.

I was on the private working floor of the soon-to-be new Sparrow organization—our new command center.

It wasn't my location that made me uncomfortable. This was now my home. I had an apartment one floor up, the same floor as Reid's and Patrick's. Sparrow had the big-ass two-floor monstrosity above ours.

There wasn't any jealousy on any of our part. He'd been the one born with the fucking silver spoon. If you asked him, that wasn't a gift. He'd tell you it had been tarnished since day one. Either way, it didn't change the fact that the money behind our lives, plans, and living arrangements came from him. Oh, hell, we all worked to make it. We all had abilities, and soon, the fortune his father had sown would be his for the taking.

Our unlikely family came together courtesy of Uncle Sam. We met in basic training and stayed together through literal war. I remembered every detail of what we'd done.

I wished I didn't.

When I first heard Sparrow's name, working with or for him was the last thing on my mind.

Killing him was the first.

Now, I'm wearing out a path in the concrete floor as I watched the large screens overhead, the ones rotating the images of surveillance scattered about the city of Chicago.

"I should be with him," I said to the only other person present, Reid Murray.

"Man, Sparrow has his reasons."

Ever since we'd all moved back to Chicago, that was the way it had been: Patrick and Reid, Sparrow and me. It took time for Sparrow and me to get on the same page, but once we did, we were like glue.

There was one time we were separated. It was after the others stepped away from the war.

Stepping away made it sound like they took a fucking stroll. That wasn't it. They took the out they were offered after two tours. They did it because they had plans.

We all did.

Uncle Sam made me another offer.

I thought I was ready for civilian life. And then at the last moment, I changed my plans and took one more tour— making it three.

After the three of them came back, Sparrow went to the University of Michigan, Patrick studied business and finance at the University of Chicago Booth, and Reid studied computer engineering at MIT. We all knew Sparrow somehow arranged the admission and financing. The GI Bill only went so far.

Education was part of our plans.

Accomplishing our goal took more than muscle. The world was changing. To get on top and stay there took brains as well as brawn.

Instead of going the way of college, I chose twelve more

months to hone the skills Uncle Sam taught me. At least, that's what I told everyone. The truth was simpler. They made me an offer and I wasn't ready to go back to real life.

The extra time without these other assholes made me realize that while I was part of a team, part of a company—I missed the camaraderie that the four of us shared. The television news made it look like all we did was combat, day in, day out. The combat was the easiest part for me. It gave me a purpose, a focus. The downtime was the real hell. That was the time when I lay in my bunk and my mind wandered.

I wasn't alone, but I was.

Without Sparrow, Reid, and Patrick around, the downtime was worse.

The four of us had gotten to know one another. Over time, we'd shared shit.

Sparrow's fucked-up father.

Patrick's time living on the streets.

The unexpected death of Reid's grandmother—his only family and the woman who raised him.

The disappearance of my sister Missy.

During that third tour, I kept things under wrap. I didn't want to come across as some pussy who still mourned the loss of his sister, something that happened when I was just a kid.

Did the time really matter?

Weeks, months, or years didn't lessen the trauma that came with having your sister disappear on her way home from school. Two years younger than me, Missy depended on me. I should have been with her. I should have protected her—I failed.

That failure never left me, pushing me to work harder, to succeed at any cost.

When I made the decision after the third tour not to reenlist for a fourth, my expertise was more than that of a sniper with Special Forces. I also excelled in linguistics. For a kid from South Chicago, it was an unusual skill.

Iraqi, Arabic, and Kurdish were the recognized languages of Iraq. However, the places and towns where we went, the people spoke many variants: Armenian, Feyli Lurish, Mandaic, Persian, and Shabaki. To this day, I have no idea how I understood them and why I could read as well as write them, but they just made sense to me.

From our first tour, I understood the local kids—the ones who would come to us wanting candy. I understood their parents and the signs. That sought-after skill made me an even greater asset to Uncle Sam. That's also part of the reason why when they made me an offer to stay that third tour, I took it.

The offer was even better for a fourth. Nevertheless, I couldn't do it.

I had other plans.

I did what I should have done months earlier. I came back to Chicago and studied the shit Reid did. With the computer skills and the ability to read without a translator, there weren't many places on the web or the dark web I couldn't access.

The four of us had plans for Chicago, and I was ready to

get down to business. I'd achieved my goals in the Special Forces. I needed to do what I could to bring Sparrow's father to his fucking knees.

While it would have been simple to put a bullet between his eyes—from the twenty-fifth floor of a neighboring structure while he walked from the doors of his office building on Michigan Avenue to his waiting car—that wasn't the plan.

We weren't just taking out the motherfucker for what he'd done; we were bringing down his ring of child exploitation. That meant we had to not only be efficient but also smart. We spent time laying the groundwork for Sparrow to take over.

The old realm was going down. Our time was now. Shit was happening tonight.

For three impoverished youths and one rich kid, we'd made ourselves an unstoppable team.

My pacing ceased long enough to watch Reid's fingers flying across the multiple keyboards. I could do what he did, but the reason for my anxiety was that I preferred to be in on the action. It didn't matter if it was in the field or on the street.

That was where I should be right now.

"Are you sure that will hold up when they look into it?" I asked, looking at the screen with the broadcast from within the senior offices at Sparrow Enterprises. From the look of it, Sterling Sparrow was in his office, periodically moving from his desk to the window, the window to the desk. The time stamp was right, but we knew the picture was wrong.

Sparrow wasn't in his office on Michigan Avenue. He was at a very important meeting.

"Yeah, there's nothing to stand out. They won't even question it."

I stretched my arms over my head, bringing my hands to the back of my head. "I should fucking be there. I would do it. I told him I would. Killing that motherfucker would be the highlight of my life."

Reid looked up and smiled.

Really? A smile?

"If that's your highlight," he said, "you need to get out more."

Ignoring his comment, I walked over to a nearby weight bench and lay back on the vinyl. The free weight above me, resting in the cradle, had two one-hundred-pound weights on each end. Gripping the silver bar, I positioned my shoulders, tightened my abs, and took a deep breath.

It was the unknown that was eating at me. We'd purposely run a loop at the construction site as well as the offices. If I could see the fucker die with my own eyes, maybe I'd feel better.

Reid appeared over me in my line of vision.

"Shouldn't you be over there?" I asked with a tilt of my head toward the computers.

"You're too antsy. I'm spotting you if you're going to pump iron."

"I don't need a babysitter."

"Not babysitting," he said. "Sparrow doesn't need one

either. This is his battle. He's wanted this his whole fucking life."

"For Missy..." I began, unwilling to allow myself to finish the sentence.

"We don't know for sure. It could have been McFadden or..." He shook his head. "...can't kill them all."

With a grunt I lifted the four hundred pounds, straightening my elbows. The muscles in my shoulders and arms pulled taut. My abdomen tightened, doing its part to hold the weight steady. The bar within my grip trembled as I counted to ten.

One.

Two.

Steadily the seconds passed.

It felt good to exert myself.

Letting out a breath, I returned the bar to the cradle. The metal upon metal clanked through the tension crackling in the air. Standing, I met Reid eye to eye. "Kill every fucking one." My head shook. "I can sure as shit try."

He looked up at the screens. "It should be done."

"Let me know when you get the final signal from Patrick."

It didn't take long until we both let out a long sigh.

"It's done," Reid said.

Allister fucking Sparrow was dead.

"Hell no," I said. "It's only just begun. We're going to own this city."

"You mean Sparrow will."

Technically Reid was right. However, for Sparrow to take

and hold the position his father just unwillingly abdicated, Sparrow needed a trusted team. We were young, knowledgeable, intelligent killing machines. The old guard had let down their defenses. They'd grown soft and comfortable with the world around them. The organization was primed for a takeover. If it hadn't been us, it would have been someone else.

Imagining the possibilities of our future allowed satisfaction to come to life, washing away my earlier unease and filling my chest with a sense of pride. "This time it will be the right Sparrow. He's good, but not good enough to do it all on his own."

"We'll all have his back," Reid said.

"We'll have everyone's back. Chicago won't be the same."

It would be better.

The illegal world would still exist, only now the Sparrow organization had a new leader. Transitions were a dangerous time. It was up to the four of us and the capos we had in waiting to make this work.

The day of reckoning was at hand.

There were members of Allister's old regime who wouldn't take kindly to the coup. That was their fucking choice. Swear allegiance to the new king of Chicago or say goodbye to everything and everyone.

In this life—as in war—there was no middle ground.

LAUREL

Present day

*M*y entire body chilled in the darkness as Kader pulled me closer to his warmth. "I-I..." I couldn't think straight much less speak. I was where—only moments earlier—I'd wanted to be. Now, I wasn't certain of anything, even my next breath.

What had he just said?

"I don't usually fail when I take a job," Kader continued, his deep voice cutting through the thundering circulation thumping in my ears. Although he'd just told me that he'd taken a job to kill me, his cadence was calm and his volume soft. "I've made mistakes in my life, but I've learned to rely on my gut. You could say it's my compass. That isn't to imply that I do the *good* thing. I don't view what I do or the assignments I accept through a good-versus-bad lens."

This was too much.

Was he actually trying to rationalize taking a job to kill me?

I pulled myself away. "This is what you do? You kill people? No..." My head began to shake as my volume rose. "You sleep with people and then kill them?" I lifted my hand between us until it came to rest over the soft cotton covering his wide chest. I wasn't thinking about his no-touching rule. My only thought was getting away. Applying pressure, I pushed myself farther toward the wall.

Away.

There was nowhere I could go.

I was within a concrete box, sandwiched between a cement-block wall and a man nearly twice my body mass.

"No, that isn't what I do," Kader said as he reached for my hand, the one on his chest. Entwining our fingers, he lifted mine to his lips.

What the hell?

His actions were not in context with the words he'd spoken a few moments ago. I never took Kader for the hand-holding type. Hell, I was shocked he'd climbed back into bed with me after we'd...

Made love was an inaccurate description. I'd asked him to take me and that was what he'd done. I asked for him and I'd gotten him.

I'd wanted and needed to feel alive, to feel connected.

Alive.

My chest ached with the memory of Russ.

Wrenching my hand away, I reached for the bedcovers and scooted farther away. Bending my legs beneath my body, I sat against the far wall using the blanket as my shield. The movement helped, yet I couldn't concentrate. There was one dominating thought.

Kader had been hired to kill me.

The man who had just taken me—fucked me—was supposed to kill me.

Silence descended upon the room, yet neither of us moved.

"When you said," I began, finally finding my voice, "that there was a price on my head and it had been accepted..." I took a deep breath. "You knew that to be true because you were the one who accepted the job."

"Yes."

Scenes over the last week replayed in my mind. "But that doesn't make sense. You said you weren't going to hurt me. That first night at the gathering you said if you had wanted to do me harm, I wouldn't have been there."

"I haven't lied to you."

"I don't see how you have been truthful. Killing me and not harming me are polar opposites."

Kader let out a long breath. "If you want me to leave, I can sleep on the recliner."

Did I want him to leave?

"I don't know what I want." That wasn't entirely true. I wanted to go back to the illusion of safety. I would say that I wanted to go back to before last Friday, but that would mean not knowing Kader—the man hired to kill me.

Come on, Laurel, that should be what you want.

Instead of voicing any of that, I asked, "Will you explain what you do or what you did? Who hired you?" A new thought registered. "Do you think whoever it is also put a price on Russ?" New sobs grew in my chest at the memory of my partner, my friend, and my sometimes-lover dead on my bedroom floor.

Kader's hand patted the top of the blankets, coming closer to where I sat.

"Come over here," he called through the dark.

"You said I can't touch you."

"But I can touch you. Come here. I'll tell you what I can."

"You never lied?" The question came between hiccups that my new round of tears had created.

"No, Laurel. I was hired to kill you. I took the job because from the first time I saw your photo, I knew there was something about you. Fuck, there is still something about you. I can't explain it. I took the job intending to complete it. I don't fail. That's my reputation."

My body trembled as I continued to clench the blanket over my breasts.

Finally, his large palm found my knee. His fingers splayed. "That's not my goal any longer. Even so, I will not fail."

Oh dear God.

Kader's grasp of my knee tightened. "I'm not going to fail, but I'm also not going to carry out the assignment as it was ordered. People hire me. I kill for a living. It's a good living. You were right that the pit upstairs isn't my standard either. I make a better-than-good living. It's not always people. I also kill reputations, companies, and ideas."

"Like my formula?" I asked.

"Yes, like that. I can hack into even the most advanced systems. I can breach firewalls like they're tissue paper. I have an innate ability to understand languages. There isn't much I can't access. I'm hired for all kinds of jobs. In most cases, I don't make contact with my target. I also don't know who hires me."

I tried to swallow, but my mouth was dry. "Is that water bottle still here?" I asked.

The mattress shifted until he was back with the bottle.

I reached through the darkness, opened the cap, and quenched my thirst. Once I handed it back, I asked, "So what does that mean for me and the formula?"

"It means that while I was hired, I'm my own boss. I answer to no one." He exhaled. "I was hired to stop the research. I made the decision not to kill you before you ever saw me. That was why I offered you money, asked your price for the research. That payoff wasn't from my employer. They weren't willing to pay you. I was."

"Why?"

The mattress shifted again. No longer holding my knee, Kader was beside me, leaning against the wall. "I have no fucking idea. I don't. Sometimes I wonder if we...if there could be something..." He let out another long breath. "What

I mean is that I determine destinies. Laurel, when I saw your picture, I think I knew." His fingers again splayed over my knee, resting on my thigh. "I knew that I would accept the assignment of your destiny because I couldn't allow the job to go to someone else."

Warmth radiated from his touch.

Slowly, I placed my hand over his. His turned until we were palm to palm.

"You're not going to kill me?"

"I'm not..." The sound of a scoff filled the air. "...although, I'm beginning to think you'll be the death of me before this is over."

Leaning toward his shoulder, I shook my head. "No. I don't want to lose anyone else."

I wasn't certain how long we sat in the dark. Over time, his sleeve dampened with my on-again, off-again tears. It was as he wrapped his arm around me and pulled me toward the pillows that I gave in to the warmth of his hold. The clean aroma of his recently showered skin, combined with the lingering scent of our union, created a reassuring scent that permeated the musty basement, settling over us as I curled closer.

It wasn't until he woke me later that I realized I'd been touching him. Not him, per se. There was a cotton barrier between us, yet he hadn't told me to stop. In many ways, he seemed to encourage it, such as following me to the wall when I refused to go to him.

Kader's fingers splayed over my skin, pulling me closer. In

the darkness, his lips found mine. Softer than before, he was no longer staking his claim or pillaging a foreign land. This was different—reassuring. The declaration had been made.

I was his for the taking.

He didn't need to tell me what he wanted. The hardness of his cock against my tummy wordlessly revealed his intentions. In unison as if choreographed, we moved as one until this man who controlled destinies was above me, his body now my shield. His lips and teeth were his tools as he worked me higher and higher.

We weren't in a basement.

My life wasn't at risk.

We were flying above the clouds.

From sleep to ecstasy, the road was long and strenuous.

Perspiration covered my skin as I held tightly to the arms and shoulders above me. I clinched the soft cotton of his shirt in my clenched fists as we became one. My back arched while my shouts echoed off the walls. As he had the first time, Kader stilled, allowing me to adjust. Unlike before, my body recalled his length and girth, giving less resistance to his invasion.

"You feel so fucking good." His proclamation sent a warm breath over my skin and a smile to my face.

"I do." It wasn't a question but a statement.

Slowly at first, he began to move. Each thrust was controlled as my nails clung to his shirt and we found a rhythm. This wasn't a race to the top. It was a marathon—no, an Ironman contest. With every touch, each kiss, and the chorus of sounds, I was expending every ounce of energy. It was all-consuming. My mind and my body were focused on the man making love to me.

I wasn't certain how many times I cried out as my body convulsed around him or my teeth sank into the material covering his shoulder as I tried unsuccessfully to stifle my shrieks of pleasure. All I knew was that by the time the muscles beneath that shirt pulled taut and Kader came undone, I was shattered beyond repair. The only reason I was not in shards on the floor was the man holding me. Breaking our union, Kader settled beside me and wrapped me in his arms, gluing my broken world back together.

I was too tired to think of anything else. For a moment in time, my life wasn't in shambles, my life's work wasn't in jeopardy, my friend wasn't dead, and I wasn't in danger. His even breaths lulled me back to sleep.

A shrill ring ripped through the darkness, waking us both and splintering our reprieve.

Before I could say a word, Kader bolted from the bed.

"Fuck."

It was the last thing I heard as he hurried from the bedroom.

KADER

*T*he alarm sounded, echoing through the room, originating from my smart watch. It meant something had changed on my surveillance feeds. I'd bolted from the bedroom, flinging open the door until it bounced back against the wall. Using my fingers, I raked back my untethered hair and rushed toward my computer setup.

What the fuck was wrong with me?

That was a rhetorical question.

Literally, I had many answers.

I needed to step up my game. Fuck, I shouldn't have been asleep.

Turning off the alarm, I'd noticed the time: 10:10...in the goddamned morning.

When had I ever slept for that long?

I couldn't come up with one instance, not even when I

was home on my ranch and not working an assignment. Hell no. There were too many things to do on the ranch, too many possibilities. Usually when I was there, I was up before the sun. Watching it rise over the distant mountains was one of the few normal activities I enjoyed. Fly-fishing in the stream that ran through my property or big-game hunting were also possibilities I enjoyed when I wasn't locked away in my office monitoring possible jobs as well as my investments.

Reaching for the mouse, a quick movement of my wrist brought the computer screens to life as I pulled up the big chair and settled upon the edge. Although the monitors were beginning to light, I wasn't seeing what was before me. Instead, my thoughts were filled with the reason I'd slept so late.

My mind uncharacteristically shifted from my work to Laurel.

When the alarm sounded, she'd also been asleep. The simple realization amazed me.

Hell, I'd told her the truth about who I am and what I do, and yet she'd remained. It wasn't as if she could unlock the padlock at the top of the stairs, but she hadn't even tried. She hadn't gone out to the recliner or sofa. She'd stayed, her warm curves curled beside me as her even breaths filled my ears, sending tiny puffs over my skin. It was the proximity that had prompted me to wake her sometime during the night.

I wasn't certain if I was infatuated with her because she stayed—or more infatuated, I should say—or if I was simply shocked.

What woman stays in bed with a professed killer?

Hell, not only stayed in bed but slept, fucked, and slept again.

Pushing the thoughts of her—her body, her noises, her scent, her soft skin beneath my touch, and even her tears—out of my head was impossible. Those mental images would be there for the rest of my life.

For a lingering moment, I had an interesting thought.

No matter how this assignment concluded, Laurel Carlson had given me something I'd never previously had. Since my rebirth, I'd accumulated what was necessary to live in a manner I found acceptable. Through the years of determining destinies, I'd earned both money and power. Those commodities allowed me a lifestyle I preferred, one of seclusion. To that end, I owned over 1,200 acres of freedom in nowhere Montana. Other than a few trusted seasonal ranch hands and a well-paid manager, my closest neighbors were elk, deer, antelope, and moose.

Solitude had been my goal. That ranch was my haven.

Yet none of those accomplishments gave me what Laurel had given me—and in only a few days.

In a short period of time, she'd given me memories—pleasant memories involving a person, not a successful assignment or the isolation of seclusion.

As thoughts of her spun around my head, a smile threatened my cold stare.

Laurel Carlson had given me...memories, something I'd never before been willing to acknowledge that I lacked.

Shaking my head at the revelation, I pushed the sleeves of my t-shirt up to my elbows and forced myself to focus. Taking inventory of the screens and subsections before me, I searched. It would take a major change in one or more of the locations to set off the alarm. A person could also set it off if facial recognition occurred.

I isolated the feed responsible for the alarm. It was Laurel's lab at the university. Apparently, the lights were no longer out.

"Well, look who's back," I said aloud to myself.

Shit, it wasn't only that. There was someone in her house.

Damn neighbor.

Laurel had said they had an agreement. Mrs. Beeson better watch out. Borrowing sugar would place her fingerprints and DNA there and get her more than she bargained for.

The sound of a closing door, refocused my attention to the other side of the Plexiglas wall.

The open bedroom door obstructed my view of the hallway. Nevertheless, it wasn't difficult to infer that Laurel had also awakened and was now out of the bedroom and in the bathroom.

I spent a few more minutes taking inventory of the people present on the fifth floor at the university. There seemed to be extra traffic and attention to both Laurel's and Cartwright's offices.

It made me wonder what those individuals believed to

have happened to the good doctors. Placing an ear bud in my ear, I turned on the volume.

My empty stomach didn't bother me as I worked. I'd often go a day or two without eating. And then I remembered the woman down the hallway. She couldn't afford to miss too many meals. As it was, we hadn't had anything after lunch yesterday. That was almost twenty hours ago.

There wasn't anything happening on the feeds that demanded my immediate attention. Besides, everything was recorded for later viewing. Kicking off my sleeping pants, I stepped into blue jeans, donned socks and boots.

Retrieving my black coat, I pushed my arms into the sleeves. With my gun in the band of my jeans, I started toward the door when I stopped.

Shit.

I wasn't used to reporting to anyone, but then again, I didn't want Laurel to come out and realize I was gone. Changing my direction, I headed down the hallway. The sound of water coming from the shower was like instant Viagra to my dick.

No longer were my images of her sensual body conjured by my imagination. I had life experiences. Each and every memory was coming at me at record speed. All it would take was a twist of the knob.

No.

We'd established that boundary. If I expected her to honor it, I needed to also.

Standing taller, I swallowed and making a fist, knocked on

the door. "Laurel?"

No response.

Reaching for the knob, I found myself wrestling with another unusual conundrum. There was no doubt she was messing with my mind. I have broken into and entered secure establishments, businesses, and residences without reservation. I'd placed cameras without one single thought of morality. And now I was considering if it would be wrong to open the door.

I shook my head and pounded louder. "Laurel."

The water's spray ceased to be heard.

"What? I'm in the shower."

"I'm going out for a few minutes to get us some food and coffee. The top of the stairs will be locked. I won't be long."

"Okay."

Adjusting myself as I walked away was easier than getting the thought of her naked body out of my head.

"Kader?"

I spun around. Laurel's face peered my way, her blue eyes wide and her dark hair wet and dripping. The rest of her was hidden behind the door. "Yes?"

"Be careful."

Her warning returned the uncharacteristic upturn to my lips. "Don't try to go upstairs."

She shook her head. More droplets of water dotted the concrete floor near the partially open door. "Not without you." Her chin tilted upward. "I'm not too proud to admit that upstairs scares me."

Damn, I needed to walk away, but for some reason my boots were walking back to her. Stopping at the doorway, I could see a bit more of her, yet the door still had her covered from the middle of her breasts down. I ran the coarse tip of a finger over her cheek, and as I did, the blue of her eyes disappeared behind lowering lids. "Upstairs is a pigsty but it shouldn't scare you. You should be scared of something or someone else."

"I'm not afraid of you."

I moved my hand away from her soft, warm skin and gripped the doorjamb. I was too fucking close to pushing the door away and seeing her in the light. I shook my head. "If you could read my thoughts, you would be terrified. Even without them and with what you know about me, you should be."

Her delicate shoulder shrugged as pink filled her cheeks. "I'm not. Please come back."

"That's one thing you don't have to worry about. The devil himself couldn't keep me away from you."

Laurel's cheeks rose higher as she began to close the door.

I stepped forward, my boot blocking the closure.

Her smile grew. "Hurry, I think we missed dinner last night. What time is it?"

"Around ten-thirty." I ran my finger again over her soft cheek and traced down her neck to her collarbone. Using all the self-control I could muster, I pulled my hand away and stepped back. "I'll hurry because if I don't leave right now, I foresee another missed meal."

Her eyes shone as she closed the door. A few moments later, the water again began to spray against the plastic stall.

Making my way upstairs, I noticed another oddity.

My fucking cheeks were up—risen in an uncustomary way. It was a full-blown smile.

I didn't smile.

My body liked this rare feeling. My dick was ready for me to turn around. It was my mind that said this assignment needed to end.

The question was how would it end?

As I locked the door from the outside, setting the padlock, I looked around at the filth. There was no question it was disgusting. I stepped over debris as I made my way to the garage and truck. As bad as it was on this level, it wasn't scary. I'd secured the boards over the windows and doors. No one was breaking in without making one hell of a racket.

Me on the other hand—I was the fucking boogeyman. Laurel Carlson should be afraid of me.

Why wasn't she?

As I drove, my thoughts centered on the assignment I'd taken—the job, not the woman.

I was in possession of both of the flash drives. Russell Cartwright was dead, and his body would never be found. Laurel could be the same. Not literally but presumed dead, as in missing.

She didn't realize it yet, but staying hidden was going to happen. She didn't have a choice.

Until I learned the identity of the person who hired me,

she wouldn't be safe.

At a nearby drive-thru I gave the speaker my order. I'd secured my hair with a rubber band. I only used cash, small denominations, nothing to stand out. With the sunglasses and black jacket I was wearing, my image accomplished my goal of being nondescript—nothing more than a passing thought, a ghost—the boogeyman.

Memories of me would be forgotten as soon as I drove away, not because I could control what other people thought, but because forgetting me was what other people wanted to do. Their rational minds didn't want to recall what made them feel uncomfortable. It was easier to dismiss it and move on.

I made my decision.

I wasn't going to keep her—I couldn't—but I sure as hell wasn't giving her back to have someone else do the job. No, I wouldn't admit to my change in plans, not yet. I'd get her out of that hellhole and out of this city, and then I'd message my employer and say the job was complete. No details needed until I learned more about who was on the other end of the agreement and who was willing to pay big bucks for the formula and compound.

The decision gave me purpose as I locked the door at the top of the stairs from the inside. Entering the basement, I stopped in my tracks. Laurel was sitting at the computers, her dark, damp hair combed out, hanging over her shoulders in waves that cascaded down her back. I filled that chair, but not her. Her petite frame, wearing a t-shirt and skin-tight, soft pants, took hardly any space as she sat with one leg tucked beneath her and her arms wrapped around her other knee in front of her chest.

My first reaction was to ask her what the hell she was doing.

Before the words left my lips, I found myself enthralled with the vision of her and the reality that she was here as she'd promised. I also recalled asking for her help, making her sit at that same chair and read the email. Closing the door with my foot, I said, "Tell me you didn't touch anything."

Laurel spun my way as if she hadn't heard me enter, not until I spoke. Her blue eyes were glassy and wide and she hugged her knee closer.

"What does this mean?" she asked.

"What?"

She pointed to the screen as I laid the bag filled with food and cups on the table. Throwing my coat onto the sofa, step by step I made my way back to what she was seeing. When I turned back to her, she was no longer looking at the computer screens but at me—no, specifically at my exposed forearms.

"Shit," I grunted as I pushed down the sleeves to my wrists. "Forget you saw that."

Laurel stood, coming closer with her blue gaze fixed on me. Looking directly at me, our eyes locked. "Kader, they're so beautiful. Why won't you let me see them?"

"They're not beautiful."

She reached for my hand and for my sleeve.

"No, Laurel. Nonnegotiable."

LAUREL

*T*he display of colors on Kader's arms caused me to rise from the chair, removing me from what I'd seen on the screens.

"No, Laurel." His voice grew gruff. "Nonnegotiable." He pushed my hand away.

While he tugged harder on the cuff of his sleeve, I pulled my hand back to my chest as I'd done the first time he told me not to touch him. There was something in his expression that pained me, a sadness I hadn't seen in him before.

"Kader."

He shook his head, his jaw set as the cords of his neck grew taut.

"I-I really didn't see much, but what I did see was beautiful."

The lighting wasn't great in the basement, and yet what I'd

seen appeared to be a kaleidoscope of blues, teals, greens, and purples—vivid intertwining colors, bold and animated. From a distance, the markings even seemed to hold depth as if I would be able to feel them as well as see them. Although it had only been a fraction of a second before he'd covered them, I knew in that short time that he was wrong. His tattoos were beautiful.

Would they also reveal what he wouldn't say?

Does Kader have secrets hidden in his ink?

I swallowed as our gazes stayed locked.

"Forget what you saw." His tone didn't suggest I do what he said. It demanded.

"Why? The colors were...are so bold. I want to see them."

He turned away with a scoff and began walking toward the table.

"What?" I asked.

"You keep asking for things you shouldn't."

"If that comment was about last night, I have no regrets."

He spun back toward me. "You mentioned the tats, well sort of. You said something after you took the sleeping pill. You were delirious, not knowing what you were saying then, and you don't know now." He began removing food from the paper bag. "I'm getting sick of shitty fast food. We won't have to put up with it for much longer."

I came up to the table, my stomach more demanding of food than I was about arguing about Kader's tattoos. That didn't mean I was giving up. Sitting, I looked up at him. "Before a few minutes ago, I'd only seen the edges. The first time was on your wrist the night of the gathering when you raised your hand to quiet the crowd. The second was a little bit on your upper chest. You had left buttons undone when I'd first woken up." When he didn't respond, I went on, "Most people are proud of tattoos. I mean, they get them for a reason."

Sitting, Kader shook his head as loose strands of hair framed his face. His green gaze stayed fixed on me as he unwrapped and lifted his breakfast sandwich. "Drop it." His chest expanded with a deep breath. Without taking a bite, he tossed the sandwich back to the paper. "Un-fucking-believable."

"Is that why it's so dark in the bedroom."

He stood and paced back and forth. "Cartwright is dead. Someone put out a contract on you and your work." He stopped and gripped the back of the chair. "Don't you think there are more fucking important topics than my ink?"

I unwrapped the breakfast sandwich he'd gotten for me. While I hadn't eaten one of these in years—I couldn't recall when the last time was—damn, it smelled fantastic.

"Tell me what had you upset." He tilted his head toward the plastic wall.

I brought the sandwich to my lips and hesitated. "Eric is back at the office and so is Stephanie."

Kader nodded as he spun the chair and straddled the back.

"You knew that?"

"Not until this morning." He took a bite of his sandwich. "They were the ones that set off the alarm that woke us."

"What else did you see?" I asked between bites.

"More heard than saw. There was a conversation between Olsen and someone on the phone. Neither you nor Cartwright has been seen since Monday night at the office. From what I heard, Olsen was trying to convince the other person that the two of you wouldn't abandon the research or abscond with it."

"So they don't know what happened to Russ?" The question added a bitter taste to my breakfast.

Kader shook his head. "No one will know for sure—ever."

"Of course, they will. He's..." I looked down, not allowing myself to finish the sentence, not allowing myself to say the word.

"Laurel, only you and I and the person who killed him know about his fate. If anyone in that facility knows that he's dead, that individual either killed him or had him killed."

After a sip of my coffee, I stood. My sock-covered feet paced the cement. "How can you discuss this so casually?"

When I turned, Kader was right in front of me, bringing my walk to a halt. He reached for my chin and brought my gaze from his chest to his vibrant green eyes.

"I've been thinking about it. Their current assumption is your best option."

"What are you talking about?"

"Someone thinks that the two of you took off. I would assume they wouldn't want to publicize that theory without evidence. Their diversion will give us time to get out of here."

"Out of here?" The edge of panic infiltrated my tone.

"Yes, out of here. This basement is secure, but we can't stay here indefinitely. Someone paid me to kill you. That someone is still out there. My computer equipment is far better at my house. I live in the middle of nowhere. No one will see you there. You can go outside and not be locked away underground."

My nose and eyes scrunched as I listened. "I can go outside?" My hands, now balled into fists, hit my hips as I took a step away from his touch. "Am I a damn puppy? I have my life's work on the line. Going outside to play isn't my concern."

Kader let out a long breath and smoothed his palm over his hair as he turned a complete circle. The bicep beneath his t-shirt flexed. "Laurel." His tone had hardened. "Just so we're clear, what I said about leaving wasn't the opening of a discussion nor was it a request for your input. You are going with me. We're getting the hell out of here before it's too late." He came closer and reached for my shoulders, again forcing me to raise my chin to maintain eye contact. "Russell's body will not be found or identified. It's too bad because without that evidence his killer will also never be caught. And there's a chance, if I don't call my job complete, that same person will come after you." Letting go of my shoulders, he continued, "If it was a professional hit on Cartwright, they wouldn't have left him at your house unless..."

"Unless what?"

His lips came together. "Unless you were being set up."

My forehead fell to his chest as I closed my eyes. The

thumping of his heart reassured me as his hands encircled my waist, pulling me toward him.

His deep voice filled the space. "I have issues with a professional hit. Someone like me doesn't get invited into my target's girlfriend's home."

"I wasn't his girl..." I didn't finish.

"That means that Cartwright probably knew the person with him. He probably trusted him or her. I can do more work on recognition at my house."

Staying in Kader's embrace, I pushed against his chest, unable to stop listening but wishing I wasn't hearing. My temples throbbed in rhythm with his heart.

"If the people at the university are certain that the two of you are on the run," he went on, "they're going to try to find you. Hell, Sinclair Pharmaceuticals may try to find you. I'll run some programs when we're home to pull up the phone records and find out who Olsen was speaking to. The person who hired me or the person who killed Cartwright may try to find you. There are a million possible scenarios and all of them mean that our time is running out.

"As it is now, we can't go to the airport. I could charter a private jet, but that would require false identities, identifications, and a shit ton of money transfers. The airports, even private ones, have cameras. It's more difficult to go unnoticed when you drop $8,000 an hour for a flight. The convenience isn't worth the risk. The best way to get out of this city is the same way we've been in it—hiding in plain sight."

A new thought came to mind as my eyes opened. "I have to tell my parents I'm safe."

His head moved from side to side. "Their concern has to be real."

I took a step back. "No, they're old. I mean, not like ancient. My father is sixty-eight and my mother sixty-seven. I can't make them go through the worry. What if people question them?"

"Then they will respond honestly. It's the best answer for their safety. One hundred different scenarios could include the thought that they are helping you hide."

My stomach knotted at the thought of anyone accusing my parents. I looked up at Kader. There were small lines next to his eyes and his brow was furrowed. "Can we do anything to keep them safe?" I asked.

"Letting them respond honestly is the best thing for us to do and for them."

It was my turn to spin as I slapped my thighs. "I hate this. Putting them through that will break them."

"Identifying their daughter in a morgue wouldn't be easier."

My spin came to a halt as I stared incredulously at Kader. "What if I say no?"

"Same option as when you asked that question in your bedroom."

Tranquilizer.

"What about all this?" I gestured around.

"Most of it we leave. It's trash. The computers I'll destroy.

The feeds from the cameras will continue to go to a well-secured cloud. I can access it all from the ranch."

"The ranch? Where is this ranch with an outside playground?"

Kader scoffed. "You know that you can be a real pain in the ass?"

I tilted my head.

It takes one to know one.

I didn't say that though my expression may have conveyed the message.

He let out a long breath. "I'm not telling you where we're going."

What the hell?

"You expect me to agree to driving in that old heap of a truck to an undetermined destination that could take hours to get to?"

"The destination is determined. The length of the drive is more like a day. Two if we stop."

"I am not riding on those back seats."

"I have a plan."

LAUREL

I opened my eyes as the truck's tires bounced along the uneven packed-dirt road. Classic rock music played within the cab, a background to the rocks and ice pelting the undercarriage. My mind was fuzzy and my body ached, both the result of over twenty-four hours in the front seat of Kader's truck. Granted, it wasn't the most comfortable or efficient means of transportation, but it was effective. It was his plan—disappear in plain sight. That meant covering my head with the hood of his giant sweatshirt whenever we stopped or went through tolls.

Stretching my sore muscles, I peered out to the scenery. At some point while I slept we'd exited the nearly deserted highways and made our way onto more rural roads. Using the word *road* to describe the surface upon which Kader was driving was a stretch. The truck's shocks, as well as the springs beneath the vinyl bench, groaned as we moved forward, our bodies—despite the seat belts—tossed to-and-fro.

We may have left Indianapolis in the spring, but we'd arrived to Montana—yes, I could read signs—back in winter. The mountains visible in the distance were topped with snow-covered peaks and the ground for as far as I could see into the setting sun was mostly white with a few scattered patches of green grass. The sky above us went on forever with darkening clouds accumulating over the mountains.

"Are we close?" I asked, turning from the majestic view to the man beside me, the one who'd been driving without sleep for over a day.

While I was probably a mess, Kader appeared as he always did, jaw clenched, back straight, and shoulders broad. Though he had a black coat, it was currently being used as a blanket over my legs. He was wearing another long-sleeved t-shirt, blue jeans, and his customary boots. His hair was secured at the nape of his neck, and his long fingers held the steering wheel with the composure of a professional driver. Despite the journey, he appeared unaffected by the lack of sleep.

"Technically, we're here," he said. "This is all my land."

"For how far?"

"Twelve hundred acres in total."

I pushed myself up, sitting taller. "Aren't you exhausted?"

His wide shoulders shrugged. "Success gives me more satisfaction than sleep does. I accomplished my goal. You're out of Indiana and more importantly, you're alive. I'll let my employer know that the job is finished. Then I'll take my offer to the dark web."

"What offer?"

"I'm going to put the research and development of your formula up for sale."

The meaning behind what he said prickled my skin. I shook my head. "You can't."

Kader's green laser stare momentarily turned my way. "Laurel, I work alone for a reason. I don't ask permission or seek recognition. I make a decision and I stick with it."

"You can't offer to sell something you don't have. And I won't let you sell my half."

"Again, Doc, not your choice. I have given this a lot of thought while you dozed in and out. My employer wanted the research stopped. Eliminating both you and Cartwright does that. Someone associated with your research wants to make big money on what you've created. It isn't like I will put up a neon sign. It's a fishing expedition and I have two baited hooks."

I swallowed. "Won't whoever is currently trying to sell it be upset?"

"That's the point. I need to make it clear that I have the latest data. You can help me state exactly what you have."

"Again, even if I agree, we only have half."

"I didn't mention it before, but I have Cartwright's flash drive."

Sucking in a breath, I leaned toward the outer door, turned toward Kader, and opened my eyes wide. The image of

Russ lying on my bedroom floor skirted across my memory. Just as quickly, I tried to blink it away. Looking at Kader, I said, "You said you didn't kill him. You said the external hard drive was gone."

"I haven't lied to you, Laurel."

"Then how do you have it?"

"I found Cartwright's body. When we were at your house, the stone was removed from your fireplace and the external hard drive was missing, just like I said. It was when I went back. The hard drive was gone, but when I cleaned up, I found his flash drive was in the pocket of his blue jeans."

The thought of Kader going through Russ's pockets or of what he did to dispose of the body and clean my house created acid bubbling in the pit of my stomach.

Kader's hand came over to my leg. "Don't think about it."

"How can I not?"

Through the leather coat, he squeezed my thigh. "If I could do any of this job differently, it would be not taking you with me that night."

I laid my hand over his. "Why didn't you tell me about the flash drive?"

"Because I've been trying to decide what the best course of action is going forward."

My neck straightened. "It isn't your decision. It should be mine. It should be Russ's." My head was shaking, my mind vying between gruesome images and wondering not for the first time why Russ would bring someone into my house and reveal the external hard drive. It didn't make sense.

Why would he offer the hard drive if he hadn't given up his own flash drive?

Tears prickled the back of my eyes. "Kader, I think that Russ still having possession of the flash drive means that he didn't plan to give it up. He was sacrificing the old data to save the current." I brushed a tear from my cheek. "Oh, thank God. He wasn't selling us out."

"You're jumping to conclusions."

I pulled my hand away. "No, I'm not. Don't you see? Russ must have realized he was in danger and hoped that the backup would suffice to save him—save our work. Maybe even to save me."

Turning away from Kader, I moved my gaze back out onto the scenery around us, forcing myself to think of something else. We'd been driving on the dirt- and snow-covered excuse for a road for some time. In the distance, the setting sun—sandwiched between the mountain peaks and the darkening clouds—cast long shadows on the plains. The bouncing ceased as the truck slowed and stopped. It took me a moment to realize the engine was off.

"What's happening?" I asked.

"I want to show you this vista."

Opening the door, the cool wind blew my hair about my face. With a shiver, I buried my hands in the single pocket of Kader's oversized sweatshirt and stepped down from the truck. Slush and mud oozed under my shoes as if the ground couldn't decide if it should freeze or thaw. When I looked up, Kader was there with his hand extended.

Beyond him in the distance, the setting sun's rays shone upward to the growing dark clouds. As if a paintbrush was applied to canvas, what had been gray now shimmered with hues of reds and oranges—gemstones or flames. With the vast sky for a backdrop, I stood in awe at the beauty of nature surrounding Kader's handsome face as ice-cold wind swirled around us.

This land fit Kader, wild, untamed, and tragically beautiful.

I peered from the glowing sky back to Kader's offered hand. For a moment I hesitated, wondering how I'd gotten to the place where I'd put my trust as well as my life in the hands of a man I barely knew, one who admitted to taking the job of killing me.

Looking up into his gaze, for the first time I saw a new emotion—anticipation at my next move, as well as an eagerness to share what was his. The golden flecks within the green shimmered as small lines like webs formed at the corners of his eyes and his cheeks uncharacteristically rose, all working in unison to melt my uncertainty. Returning Kader's grin, I removed my hand from the warmth of the hoodie pocket and placed it in his. His long fingers surrounded mine as he tugged me forward. Within a few steps we were at the rim of a deep ravine. At the base was a river.

"This is beautiful," I said, taking it all in.

"The snow is melting, so the river is over its banks."

"Is your house down there?"

"No. That's a floodplain." With his free hand, he pointed to the other side of the ravine. My house is over there."

I gasped as I took it in. Even from this distance, I could tell his home was large, much larger than mine. As clouds moved in the sky, multiple buildings became visible in what had been hidden by shadows.

"It's like a small city."

"Hardly. It's my home base."

"Why are there so many buildings?"

"I'll show you in time."

In time.

What did that mean?

How long did he think we'd be here?

As we turned to return to the truck and the wind continued to blow, I squeezed his hand, causing us to momentarily stop walking. "Will I ever be able to go back to my house, my job, my life?" I asked.

LAUREL

$\mathcal{M}$y question floated away with the cool breeze as I waited for an answer.

Kader turned to face me, his stoic expression back in place. "I haven't lied to you. I'm not going to start now."

His image blurred as new tears filled my eyes. "I want my life back."

"I don't know, Laurel. It depends on how well my plan works."

After he helped me into the truck, we rode the rest of the way around the ravine in silence. His answer settled over me and played on repeat in my mind.

His plan.

To use my formula as bait.

I wasn't cognizant of the passage of time until Kader pulled the truck up to the front porch of what appeared to be a sprawling home. It reminded me of something out of a western yet not old. There were large barn-like structures around as well as fences.

"Do you have horses or other livestock?" Living in Indiana since leaving Chicago taught me a thing or two about rural living. Though I'd lived in cities, the country was always nearby.

"Yes, horses and steer. The horses aren't kept up here. I'm gone too often. They're corralled down by Jack's place."

"Jack?"

"He's the ranch manager. His house is closer to the entrance. You were asleep when we passed it. No one makes it back this far without clearance."

Taking a deep breath, I took in the house. "When we get inside will you find out what's happening at home? I wonder what's being said about me and Russ."

"I need a shower. Let's clean up, eat, and then we'll learn what there is to learn."

I nodded.

Kader reached behind the seats for my suitcase. Carrying it with one hand, his other hand moved to the small of my back as we walked up the stairs to the landing. It was a small gesture yet a reassuring one.

To the left of two massive ornate wooden doors was a sensor similar to ones we had in our lab, except there was no place to insert a badge. Nevertheless, the technology was revealing. Like the man beside me, the house's appearance was deceiving—rustic at first glance yet technically advanced upon closer inspection.

Putting down the suitcase, Kader leaned forward toward the sensor. It wasn't a badge that activated it, but him. The sensor scanned his eye.

Wow. Advanced.

"Welcome home, sir."

The door began to open, moving inward.

Being caught off guard by the female voice, I stood taller. "Who was that?"

Kader scoffed as he again lifted my suitcase. "No one. It's the house."

As we stepped inside, my feet came to a stop and I scanned all about.

We were in an open area with a large staircase that led to a landing above. On the level where we'd entered were archways leading to other rooms. The feel was rustic with natural tones. The minimalist furnishings appeared high quality. Every room I could see was lit in a soft golden hue.

"Do you leave the lights on? Have timers?"

"When we were approaching, I told the house I was near."

I shook my head, wondering what else he could tell the house to do.

"I'll show you to your room," Kader said, "and after a quick shower, I'll get us something to eat. Tomorrow, I'll show you around more and maybe even some of the outbuildings. Tonight, I think we're both tired."

I wasn't certain why the idea of having my own room disappointed me, but it did. "You're going to leave me alone?"

"Not technically. Instead of a musty basement, we're in a six-thousand-square-foot house."

I spun around. "Not remotely the same."

"In a way it is. Like in that basement, we're the only two people in this house. No one can enter. You're safe. For now, stay away from my office. I'll get you set up with some computer equipment tomorrow. When I do, you'll have a new presence on the web. Nothing can indicate that you're alive."

While the idea of being alone in my room made me sad, the prospect of being able to do any work brought the seed of anticipation to life.

I looked down at my tennis shoes. "I should—they're muddy."

One side of his lips moved upward. "They're fine. You can clean them upstairs."

Not listening, I quickly bent down and removed my shoes, carrying them in my hand and refusing to leave a trail of dried mud.

As we started climbing the staircase, I remembered entering the house. "Wait, so your house talks to you and you talk to it?"

"Yes. I can go weeks without seeing another soul, even Jack. That's why I like him. I suppose that I programmed the house to talk so that instead of people, the house is my company."

"Who cooks and cleans? Does the house do that too?"

Kader stopped halfway up the stairs. "Doc, I never would have taken you for a sexist."

"Me? What? Why?"

"Men are capable of taking care of themselves. It isn't difficult to cook for one. And one person doesn't create much mess."

I scoffed. "Guilty as charged."

"However, as a disclaimer, the house is programmed to do simple tasks."

"Such as?"

He nodded toward my shoes. "Sweep and vacuum."

At the top of the landing, I paused to peer over the rail. High above the front doors was a large window, the scene beyond fading into night. Together we walked down a hallway. Kader offered no explanation of the closed doors that we passed—what they contained or why he needed so many. It wasn't until we made it to nearly the end of one hallway that he stopped and opened a door.

With a gesture of his hand, we both stepped inside. He must not have told the house we were going to this room because upon entering it was dark. For a split second before he turned on the lights, my gaze went to the gorgeous view through the large windows. This room faced the same ravine he'd shown me earlier, but now we were at the other end. And then with a flip of the switch, the room filled with light and the glass panes turned dark.

Kader sat my suitcase next to the big four-poster bed and pointed toward another door. "Your bathroom is in there. Let me know what you need. I've never had company."

I turned a circle, slowly taking in the room and the furnishings. The bed was large—I'd guess king-sized. There were matching dark wood bedside stands with tall lamps, and near the windows was an overstuffed chaise—a perfect place to read. There was also a dresser with a mirror and a chest of drawers. There was another door Kader hadn't mentioned. I went that direction and peeked inside, viewing an empty walk-in closet.

When I turned around, Kader was right there, his chest at my eye level. I looked up until I met his gaze. "This is really nice. And you've never had company?"

He shrugged. "Never."

"Then why do you have a furnished room waiting for someone?"

"I don't know. Maybe it was for you."

My cheeks rose in response to his answer. Before I could verbally respond, Kader turned toward the door leading back to the hallway. "By the way," he said, "the first room, the door closest to the landing, is my bedroom. It's my space, off-limits."

My chin jutted upward. "Is my room off-limits to you?"

When Kader's gaze met mine, the golden flecks of his green eyes shone under the overhead light. His gaze quickly scanned from my socks to the top of my head.

Each inch upward warmed my skin, twisted my core, and drew my nipples tight. Finally, our eyes met again.

"I guess not," he said as a smile threatened his customary expression. "I'm here now."

I shook my head and crossed my arms over my traitorous breasts. "Unfair."

"Do whatever you need to do that doesn't involve my bedroom or my office. I'm going to clean up and then I'll be downstairs. The kitchen isn't difficult to find. It's the room with the counters and appliances."

My lips pursed. "Thanks a lot. I'll use my detective skills."

"I'm here to help, Doc. Come down when you're ready. We'll get a bite to eat and find out together what's happening in Indianapolis. Oh, and if you get lost, you can ask the house for directions. Her name is Missy."

Missy?

It wasn't that that was an unusual name, and yet hearing it always evoked a feeling of loss. It had been a long time ago back when I was a child myself. "Why Missy?"

"I don't know that either."

Pushing those thoughts away, I reached for his hand. "Kader, can you check on my parents, my sister, and my niece?"

"I really do work alone. I don't have people to send."

Moisture prickled my eyes.

His Adam's apple bobbed as he let out an exaggerated breath. "Shit. I'll see what I can come up with."

"Thank you."

The door closed as I lifted my suitcase to the bed.

Almost an hour later, I was showered and for the first time

in days, my hair was dried and I'd applied a bit of the cosmetics I'd thrown into my bag—nothing like the night of the gathering. Our freedom from the basement felt too good to not celebrate in some way, not that a little mascara and lip color was celebratory. It was more about a sense of surviving, something I was learning to acknowledge in small victories.

In the last day, we'd survived.

We'd escaped a rudimentary shelter, and our reward was found in luxury accommodations. The giant tiled shower within the attached bathroom was amazing. If I wasn't curious to learn what was happening in Indianapolis, I might have spent an extra hour or two under odor-free hot water.

Not only was the bathroom stocked with a hair dryer, there were also soaps, shampoo, conditioner, and lotions. I even found a hairbrush and comb as well as a brand-new toothbrush and toothpaste. Though there weren't any cosmetics, it certainly seemed as though the guest Kader had prepared to house was one of the female variety.

He'd asked what I needed. Looking down at an outfit I'd already worn, I knew that I needed more clothes and a washer and dryer to clean the ones I had.

How was I to know that when I'd thrown a few things into a suitcase, they would become my only possessions?

Walking down the hallway to the landing, I listened, using the detective skills I'd mentioned. Coming from the level below were various noises, confirming that Kader was down-stairs. Before I descended the stairs, my lip went beneath my front teeth as I recalled what he'd said about the location of his bedroom.

Turning back toward the hallway, I ascertained that the door before me was his.

What would happen if I opened it?

Staring at the wooden barrier, I continued to nibble my lip as my feet moved. One step and then another drew me closer to his door.

If he was downstairs, what would it hurt for me to take a quick look?

After all, I just wanted a peek.

I reached for the knob.

KADER

"*F*uck." The sentiment ran through my mind as the image of Laurel appeared on the screen over the kitchen counter. I owned a house that talked. She should have known—or at least assumed—that it was all well-surveyed.

Taking a deep breath, I stilled the knife in my hand, the one that I'd been using to cut vegetables. The blade now lingered in midair as I continued to watch.

Laurel Carlson, it seems you like to misbehave.

That thought shouldn't cause a redirection of my circulation. It shouldn't, but it did.

On the screen, the door to my bedroom opened inward and her curious expression came into view. I should be furious, yet I was struck by her image, her simplistic beauty. Her blue eyes were wide as she took in the space around her. Her long hair was smooth, the waves she'd had in the basement gone, the length hanging down her back like a dark veil swaying over her curves with each step

Perhaps, I was as mystified by her curiosity as much as I was my own.

What did she expect to find?

Why wasn't I stopping this?

When it came to my room, I had nothing to hide—as long as I wasn't present. It wasn't like I had a sex dungeon.

I half chuckled to myself.

Hell no.

Watching Laurel inside my private space, the pitiful truth hit me with the force of a ton of bricks. Dr. Laurel Carlson was the first woman to enter my bedroom. The professionals I'd hired for physical relief didn't make house calls. I wouldn't have allowed that if they did.

Perhaps, it wasn't one hundred percent accurate that Laurel was the first woman. Before I'd moved into this house, I'd hired an interior decorator—a woman. We never met in person. Via emails, I suggested ideas and then stepped back, mostly allowing her to take over. There wasn't much I had an opinion about—colors, lighting, surfaces, none of it mattered. It was the view and the expanse of land that attracted me to this property.

The house just was.

Why did my house now feel different seeing Laurel where I'd told her not to go?

The small hairs near the nape of my neck stood to attention as I lowered the knife to the counter and gripped the edge of the granite. She wasn't being quick. No, she was lingering as she took it all in.

A bed, bedside stands, and other regular bedroom furnishings were her tantalizing discoveries. She stilled momentarily next to the glass doors, perhaps to see past the panes. It was too dark to see beyond the glass with the lights on. She'd need to go outside onto the balcony to see. The doors were closed but not locked. Inaccessible from the outside due to the steep drop-off, I rarely thought to lock them. Besides, the house would tell me if they were opened. Laurel's small hand reached out. A shake of her head and she turned, her mind seemingly changed.

My pulse increased as Laurel stepped toward the desk along the far wall. If I hadn't turned off the screen to that computer, she'd be seeing herself. Instead, she ran her hand over the glossy surface before turning and stepping toward the attached bathroom.

The cameras were motion activated, following her movements as if I were in there with her. My heart thumped behind my breastbone as the air around me warmed. My mind was at odds with my body. I could be upstairs in less than a minute, catch her in the act.

And do what?

Yell at her.

Punish her.

Lock her in her room.

It wouldn't be unwarranted. I'd stated the rules clearly.

What I'd earlier considered curiosity at entering my bedroom was more accurately disobedience.

How fucking hard was it for her to follow directions?

My breath caught in my chest as Laurel stooped down—her nice round ass in the air. If I was a betting man, I'd say there were no panty lines beneath the pants she wore. Shit, she picked up the towel that I'd used after my shower and after folding it, placed it over the rack.

Fine. I wasn't immaculate.

Didn't it occur to her that I'd know it had been moved?

Did she care?

This woman on the screen and in my house should be afraid of me, and yet not only wasn't she scared, she had no problem openly defying me. I wasn't certain if that pissed me off or turned me on. The hard-on growing in my jeans led me to believe it was the latter.

Clenching my jaw, I looked around the kitchen. There was a salad large enough for two on the center island beside a bottle of wine I'd retrieved from the cellar on a whim. Though the flame of the burner wasn't turned on, the mushrooms and onions were nearly ready to be sautéed in a waiting frying pan, and on a platter, were two raw filet mignon steaks ready to be grilled.

Fuck it.

Dinner could wait.

Wiping my hands on a nearby towel, I knew what I needed to do.

LAUREL

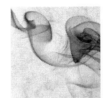

*T*he magnitude of what I was doing—going against Kader's earlier decree—hit me as I stood at the entry to his closet. This was his private world, and I was witnessing it firsthand—no, I was trespassing. The racks of clothes before me made my chest ache, rows of long-sleeved shirts and long pants.

Kader told me that he'd never had a guest and that he would sometimes spend weeks alone. Yet even in private, he kept his colors hidden.

Why?

That discovery combined with the total lack of personalization of his bedroom affected me more than I'd anticipated. Unlike the dresser in the bedroom he'd declared as mine, Kader's didn't have an attached mirror. The only mirror in his space was a small oval one over his vanity in the bathroom.

There were no pictures of family or friends. No remembrances of days gone by.

I thought about my bedroom at home, the one I would never be able to return to without thinking of Russ. On the mantel of the fireplace were pictures, wonderful memories with my parents, my niece, as well as me and my sister. There were photos of friends from different times in my life.

Kader didn't have one, not one.

The sorrow was overwhelming as the atmosphere shifted.

A more powerful aroma of Kader's cologne filled my senses. I'd noticed it when I first entered, but now it was stronger. My senses were on alert—the small hairs on my arms standing tall, the sound of my breathing magnified.

What had earlier been curiosity was now crushing remorse.

My reaction was not limited to my thoughts—my entire body reacted. Holding onto the doorjamb to Kader's closet, my hands began to tremble, perspiration coated my recently cleaned skin, and tears formed in my eyes. Blinking them away, I worked to slow my increasing pulse and catch my breath before a full-blown panic attack overwhelmed me.

I had one thought. I needed to get out of Kader's space.

Now.

Taking a deep breath, I spun toward the door to the hallway.

"Oh!" My hands reflectively came to my chest, grasping one another.

Shit.

Kader's dark stare sabotaged my escape. The taut cords in his neck and the fisting and unfisting of his hands were the most notable signs revealing his displeasure.

"I-I'm sorry." An apology was the only thing I could think to say. It wasn't a lie. I was sorry I'd gone against his wishes. I was sorry for what I'd seen. There weren't words capable of articulating my remorse any further or more elaborately.

I was sorry, period.

His lips twitched before his head tilted. "Everyone says that after getting caught." He took a step toward me and then another. The boots he wore tapped against the hardwood floor, his height dwarfing me with each step. He ran the tip of his finger over my cheek and feigned a smile. "Do you know how many people resort to meaningless apologies when they realize their time is up?"

I took a step back, holding his gaze. "You're trying to scare me."

Another step closer, another step backward. Together it was a waltz.

"I'm not trying," he said, "but you should be."

The rich birch cologne that had been lingering in the bedroom grew even stronger as he neared. His hair was combed and tethered at the nape of his neck, but unlike earlier, his cheeks were now smooth, making his clenched jaw and the tenseness of his facial muscles more pronounced.

I stood taller. "I'm not."

Kader's head shook from side to side, yet our battle of wills continued, neither of us willing to break eye contact.

Within his stare was something different than he'd shown me before. There was a battle raging within his green orbs, one that only he was fighting. Its presence rippled around us in waves.

"Why, Laurel?"

"I was...I'm curious by nature. You said not to and well, I wanted to know why."

"No," he said. "Why the fuck aren't you afraid? Grown men have emptied their bladders when confronted by me, often without a damn word from my lips. When I meet their stare, they know. They instinctively know the truth about what I do and what I'm capable of doing. They know that their destiny has been set." His Adam's apple bobbed as he momentarily closed his eyes. "Why don't you fucking see it?"

My head shook in confusion. "I don't know what you're talking about."

His masseter muscle grew prominent with the increased clenching of his jaw. Kader reached for my shoulders, his grasp progressively tightening as my answer floated away.

"I told you," he said. "You know what I do, how I found you, and why I found you."

The battle behind his eyes pained me more than the vise grip on my shoulders. Instead of answering, I leaned into him, pushing against his hold until my cheek met his chest and my arms surrounded his torso. Beneath the softness of his shirt, Kader's heart thumped like the beat of a drum, its cadence calling to me as either a song of peace or a battle cry. I wasn't sure which.

I wrapped my arms tighter, and yet beneath my embrace, his stone-hard muscles tightened, transforming from a man to a granite statue, one with a heartbeat and warmth. This man, for some reason, wanted to believe that he wasn't a person with emotions and needs. He wanted to believe he was a cold sculpture, but that wasn't what I saw.

Finally, his grasp of my shoulders loosened and his strong arms encompassed me, holding me to him as I was him to me. I closed my eyes. Time passed. We stood that way in silence, surrounded only by the sound of our breath and heartbeats until finally I let go of his torso. The mascara I'd applied now smudged his blue shirt and probably created circles under my eyes. I looked up. "Kader, who are you and what happened?"

His nostrils flared as he exhaled, and his lids closed, taking away the embattled green. "Listen, Laurel, don't."

I swallowed. "You told me what you do and why you found me. I'm not afraid of you. I want to know you, to help you, as you've helped me."

He shrugged. "I'll let you know if I have a dead lover for you to clean up."

I staggered backward as if instead of using cruel words, he'd physically assaulted me. My neck straightened while the shutting of my eyes prompted another tear to descend my cheek.

"Fuck, that was a shitty thing to say," Kader said, reaching for my chin and wiping the tear with the pad of his thumb. "I've told you. I'm not a good man. I'm not sure why you don't see that. The fact that you don't is fucking with my head. It needs to end. You want your life back. So do I.

"I'm going to do my best to either get you your life back or get you a new one, somewhere where you are safe." His head shook. "That sure as hell isn't with me."

The crushing ache in my chest was back. My temples throbbed and stomach churned.

With my lips together, I gave him one last nod and took another step back. The new position cleared my path to the door. Taking it, I walked past him and began my escape. "Fine, get rid of me. I didn't ask to come here." My ire grew with each step.

How dare he throw Russ at me like that.

I spun back toward him, my fist coming to my hip and volume rising. "If you ever decide to lose the tough-guy act— or maybe understand that in reality it's a shield, one so damn big you should be exhausted from carrying it day in and day out..." Opening my fist, I slapped the side of my thighs. "Whatever, in the meantime, I'm here if you ever want to talk."

It could be called women's intuition or even a scientist's gut. All I knew was that I specialized in traumatic memories and identifying common coping mechanisms and cues, such as isolationism and insomnia.

Kader had both in excess.

"I'm not one of your clients or participants, Doc."

"I never said you were." I swallowed. "It doesn't matter. I'm still here and not because I want to be. Nothing has really changed since the basement. I'm still caged." I gestured around. "Sure, it's bigger and there's an outside, but I can't leave, which I believe is the definition of being held captive. Kidnapping across state lines is a felony offense."

He shrugged. "You need to start listening to what I say. Illegal activity is what I do. Stop trying to analyze me. You wouldn't like what you find. It's not a pretty story with a happy ending."

"Kader, I'm not...I just thought..." Swallowing back tears, I let out a long breath and shook my head. "You know what? Obviously, my thoughts don't matter. I'm going to bed." I turned away, no longer wanting to see him.

Fuck him and his obsession to hide his secrets.

"You need to eat."

His voice floated down the hallway. I didn't respond. My steps grew faster as I turned away from the stairs and ran toward my room, suddenly grateful that I had my own space.

"Laurel?"

KADER

I repeated her name, "Laurel." It didn't matter. She wasn't turning back.

Fuck me.

I ran my hand over my hair, tugging at the rubber band and shaking the length loose. My skin felt tight, tighter than the scars, as if it were being pulled taut from the inside. I yanked at the collar of my shirt and again tugged on my hair. Hell, it wasn't enough. If only I could do more—pull the damn hair from my scalp. Rip it out from its roots and leave bloody chunks to dry on the damn floor. My goal was to inflict the pain on myself that I'd given to her. I wanted to feel it, to drown in it.

These foreign sensations had me in uncharted territory.

Mentioning Cartwright was a shitty thing to do. I knew

that as soon as the words came out of my mouth. Yet I didn't care until it was too late.

Because I didn't care—about anyone or anything.

That was the lie that I was finding more difficult to believe. Even now, I knew it was wrong, but I craved more—more stimulation, more something, more of what I couldn't have.

Stalking to the bedroom door, I slammed it shut. The sound echoed in my ears as I stared at the neighboring wall. My hand balled into a fist. For longer than I care to admit, I contemplated the possibility of punching through the plaster. In my mind's eye I saw it happening. The plaster turning to dust as my fist made contact, breaking through the surface while my knuckles ached.

Would that give me the pain I sought?

Would it take the anguish away from Laurel?

Would I find relief?

It wouldn't. I wouldn't—ever.

Taking a breath, I ran my palm over my face—over my forehead, eyes, nose, and mouth. The skin of my cheeks was uncharacteristically smooth, absent its normal facial hair.

Fuck me.

I'd showered, shaved, and put on cologne before going downstairs and preparing to cook our dinner. I scoffed at myself, recalling the bottle of wine.

A sarcastic laugh bubbled from my throat.

What a fucking joke to think that Laurel and I could dine like a normal couple, even like two normal individuals. I wasn't normal. In a few long strides, I was within the attached bathroom. My gaze went from the towel she'd hung up over the rack to the small mirror over the sink. The decorator had wanted a larger one, saying this one was disproportionate to the vanity.

It was one of the few things I insisted upon.

As my eyes met my own, I spoke through gritted teeth. "Get this assignment done. She's fucking with your mind. Stop pretending that there's something special about her or about you. You are *not* special nor will you ever be—never again, *even if maybe once you were.*" I mumbled the last part or maybe I only thought it.

Laurel Carlson had me wondering about things I'd never before cared to know. It was a dangerous trail. One thought led to another. The look on her face when I mentioned Cartwright came crashing back.

My fingers blanched as I gripped the edge of the vanity and doubled over. Fuck, her hurt expression. The words I'd spoken hit like a damned sledgehammer to the gut. The memory wasn't any kinder.

Lifting my chin, my stare returned to my own.

No. This is wrong.

Turning off the light, I returned to my bedroom and scanned the room, looking for something.

What the fuck did she see?

There was nothing out of the ordinary, nothing different from millions of other bedrooms.

Again I tugged at my collar. I'd rip the damn shirt off if I could guarantee we wouldn't run into one another. She'd been right. This wasn't different than the basement. It had been fine before—now I was claustrophobic.

Going to the glass doors, I opened one inward. The cold, fresh air hit me with a cooling gust as snowflakes swirled through the air. There was probably at least three fresh inches on the railing, all accumulating since our arrival. The view beyond was shrouded in darkness, only the new coating of white visible. The new snow didn't surprise me. The dark clouds over the mountains as we'd approached warned of the impending storm. Even in the springtime, this area was susceptible to snow accumulation measured in feet not inches.

Inhaling and exhaling, I filled my lungs with the icy air as I tried to make sense of what had happened.

This wasn't like me.

I didn't get upset or regret my actions or words.

"What the fuck are you doing to me?"

Though my question was audible, no one was close enough to hear as the words were carried off by the wintry winds.

Going back inside, my desk caught my attention. Hitting the button on the screen, I shook the mouse and brought the house cameras into view.

Hey, asshole, how is watching her through a camera any less a violation of her privacy than her walking into your bedroom?

I wasn't in the mood for reasoning.

The camera in her bedroom broadcast on my monitor.

Still standing with my weight on my hands, I bent over the desk and clicked on her feed, keeping it from rotating to another location. I wasn't sure what I wanted to see.

Her—Laurel.

I wanted to see her.

The lens adjusted to night vision. Her lights were turned out.

Where was she?

The green hue created a grainier view as the camera panned out and Laurel came into view. There was no motion to detect. She was sitting up in the big bed, the blankets covering her breasts and her arms crossed over her chest. Her expression was devoid of emotion as she stared into the darkness. The pain I'd inflicted was gone—or maybe simply suppressed.

I fell back into the chair.

I'd come upstairs because Laurel Carlson had violated the boundary I'd set, plain and simple. I came up to call her out and reinstate my dominance in this relationship. She was out of her league with what was happening and had already occurred. I set the rules. If this was going to work—if I was going to get her to a safe place—she needed to follow them.

It wasn't simply that she'd gone into my room. I wasn't here. I was concerned about the fact that she'd blatantly disobeyed. Rules were like railings on balconies—respect them and they kept you safe. Ignore them and be prepared to accept the consequences.

My chest filled with air as I inhaled and stood. Yes, I'd

come up to deliver a consequence. It didn't matter that it was somehow turned into me being wrong.

Was that what all women did, turned the tables?

No wonder I'd avoided them for years.

My boots slapped the planks of the floor as I stepped determinedly toward the door.

Fuck this.

This is my house.

She was my assignment.

I made the rules.

I flung open the bedroom door to the landing.

Twenty minutes later, I was back upstairs, my long, determined strides passing the door to my bedroom. I barely hesitated, not bothering to knock, as I twisted the knob and pushed Laurel's door open. The hallway light streamed into the room, yet the bed where she was now sleeping was still in the shadows.

Her lack of movement meant she hadn't heard me enter.

Walking to the edge of the bed, I reached for the covers and threw them back.

"What the—?" Her groggy question came in unison with my shocked one.

"Fucking hell?" I asked. The vision before me was not at all what I'd expected—not that I was complaining. No longer wearing what she had been in my bedroom, Laurel was stark nude, every fucking curve and valley.

She reached for the blankets.

Nice try, sweetheart.

I lifted them higher as a grin transformed my expression. There was no way I was giving them up. "Dinner is almost ready. You have five minutes to get your sweet-looking ass downstairs or the over-the-shoulder threat still stands." My cheeks rose higher as she scooted away, lifting a pillow and pulling it over her.

"Kader, this is...unacceptable."

"No, Doc. You breaking my rules is unacceptable, and it's not going to happen again. I told you to stay out of my room. You disobeyed. I said that you needed to eat and you walked away from me. That shit isn't going to happen. Not in my house. Not ever again." I dropped the blankets near the end of the bed, leaving the pillow as her shield. And yet I couldn't contain my curiosity. "Did our little discussion make you so hot and bothered you couldn't wear clothes?"

Laurel had reached down and pulled the sheet up, covering from her breasts down. Her arms were crossed defensively over her chest, her hair was slightly mussed, and her blue eyes were sending daggers my way.

She was hot as shit.

"Did you get off?" I asked, my tone laced with amusement.

"Stop it." She slapped the bed beside her. "I took off my clothes because I don't have any that are clean. I didn't want to sleep in dirty clothes on fresh sheets."

Fuck. It seemed as though my track record of making dick comments was still intact.

"Wait a minute," I said, shaking my head.

Hurrying to my bedroom, I grabbed two t-shirts and a button-down from the closet. Hell, they'd be dresses on her. I also grabbed a pair of boxer shorts from the dresser. When I made it back to her room, she was standing, holding the sheet around her. I had visions of Roman goddesses in togas. Those images paled in comparison to the one before me.

"Here," I said, tossing the clothes on the bed. "Four minutes. And after what I just saw, I hope you don't make it. That bare ass over my shoulder would be more fun for me than it would be for you."

"Get out. You're not touching my ass."

With a scoff, I turned to leave, but before I reached the door, I stopped. "Thought you should know; it's over. I sent the message to whoever hired me. You're dead."

MASON

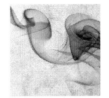

Over seven years ago in a mansion in Lincoln Park,
Chicago

Sterling Sparrow replied to the Chicago police detective, "My mother needs time to come to terms with the loss of her husband before you or anyone else will be able to speak with her."

From the distance of the attached parlor, Genevieve Sparrow nodded. Sitting daintily on a velvet sofa, she appeared to be in deep thought about something on her lap. Truth be told, before allowing the detective to enter, Sparrow told his mother to be in sight and remain silent. There were too many moving parts right now for her to add any unnecessary information.

Newly promoted from patrolling the city streets, Detective James was a recent assignment to the Chicago Police Bureau of Organized Crime. Though he thought he was a shark smelling blood, he was sorely mistaken. If keeping with the fish analogy, he was merely a simple herring flopping helplessly within a school of barracuda.

The detective shuffled his feet over the shiny marble floor and straightened his neck, doing his best to see beyond the entry of the Sparrow mansion. It wasn't going to happen. Sparrow and I were standing shoulder to shoulder in the foyer, gatekeepers refusing his entry.

The detective swallowed. "Mr. Sparrow, why are you here?"

"That question seems a little elementary coming from a detective. Perhaps the department needs you back on the streets directing traffic." Before Detective James could respond, Sparrow went on, "Officers from the great Chicago PD came to my office this evening and informed me of my father's passing. It shouldn't take a detective to assume that comforting my mother, the alderman, and protecting her from unknown threats would be my top priority."

"Is she your top priority?"

Taking a step forward, I decided that I'd stood silent long enough. "Good evening, Detective James. It's time for you to go. Mrs. Sparrow will be available after her husband's funeral has been arranged and completed. This is not a good time." I took another step closer.

Detective James lifted his hand. "Out of respect for the alderman, I won't persist. I will, however, be back."

"Be sure to have the proper documentation," Sparrow said. "This house is private property and my mother is a government official."

The detective returned a quick nod, his gaze going beyond the two of us to the parlor where Sparrow's mother was dabbing her eyes with a lace-trimmed handkerchief. Her unusually pale complexion was visible in the ring of light from the lamp on the nearby table. Her long robe split near her feet, exposing what she would refer to as slippers, revealing the late hour.

Who the fuck wore heels as slippers?

I'd never been a Genevieve Sparrow fan.

That wasn't why we were here. We were here for this exact reason, keeping her away from the police and protecting what now belonged to the new Sparrow organization. The large limestone monstrosity was currently being protected by men *we* trusted. Many of Allister's men would be out. There was a war happening on the streets of Chicago that wouldn't make the newspapers or social media.

The detective cleared his throat. "Mrs. Sparrow, you have my condolences." He turned back to Sparrow. "And you too, Mr. Sparrow."

Genevieve responded with a simple nod of her head.

"Thank you, Detective James," Sparrow said. "I trust you and your department will leave my mother in peace. Contact me when you're ready to speak to her." He removed a business card from the inside pocket of his suit coat. "I won't allow her to be questioned without support."

"Sir, it isn't questioning, per se. We simply have some things to clarify. Like why would your father be at a construction site late this evening?"

"That sounds like questioning to me."

"Did your father keep items here, business items, files, documents, or ledgers?"

Sparrow inhaled. "Sparrow Enterprises is located on Michigan Avenue. I'm certain you've seen the building. There is an entire department that oversees those items. Sparrow Enterprises is fully transparent. If presented with a warrant, we will, of course, comply."

"I was simply curious if there might be more—"

"I'll say good evening one more time," Sparrow interrupted, "and then I'll make a call to the mayor and tell him about the inconsiderate behavior of one of his detectives. I'm certain he'll take my concern up with the superintendent, first deputy superintendent, and eventually the chief of your department. You understand that while perhaps acceptable in the Bureau of Patrol, in your current appointment, harassing grieving widows is intolerable. And doubly so when the widow is an alderman..."

Detective James nodded again as I stepped past him and opened the front door.

"I'll be in touch." It was the last thing the detective said before crossing the threshold and stepping out into the cool rain.

We all stood in silence until Reid entered from a back hallway. In his hand was a device capable of detecting unwanted monitoring devices. We couldn't take the chance that Detective James had covertly left one behind. Once everything was cleared, Reid lifted his hand. "We're good."

Genevieve looked up from her perch. "Sterling, your ring..."

"That's right, Mom, it's mine. It's all mine."

"The house?" she asked, her chin raised and proud.

"I don't want this house. You keep it. Burn it. I don't give a fuck."

"Language," she replied as if she hadn't just scolded the new king of Chicago's underworld.

Sparrow turned back, facing toward me and Reid. "I want this place crawling with Sparrows. Out of sight. No one is getting in here until we rid my father's office of everything that's now ours."

"What about him?" Reid asked, nodding toward the place Detective James had been.

"He'll back down," Sparrow said. "He thinks because my father is gone that he can come in here, act tough, and I'll reveal secrets. What he's too stupid to understand is that those secrets involve people in his department and in positions over him. Hell, there isn't a department of the police that isn't involved. I'll make a few calls. I'll let them know that there's been a change in leadership, and I'm now in charge. I'll assure them that even better than my father, I'm capable of keeping secrets. I'll help *them*..."

"They'll help you—us," I finished.

"I'll see you in the office," Reid said. His dark eyes grew wide. "Let me just say—shit."

The house phone rang in the distance. A moment later, a woman in a maid's uniform appeared. "Mrs. Sparrow, Mrs. McFadden has called twice. She's currently on line one and insists on speaking to you."

Pauline McFadden was the wife of Rubio McFadden, senator as well as the don of the other ruling organization in Chicago. It took fucking balls for her to attempt to reach Mrs. Sparrow on the same night as Allister's death. That was what these women had to have—balls of steel—to survive in this world.

All polite and genteel on the outside, the women of the underworld hierarchy were piranhas on the inside. The men who lived this life were at least honorable enough to call a rat a rat. These women, they were fucking sneaky. I wouldn't trust a word of condolence from Pauline McFadden.

"Molly," Sparrow said before his mother could respond, "my mother is not taking any calls tonight. None. Take a message. Accept condolences from anyone who calls but..." He turned to Genevieve. "...no talking to anyone. Tell me you understand the importance of this transition."

His mother inhaled and turned to Molly. "Sterling is right. It would be best for you to tell anyone who calls that I'm too distraught to speak at this time."

"Yes, madam."

As Molly walked away, Sparrow asked, "Mom, where is

your cell phone?"

"Upstairs. It's charging."

"I want that too."

With another sigh, Genevieve rose and came toward her son, her slippers clipping across the floor. "What about Rudy?"

Rudy Carlson was Allister's consigliere, a man now without an organization. There was no way in hell Sparrow could trust him.

Sparrow shook his head. "He's out. He won't be coming here again."

Genevieve nodded.

From her reaction, I wasn't certain if she was relieved or disappointed. As long as she wasn't fighting her son, I didn't care.

"How can you get your father's things out of here without being seen?" she asked. "I want it all gone."

"The tunnel, and when we're done, that entrance will be cemented shut. No one will be coming and going from your house without using a visible door."

You'd think a mansion like this would be on a sprawling estate. It wasn't. There were other homes and buildings nearby. One of the less assuming homes in the area was connected to the mansion via an underground tunnel. It was how Allister Sparrow conducted business without the appearance of people coming and going from his residence.

Mrs. Sparrow's eyes fluttered as she laid her hand on Sparrow's arm. "Be careful. I don't want to lose you, too."

He scoffed. "Don't worry, Mom, the money won't stop."

"It's not—"

"Go to bed," Sparrow said, tilting his chin toward the staircase. "I'll put a guard outside your door. This place is surrounded. No one will get to you or Molly. And tomorrow, have your assistant work on planning the funeral. You need to appear the grieving widow, doing what any widow in your position would do. You oversee what she does. Once you're content, the plans need to be cleared by me. We will assure security."

Mrs. Sparrow nodded.

"One more thing," he said, "before you begin to return phone calls, I need to see the list. Things are happening as we speak. Tomorrow, some of those old biddies will also be—as you said about yourself—too distraught to take your call."

Her shoulders slumped. "Sterling, please."

"Don't," he said with a shake of his head. "From the time I was a fucking kid, they'd made their beds. It's past time for them to lie in them. Permanently." With her hand still on his arm, Sparrow walked his mother to the staircase. "Good night, Mother. Go up to your suite. Have Molly bring me your cell phone."

Genevieve brushed her lips over Sparrow's cheek. "Good night. I won't interfere."

"That's for the best."

With her departure, I moved closer to Sparrow near the bottom of the stairs.

Standing shoulder to shoulder, we watched as Sparrow's

mother walked regally up the giant staircase. The sweeping spiral design led to the second and third floors. Her long robe flowed behind her as she climbed with her chin in the air.

The woman had always acted like a fucking queen—better than everyone.

She tolerated Reid, Patrick, and me, but rarely acknowledged anyone other than her son even when we were all in the same room. Prior to the transition, the four of us had discussed how she would take the news. She should have suspected that something was going to happen. It was either her husband or her son. Sparrow was confident that she would do whatever was necessary to maintain her wealth and standing in the community.

If the secrets in the back office were brought to light, Genevieve's reputation as well as those of hundreds of other people would be ruined. The news channels would go wild fighting for the exclusive rights to all of the stories. While the idea of Allister's reputation in the shitter was appealing, for the Sparrow organization as well as Sparrow Enterprises to remain unscathed, we'd keep the secrets. We'd move every damn document, every hidden ledger, everything that could be connected to the Sparrow organization to our new headquarters in the sky.

And then over time, Reid, Patrick, and I would scan, classify, and destroy.

Secrets were best when they were held in keeping—just in case.

It was past time for the Sparrow organization to step up

its record keeping. Paper ledgers and files were a thing of the past. We'd have a fucking bonfire in celebration of the new regime.

As Genevieve disappeared onto the second-floor landing, I asked with a grin, "Did you just send your mother to bed and take away her phone?"

Sparrow shrugged, a half smile coming to his face as he slapped me on the back. As his hand moved away, I took another look at the ring on his right hand, the gold one that bore the Sparrow family crest.

As recently as this evening, it had been on Allister's finger.

Now the corpse lying in the morgue was without a family ring, and after what Sparrow showed us, without a finger. Sparrow's willingness to wear that ring, openly and this soon, was another example of his power in this city.

"I'm relatively certain she had dinner though," he said with a brief smile. "That detective won't be back, but I want everything out of this house, anything that could be a threat to my mother. She's a bitch, but she's a Sparrow. We protect what is ours."

"Let's get busy," I said as we walked the hallways of the Sparrow mansion to join Patrick and Reid in the back office.

Sparrow stopped at the threshold, looking inside the dark paneled room. "I fucking hate this office almost as much as I hated him. Maybe we should burn it."

Reid looked up from where he was crouched on the carpet with a file drawer in front of him and stacks of files to his side. "Not until we scan this shit. Holy hell, the names..."

LAUREL

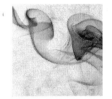

Present day

*W*earing Kader's button-down shirt with the sleeves rolled up, I walked silently down the staircase, ignoring the door to his room on the way. It wasn't only the fear that he'd carry out his threat—literally—it was that after he'd wakened me, I realized that I was hungry. I wasn't certain what food he'd have here, seeing as we'd recently arrived. Nevertheless, I was willing to find out.

The boxer shorts were a joke. I would need a belt of some kind to keep them from falling to my ankles, and as it was, the shirt I wore went to nearly my knees. The shoulder seams were near my elbows and the bulk of the sleeves were rolled over itself. The clean material held the lingering scent of his cologne, the aroma permeating everything within his closet.

Even though I wasn't happy with the man in the kitchen, I appreciated the gesture.

I'd combed out my hair and reapplied the small amount of makeup. The way I told myself to approach this command performance was that we were stuck together, and now that I had been declared deceased—that was a thought I refused to dwell upon—we needed to learn how to coexist.

I also assumed that Kader had information from Indianapolis, and I would only learn what he knew by coming downstairs willingly.

At the bottom of the staircase, I stilled. Even if I couldn't hear him, I was certain I could find the kitchen from the amazing aroma alone. A loud growl came from my empty stomach as I crossed the wood floor in my bare feet and stopped within the archway to the kitchen.

The room before me was big and beautiful, something out of an architectural magazine on kitchen design. There was a large fireplace that took the expanse of one wall with a raised hearth. Windows above a sink and counters filled another. The walls and ceiling were covered with weathered wood planks. White cabinets contrasted the black glossy hard-surface countertops and the red-brick backsplash that matched the fireplace. There was a large island in the middle of the work area with a breakfast bar and tall stools as well as a long wooden table with eight chairs where the windows went from the floor to the ceiling.

The view beyond the windows was lost to the darkness. It was the view within the kitchen that had my full attention.

Kader was attending to two steaks sizzling on the surface of a grill in the middle of his large range. On a side burner was a frying pan emanating the delicious scent of onions. On the island there was a glass bowl with lettuce and other fixings. On the long table were two place settings complete with wine glasses. And on the table was a bottle of wine, the cork removed.

If this was his way of apologizing, I would accept it.

Just when I didn't think he could be handsomer or sexier, Kader blows off his dangerous persona to don that of a master culinary artist.

A good cook and pretty damn great between the sheets.

That thought had me considering more than food.

My stomach again made a noise demanding me to move forward.

Flipping the steaks, Kader turned my way, a small smile threatening to break his stern facade. "Damn, I was almost ready to carry you down." His green stare scanned from my bare toes to the top of my head. "We need to get you some clothes, but I like what I see. Maybe I should let you wear more of my shirts." With a large barbeque fork, he checked the meat on the grill, the large stainless-steel hood above the range taking away the delicious-aroma-filled smoke. Laying the fork on the counter, he took two long strides and then we were inches apart, his arm snaked around my waist as he pulled me closer. "I swear you're fucking hotter in this shirt than you were at the gathering, and you were smoking that night."

Warmth filled my cheeks as a twinge of sadness reminded me of the life I'd lost. Pushing that emotion away, I concentrated on the hard body before me. My nipples tightened against his chest. My body was at war over which sensations should dominate. While there was no doubt I was hungry, being this close to Kader had other needs coming to mind.

Looking up, I concentrated on nutrition and said, "This all looks delicious."

"I can say from experience, you are too."

I closed my eyes, my thoughts of his expertise between the sheets sending a bolt of electricity to the part of me that was currently without panties.

"Stop." I pushed myself away and took a step around him, inspecting the contents of the frying pan.

Kader appeared at my side, moving the steaks from the grill to two waiting plates and spooned sautéed mushrooms and onions over each one. "I hope you're not a secret vegetarian."

I shrugged. "I don't eat a lot of red meat, but after all the junk food in the basement, this is a feast."

When he started to lift the plates, I stopped him, laying my hand on his arm, mindful of touching his sleeve. "You were an ass."

His eyes opened wide. "You purposely defied me."

"Do you think that makes us even?"

"Do you?" he asked.

"I guess it makes us human."

Kader shook his head. "Give it up, Doc. That doesn't

describe me. It describes you. Let's eat and figure out what's happening next."

I wanted to argue, to tell this beautiful man that he was human. Lashing out, yelling, fighting, and even saying hurtful things were all part of the humanity. They weren't the pretty parts, but without them, there wouldn't be a whole.

Watching him carry the plates to the table, I gave that more thought. Without those parts, there would be a hole.

It was the premise Russ and I had been working on with our research and development, removing and redirecting the traumatic memories so they wouldn't incite their usual psychological and physiological responses, without taking away all responses. If we removed response to stimuli, we would leave a hole.

Did Kader have that hole?

Why?

"A 2012 shiraz," he said, redirecting my thoughts as he lifted the bottle. "I've been letting it breathe. Would you like a glass?"

A feigned smile came to my lips. "Sure, thank you."

After carrying the salad to the table, I sat and took another look out the dark windows. "Is that snow?"

"Yes, we've gotten three or more inches since sundown."

I shook my head. "Isn't it late in the year for snow?"

"Not at this elevation. I've seen blizzards in June. The accumulation won't last long. That mud near the ravine means the ground is warming during the day."

Blizzard in June.

Where would I be in June?

I refocused my thoughts on the food before us. "How did you get this food so fast?" I asked as I scooped salad from the bowl to my plate. "It's fresh. Did you stop somewhere and shop while I was asleep?"

His gaze found mine. "I told the house we were coming."

My cheeks rose. "The house bought you fresh food?"

"No, that would be Jack."

"Someday, I would like to meet this Jack of all trades." I plucked a grape tomato from the salad and put it in my mouth.

"Sorry, Doc. Remember, you're dead."

LAUREL

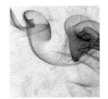

*E*xhaling, I lowered my fork to the table. "I'm trying not to think about that. I'm worried my parents will hear."

"That's the thing. If they do, they're in contact with my employer. It's not like they'll find your body."

My pulse quickened. "What do you mean in contact with?" My stomach churned with the little bit of food I'd eaten. "I'm so scared for them."

"In my experience, I can tell you that you don't need to be. I was the one hired to kill you. A threat to them would have come from me. I didn't threaten them." One side of his lips curled upward. "I took you instead."

"I told you it was kidnapping. What happens next?"

He nodded toward my plate. "Eat."

"You do know that I've managed to survive for most of my life without starving."

"You weren't my assignment then. Now you are. Eat and drink. The wine will help you sleep."

"Are you trying to get me tipsy to take advantage of me?"

Kader didn't answer, but the gaze he sent my way told me that it wasn't beyond the realm of possibility. I could tell him that getting me tipsy wasn't necessary. Instead, I scoffed and said, "Well, it's better than that sleeping pill."

"Don't worry. There's no way I'm giving you another one of those."

"I wouldn't take it." I lifted my fork and took a bite of the salad. "After eating and drinking...?"

"We'll check the recent feeds from the university, your house, Cartwright's, and anything else we can find. We'll check the local news outlets, and we'll get some sleep. For the next few days, our job is to watch. It will be more efficient if we divide and conquer."

"My parents, sister, and niece?" I asked again. "I don't mean to keep bringing them up, but Kader, you have to understand, they're my family."

"Logically I understand. Being without one myself, I think your concern is unfounded, ill-timed, and emotionally biased."

My eyes widened. "I'm emotional because I'm worried?" I tilted my head. "Tell me, what makes you emotional?"

Kader lowered his fork to the table. "You're doing it again."

"What?"

"Analyzing." Kader lifted his hand, revealing a small bit of color near his wrist. "Back to your family, I've been thinking about your request—for logical reasons. Do they have any set schedules or routines?"

My lower lip slid under my front teeth as I gave his question some thought, wishing I had been closer to them. "I'm not sure, but I'll think about it. Why?"

"Without leaving you—which I won't do—and seeing that they're safe with my own eyes, I had an idea to hack into traffic cameras, stores' security, school security...hell, doorbells or home security systems—anything that could find them and ease your mind that they're safe."

My head was bobbing. "Yes," I answered excitedly. "My dad has cameras on his property. It's weird because he always talks about how safe Iowa is, and that's why they moved there. He claims the cameras aren't for security but to see the wildlife." I tilted my head. "He's into birds."

"Why did you go to school in Indiana if you were raised in Iowa?" Kader asked as we were continuing our meal.

"I wasn't raised in Iowa. I've never lived there." My gaze narrowed. "I thought you knew everything about me."

"Everything for the assignment. Most of it recent. Where did you grow up?"

"A neighborhood in Chicago and moved to Indiana for school. They offered me the best scholarships. From there, my grades and studies funded my education."

"Impressive. What neighborhood in Chicago?"

"Wicker Park."

"High rent," Kader said, cutting another piece of his steak.

I shrugged. "Both of my parents were psychiatrists. They had a small practice in Wicker Park. Mom also had privileges at a hospital downtown, and Dad volunteered at a couple of not-for-profit organizations. Sometimes I thought he enjoyed donating his time more than working at their practice."

"Why did you and your family leave Chicago?"

"It was weird and sudden. I honestly don't think I was told the real story."

"What does that mean?"

I thought back to a time when I was in graduate school. "My sister and I had already moved away. I was in grad school. Ally was finished and recently married. Out of the blue, my parents sold their home and their practice and moved to Iowa. It was after my uncle died. He was my dad's brother. It was weird because my uncle was quite a bit older than Dad." I shrugged. "They were never close. It wasn't like we would go over to their house or they would come to ours. My mom always said it was because they never had children." I shrugged. "Mom even told Ally and me not to worry about his funeral." I gave that some thought. "Yeah, we weren't close. I haven't spoken to my aunt in years."

After we'd both eaten, we carried our dishes to the sink.

"Does the house wash the dishes?" I asked, the little bit of wine and delicious food erasing my earlier displeasure with the man beside me.

"After I put them in the dishwasher."

"If it would help, I'll put them in the dishwasher. Then tell me where to meet you to begin watching."

His chest expanded. "My office but only in my presence. I will set up another computer system, but there is too much on mine. You click on the wrong tab or icon and let's just say, you can never unsee what you saw."

My eyes opened wide as the thought of what he could have on his computer knotted my now-satisfied stomach. "I promise. I have one too many gruesome images in my memory. I don't want more."

Kader took a step toward me and ran his finger over my cheek. Curling his thumb under my chin, he lifted it higher, bringing my gaze to his. "Laurel, for that I'm sorry. And know that I don't apologize...ever."

I reached for his hand. "I know it wasn't your intention for me to see him and that you tried to stop me." For a moment we stood silently, perhaps moving on from our earlier argument or maybe moving forward. I wasn't certain. Finally, I let go of his hand. "I'll clean up. Where is your office?"

He tilted his head toward the archway I'd entered. "Through the living room, take the hallway to the left of the fireplace."

"Okay."

With the dishes in the dishwasher, the kitchen wiped down, and the remaining salad in the refrigerator, I turned off the lights and followed his directions. The path before me was illuminated with a hue of golden lighting. The large living room had more windows that looked out to the swirling snow.

For a moment I thought about my house, how my old windows rattled with the wind. Though the snow swirled in cyclones near these panes, there wasn't a sound.

The fireplace in there was larger than the one in the kitchen and made of sand-colored stones of various sizes, its chimney extending skyward. Looking upward, I noted the ceiling was high. If I were to guess, I'd say twenty feet or more.

Once I entered the hallway on the left, the partially opened door came into view as the clicking of a keyboard came into range. I'd found him.

Although I was barefoot and my steps were silent, Kader seemed to be warned of my approach. Maybe it was the house that told him. Now that I thought about it, I probably had the house to blame for him finding me in his bedroom.

Thanks a lot, Missy.

The voice was only in my head. I found it difficult to be upset at a house with the same name as the girl who a long time ago I'd considered a friend, the one who introduced me to her brother, my childhood crush.

Kader looked up at me from the many screens, his green-eyed gaze momentarily stilling my steps, reminding me a little bit of that older brother.

That was ridiculous.

I hadn't laid eyes on that boy since we were teenagers, and he went off to serve our country, and I headed to college. We'd said we'd keep in touch, but after my letters went unanswered, I stopped sending them. I still wrote letters, but instead of mailing them, I threw them away until eventually even the writing stopped.

My lips flattened as the teenager's image came to mind, nothing like the man before me. Not necessarily scrawny, my first love's body was still that of a boy's. Fighting for food day and night for him and his sisters—when he had two sisters— didn't exactly allow for excess calories.

I recalled the sadness when I received the letter from his sister telling me that he was gone. I never knew how she found me or why, and there was no return address or way to contact her.

Swallowing, I took a deep breath and did my best to send the memories away.

Maybe it was talking about my childhood with Kader that had stirred these melancholy recollections. Now wasn't the time. My life was on a collision course and needed my full attention.

"Is everything all right?" Kader asked.

I scoffed. "Grand scheme—no. Now, yes, I guess."

"Come sit down," Kader said, his voice much deeper than the one in my memory and his body bigger than the other boy with green eyes.

That was it.

I simply liked green-eyed men.

Kader pointed to a chair beside him. "Over here, there's been a few developments."

LAUREL

*T*he pleasant effect of the wine and dinner had been tempered by my recollections. That was nothing compared to how the good feelings disappeared as I stepped over the threshold into Kader's office.

He'd told me to be afraid of him.

I wasn't.

The cold reality that grew within me was that I was frightened of what he had learned, might learn, or what he would tell me.

It wasn't like me to avoid answers. Hell no, for most of my life I'd sought answers.

Now, as I approached Kader, my fingers and toes cooled with each step as a chill settled over my skin. In a short period of time—since the gathering—I'd become a woman who would rather forget than remember.

I silently scoffed.

It was too bad I didn't have some of our compound with me.

I slowly spun a full circle, taking in the entirety of the room. It wasn't only the answers that I might learn that brought a chill over me. His office was cold, not as in temperature, but as in atmosphere.

Unlike the rustic chic and golden hue of the other rooms of his house, Kader's office could be considered industrial, like walking out of a home and into a warehouse. In a way, his office reminded me of the basement where we'd been, only this one had windows.

The wood floor that spanned throughout the rest of the house stopped at the entryway to the office. I stared down at my bare feet. The surface currently beneath them was smooth, much like concrete covered in a glossy finish, the same as people had in fancy garages. The walls were covered with the same gray coating. While there were multiple computer screens on the long desk at Kader's eye-level, there were also huge flat screens mounted higher on the walls, currently dark. Beyond the computer center were other machines. Some were familiar, such as a normal printer and a 3D one as well. We had those at the university. Those were only two. There were plenty more of which I had no clue of their functions or benefits.

Unlike offices of old, there were no walls filled with bookcases full of books and trimmed with fancy woodwork. There wasn't a grand desk, a grouping of chairs, or a conference table for discussions.

It was clear that Kader worked as he'd told me—alone. I also ascertained that his information didn't come from old books, cases, or studies. Kader did his research through the internet.

As a scientist and professor, I was cognizant that by the time a textbook was published, the material was out of date. Staying up-to-date on current research meant reading the most recent refereed publications. When my parents studied psychology, staying up-to-date meant subscribing to the most respected monthly research journals. Today those publications were online and not limited to monthly postings. Every day was a race to publish first, to blaze the trail.

Mourning my loss, I admitted to myself that had been our goal—what we'd hoped would happen with our formula and compound.

With a sigh, I tucked Kader's shirt under my backside and sat on the chair he had waiting beside him.

Turning away from the screen, his gaze met mine. "It's late. There have been some developments, but they won't change by tomorrow. Maybe we should wait. You seem...tired."

"I am. But I want to know."

His gaze lowered to my lap, scanning and stilling as it reached my exposed legs. "Fuck, Laurel, you know how to be distracting."

I tugged the shirt lower. "Tell me where the laundry room is, and I'll throw a load in the washing machine before bed."

"If I don't tell you, does that mean you'll spend tomorrow in another one of my shirts?"

Reaching toward me, Kader's fingers splayed above my knee, the warmth sending impulses to areas of my body I knew would be counterproductive to learning the most recent developments. I covered his hand with mine. "This touching thing is still unfair."

"I like touching you, but if you say no..." His words trailed away.

Leaning forward, I moved my hands to his smooth cheeks, closed my eyes, and brushed his lips with mine. Though it wasn't really a kiss, the contact sent more waves of warmth through my circulation. My nipples drew tight, and without thinking, I pushed my thighs closer together. When I opened my eyes, we were nose to nose, our breathing shallower than a moment before as we inhaled one another's breaths. "I'm not saying no. I like it too." My hands were still over his cheeks. "I like touching you too."

The sound of something resembling a low growl came from his throat.

"I'll give you the same option you gave me," I said. "If you say no..."

"You have a short memory, Laurel. I've said no."

My shoulders slumped as the disappointment of his words squelched the fire that had been flickering within me. Pulling my hands away, I broke eye contact and looked toward the screens. "What's happening on there?"

Kader didn't answer. Instead, he reached for my hands and returned them to the sides of his face. As he did, the fire's warmth returned, a singular spark saved by an unanticipated fuel source. My heart began to race and my eyes widened.

"What does this mean?" I asked.

Lowering his eyelids, for a moment Kader's green disappeared, and then it returned, glowing with the light from the screens. "Fuck, Laurel, I don't know. I'm no longer saying no. I'm saying I like having you touch me too. Just keep it to my face, hands..." He lowered one of my hands to his arm, placing my palm over his sleeve. "...and clothes. I don't want to explain any more. I..." He swallowed. "...this is new for me. I don't understand it."

My forehead furrowed. "What is new? I'm no expert, but I'm confident that what happened back in the basement wasn't your first time."

"First is more subjective than it sounds. It was the first time I've wanted a woman as much as I want you. I don't remember ever being as overwhelmed as the way you overwhelm me. You're fucking with my head. You're messing with my self-control, and for a person in my line of work, that's not a good thing."

A smile bloomed across my face, growing larger with each of his sentences. "I know exactly what you mean about being overwhelmed."

His broad shoulder shrugged. "I doubt that, but I'm tired

of fighting it, especially with you sitting here with only my shirt covering you and nothing else underneath."

My neck straightened as my mouth dropped wide open. "H-how did you know that?"

His lips curled upward as his cheeks rose. "When you walked in the kitchen, the way the light hit you, the shirt was..." His eyebrows moved upward. "...transparent. With one glance, I was ready to forget the dinner and get a better look at what I'd seen upstairs."

I sat back against the chair and covered my heated cheeks. "I'm so embarrassed. I need to do laundry."

He reached for my hands. "For a doctor with your credentials, I'm certain you've been required to make a case for a thesis or dissertation and to defend that case to the committee in a convincing manner."

I nodded.

"And I would assume you were kick-ass."

"I succeeded."

Kader's hand was again on my leg, inching upward over my thigh. His green orbs glowed with a new warmth rivaling the intensity of the sun. His head shook. "If your argument for laundry is that with access, you won't walk around here like you are now, with your bare pussy inches from my touch and your hardened nipples tenting the material of my shirt, your argument has failed."

Covering his hand, I smiled. "Thank you."

"For wanting to finger-fuck you right now, right here?"

Though I was smiling, my eyes filled with tears. "You

knew I was scared about what you might tell me. Thank you for distracting me."

"Is that what you think I was doing?"

I nodded as I entwined my fingers with his, moving his away from my leg. "I do. And you succeeded." I looked up to the screens. "Are you going to tell me what you've found?"

Taking a deep breath, Kader began typing, his actions pulling up the same surveillance I'd seen on the screens in the basement. "Right now, not much. It's two hours earlier here than in Indianapolis."

The clock in the kitchen had read a little after ten at night when I turned off the lights and headed this way.

He looked up. "I did confirm that during the conversation where Olsen was defending you and Cartwright, he was speaking to Oaks."

Did it make me happy or sad that Eric believed in us?

For the next undetermined amount of time, Kader ran footage at a faster than normal speed. He started with today's and then yesterday's, making his way back in time. It was as if we were watching movies in fast-forward. The human mind was a fast learner. It didn't take much time before I was viewing the sped-up feeds as if they were in real time. He only slowed the feeds when someone would come and go.

It was as we were watching footage from my kitchen that I gasped, and new tears filled my eyes.

"Slow it down," I cried. "What is the time stamp?"

The feed paused, yesterday's date and 4:15 P.M. became

visible in the corner. On the screen was a policewoman in uniform entering my house.

"Laurel, I haven't seen this footage. I think that I should watch it first."

Though my heart was beating wildly within my chest, my fingers blanched as I held tightly to the chair, and I'd now scooted to the edge of the seat. I shook my head. "No. I want to see."

The feed began moving in slower than normal speed. The woman in uniform walked about my kitchen as the door opened and a man in a suit entered. She stepped back, allowing him to take the lead.

"Who is that?" I asked.

"I'll run facial recognition, but I'd assume an IMPD detective. They aren't going to send a patrol officer in alone. I'm surprised they didn't send a forensic team." He shrugged. "Maybe they did Wednesday night."

With my lip snagged between my teeth, I watched, enthralled by what I was seeing. They spent a few minutes in the kitchen. And then the man led as they both disappeared from the kitchen, heading the direction of my living room.

"Do you have other cameras?"

Kader typed as the screen before us subdivided. My living room, bedroom, and spare bedroom came into view. The policewoman was walking up the stairs while the man was already in my bedroom.

"I thought the cameras at my house had been disabled," I said, recalling when they went black.

"I put in more when I went back to..." Kader didn't finish the sentence.

"What do you think this means?" I asked as the two moved about the rooms.

"Based on an earlier news app I'd seen before you came in here, you and Cartwright have been reported missing. You're both nondisabled adults. The police don't usually investigate adult disappearances during the first forty-eight hours. You were last seen on Monday. The news didn't mention you being at the university in the middle of the night. I'd disabled the cameras out on the loading dock. That means that whoever was taking you or wanted you got rid of the footage from the front lobby as well as the elevator." He tilted his head toward the screen. "This was recorded on Thursday. The timeline fits."

A surreal feeling washed over me as we sat watching someone I didn't know go through my house.

Kader and I sat in silence as each room was checked and they descended the stairs going back to the kitchen.

"Can you imagine..." I stopped, trying to swallow my grief and tears. Reaching out, I laid my hand on Kader's arm.

When he looked my way, he silently covered my hand with his.

"...if they would have found...him..." I looked down.

"They didn't. They won't."

"I'm not sure if I ever said thank you."

"You did," he said.

Movement on the screen refocused my attention beyond Kader's handsome face.

The policewoman and gentleman exited; however, they didn't stay gone for long. The door opened again. My heart soared as I jumped from the chair and stifled a gasp.

"Oh my God. It's my parents."

KADER

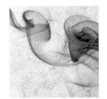

I wasn't certain at what point it happened. My memory blurred. No one's anguish affected me. I'd watched men die from a distance. I'd also been close enough to feel their last breaths and hear the crackling of the vertebrae as I snapped their necks, severing the vital nerves. Respiratory arrest was immediate; cardiac took longer. During those instances, I had even allowed the beneficiaries of my services to see me.

There was satisfaction in a job well done. To view the expression of an assignment during his last seconds of life, watching the change in his expression as the realization of imminent death settles over him was a show unlike any other. In many instances, I wanted that person to see me, to then enter the gates of hell with the knowledge that I was the one who delivered to them their destiny.

Mindless pleas spoken by a sentenced assignment—a man or more rarely a woman—never mattered to me. I was deaf to them. To be honest, they bored me. Those that haven't witnessed what I have often harbor preconceived notions about the fortitude of powerful businessmen, entrepreneurs, or even hard-core criminals. It was a general belief that the more powerful that individuals were, the more dignified a manner in which they'd face death. I could testify that in most cases that belief was untrue.

None were above pleading for their lives. The bigger the assignment, the more they possessed to offer.

Fortune.

Power.

Women—even their own daughters.

There was nothing a man or woman wouldn't put forward in exchange for that next breath.

Those promises and pleas never affected me. Those people had nothing I wanted. It was the opposite. Taking their lives meant fortifying my reputation.

Somehow with Laurel, all of that had changed.

The sight of Laurel's anguish as she watched her parents overwhelmed me in an unfamiliar way. Moved to action, I'd offered to turn off the feed, to watch it by myself and tell her what happened, or to watch without sound. Every offer was met by a shake of her head until there was nothing left to do but watch with her.

Her eyes grew red and puffy as she struggled to breathe.

Helplessness was also foreign to me.

Not certain what to do, I offered her my hand. "Come here." She wasn't far away; nevertheless, any distance was too far.

Laurel didn't move as her grip of the chair's arms tightened.

Perhaps it wasn't her decision to remain still. I would ascertain that at that moment she couldn't move. Laurel was paralyzed by the scene unfolding: her parents wandering her house, accompanied by the detective, the policewoman, and Laurel's assistant. Mrs. Carlson's tears and Mr. Carlson's constant questions filled our ears.

"I don't understand," her mother repeatedly said between bouts of crying. "You think she left?"

"Why would she leave? You have to find her," her father pleaded with the detective.

I stood, momentarily blocking the screen. If Laurel wasn't going to come to me, I was going to bring her to me. Bending down, I scooped Laurel from the chair. She didn't protest or object. Her slack body fell against me as her dampened blue eyes vied between the screen and me.

"I-I want to watch," she managed to whisper.

"We won't leave."

I'd carried Laurel before, when she was unconscious, but this was different. As I sat back in my chair, her trembling body in my lap and bare legs over mine, Laurel curled farther into my grasp, settling her head against my chest.

My mind filled with questions.

When had her parents been contacted?

Who had contacted them?

Why would they allow so much traffic within her house?

Had they decided it wasn't a crime scene?

And then as the five people left her home, the tugging in my chest accompanied by the way Laurel's hands fisted my shirt—holding on for life—I knew my questions could wait.

My lips brushed the top of her head. "Let's take you upstairs."

She nodded.

"Can you walk?"

Instead of answering my question, Laurel began speaking about what we'd seen and heard. "This isn't me." She pointed at the screen as her volume rose. "*That* isn't me. I wouldn't leave like that. They..." She gasped for air between words of her tearstained declaration. "...did you hear what they said? They think Russ and I took off—left. They're accusing us of stealing the university's research." She turned in my lap and faced me. "Kader, my reputation...my research and published papers are respected worldwide. Were. This..." She gestured about. "...has taken everything from me, *everything*." She elongated the repeated pronoun, turning back to the now-dark screen with a sigh. "And my parents are being told...lies." Swallowing, she turned back to me and acknowledged my earlier question. "Yes, I can walk."

Pushing away, Laurel moved her feet to the floor, her bare ass squirming in my lap.

Fuck, it was totally inappropriate to get hard at this moment.

My mind knew that.

When it came to Laurel, my dick and mind weren't on speaking terms. At the moment, the denim of my blue jeans was the only thing keeping my growing rod from her pussy.

How much pressure could a zipper take?

I stood beside her, needing to adjust myself before the zipper's teeth lost the war.

Laurel looked up at me. "I don't want a new life. I want you to help me save mine." Her neck straightened as she pivoted and walked toward the doorway. At the last second she turned back to me. "Or I'll do it myself."

In one stride I was before her. "What do you think you are going to do?"

"Where's my phone?"

Without verbally answering, I shook my head as my jaw clenched.

Laurel pointed back at the screens. "Were those real police? Are my parents and Stephanie in danger? How is Stephanie back at the university when she said she received the same call as I had?" Her hands cupped her cheeks. "Oh, Kader, you said the only way my parents would know about me was if they were in contact with the person who hired you. Now they're in danger."

New tears filled her eyes.

I reached for her shoulders. "I said the only way your parents would know you were *dead* was if the person who hired me was in contact with them. You heard what they said on that recording. They don't know you're dead. They only know that you're missing. Anyone could make that assumption. You haven't been to work since Monday. You haven't been to your house. Your car is in the driveway. They know you are *missing*."

Laurel nodded and taking a step out of my grasp, walked away. Instead of heading toward the stairs, she turned back to the kitchen. Pushing a panel of switches, she bathed the room in light.

"What are you doing?" I asked. "It's late. You need sleep."

"It was your idea," she said, going to the bottle of wine sitting on the counter. We'd each had a glass with dinner. Now there was a stopper plugging the neck of a half-full bottle. "Where are the glasses?"

Without speaking, I opened the correct cabinet and removed two wine glasses.

Her blue eyes shone upward through veiled lashes. "I wasn't planning on sharing."

I cocked my head to the side. "It's *my* wine."

Pulling the stopper, Laurel poured the remaining wine into the two glasses, filling them to nearly the rim. "I'm not a big drinker, but I guess that doesn't matter."

With the stem of a glass in her grasp, she turned and walked toward the windows.

Her shoulders hunched forward and face fell forward. Though her back was to me, the windows were now a mirror. In the reflection her forehead furrowed and eyelids fluttered. Finally, with a deep breath she straightened her neck and lifted the glass rim to her lips and drank.

Laurel spun my direction with new determination in her tone. "You know what else I'm not?" She didn't wait for me to answer. "I'm also not someone who cries hysterically, hides from problems, steals the university's property, abandons my friends and family, or runs away with a man she barely knows." After shaking her head, she took a bigger gulp. "I quit. I can't do this. You said you stepped in to save me. Don't. It would be easier if you completed the task that you were hired to do. That way, I wouldn't have to witness..." She let out a breath. "...all of this."

I shook my head. "No, Laurel." After placing my untouched glass of wine on the counter, I stepped to her, removed the glass from her hand, and set it on the nearby table. Wrapping my arms around her waist, I pulled her closer until her chin rose and her blue eyes were staring up at me.

"I wasn't done with that," she said.

"Dr. Laurel Carlson, I know something else that you are *not*. You are not a quitter. There's no way in this fucking world you would quit. With your formula, did you quit?"

She shrugged. "I guess I have now."

"You haven't. The research and development is on those flash drives. The flash drives are in my office. You didn't quit. You're taking a break."

Her forehead fell to my chest and I brought her closer. "I'm taking you upstairs to sleep."

"Kader..."

I'd taken a step back and reached for her hand. As our fingers intertwined, I asked, "What?"

"Tell me that it will be all right."

"I'll tell you that we will do our fucking best to make it right."

Laurel didn't argue or ask for more promises I couldn't guarantee. She didn't say a word until we reached the landing at the top of the stairs.

"Something else I'm not is needy." Her head shook. "I doubt you believe that, but it's the truth."

"These are not normal circumstances."

"Will you..." Her beautiful blue eyes had dried and were searching mine.

"What, Laurel?"

"I don't want to be alone."

LAUREL

"I'll stay with you—"

"...until I fall asleep?" I asked, finishing Kader's sentence.

"No, until I wake up. Give me ten minutes and I'll be in your room."

I nodded and continued down the hallway. An odd sensation came over me with each step. In the presence of a man who'd been hired to kill me and who I'd recently asked to carry out the job, I felt safe. It was more than the knowledge that his home was isolated—because that should be a warning—or that the house was technologically advanced. It was a sense that I was meant to be here with him.

I couldn't explain this predicament to myself much less someone else although I'd like to try. I'd do anything to call my parents and tell them the information was wrong. I hadn't run off with Russ, stealing the research and development. I had disappeared because after seeing Russ dead, I feared for my own life. I would tell them that despite all of that, I am safe.

With my hair brushed, face washed, and teeth brushed, I stared into the mirror. The reflection didn't look different. It rarely did. One doesn't see oneself age. It happens too slowly. Yes, there were good hair days and bad, makeup and no makeup, clothes that flatter and others that don't. Those superficial qualities mean less when faced with life or death.

I'd lost it earlier.

I wasn't proud of that behavior, but I was ready to move on, to continue to put the pieces together and find a way to live, to work, and maybe one day to love.

The opening of my bedroom door drew me from the bathroom. Stepping into the expanse of the bedroom, a smile came to my face as I scanned the man standing before me. He'd done the same as I had and readied himself for sleep. Instead of his normal blue jeans, Kader was wearing the soft pajama pants—similar to the ones he'd worn in the basement—a long sleeved t-shirt, and socks.

Why was he wearing socks?

When our eyes met, I asked, "Are there tattoos on your feet?"

Kader shook his head. "Stop. Remember, that subject is off-limits."

"You can't blame me for being curious."

He came closer, lifting a lock of my recently brushed hair.

After wrapping it around his finger and letting it go, he said, "I can." His head shook. "But I doubt it will stop you."

My only response was another smile or perhaps the one I'd had simply grew larger.

"It's late," he said. "I haven't slept in a while. I promise that while you're in this house, you're safe."

"I was just thinking about that. Do you have the perimeter armed?"

He shrugged. "Something like that."

"If I opened a door to the outside, would I set off alarms?"

"Internal. Let's just say, I'd know."

I wasn't certain what it was, but even in my state of exhaustion, I was drawn to him with a need to be even closer as if there were an invisible connection. I wanted more. I lifted my hand to his chest. "Thank you for not leaving me alone."

"I can't promise to be a gentleman." His lips quirked. "I can more likely promise that I won't be one."

Reaching higher, I cupped his cheeks with the palms of my hands. In the last few hours a tiny bit of stubble had grown. The prickly sensation tingled from my palm to my core. "I had no expectations when I asked you to come in here. You must be exhausted. I asked you to be here because even though this house is safe, being near you fills a hole that the loss of my..." I sighed. "...*everything* created."

Kader took a step back as his gaze did a sweep of my body. "Tell me, Laurel, are you planning to sleep as you were when I woke you?"

"I'd thought about one of your t-shirts."

Kader shook his head.

"I mean, it's soft and—"

He didn't let me finish. Reaching for the buttons on his shirt currently covering me, his lips found my neck. "The basement was dark." His words came between kisses. "I felt your soft skin and sexy curves." With the top few buttons undone, his lips moved downward to my collarbone, chest, and lower.

My eyes closed and a moan escaped my lips as he nipped my now-hardened nipple, one and then the other. Teeth, tongue, and then he'd suck. I squirmed in his hold at his unrivaled use of both ecstasy and torture.

"And I saw these gorgeous tits in your bedroom, but tonight..."

I reached for his head, unsteady on my feet, and weaved my fingers through his recently untethered hair. Kader's mane was untamed, much like the beast before me. There was nothing else I could do. Our roles were defined—as if before we'd met.

He was the beast and I was his prey.

Kader took a step back, the loss of his warmth causing my eyes to open. Though I wanted to protest, to say he'd said I could touch him, the growing cock beneath the soft pants reassured me that my fears of being rebuked were unfounded. "Kader?"

"I want to see you—all of you."

"Will you let me—?"

His finger came to my lips. "Don't. This isn't a quid pro quo."

Power and control deepened his timbre, sending jolts of energy and warmth through my bloodstream, settling between my legs.

"Do this for me. Show me your fucking gorgeous body, all of you."

He ran his finger over my cheek. Its touch, now heated, left a trail of ashes as if his coarse fingertip was steel and my skin flint. Striking them together had me ready to ignite.

"Don't expect life to be fair," he said. "It's not. Show me what I saw before dinner. Unbutton my shirt."

My lower lip slipped below my teeth while my hands moved to undo the buttons. Desire and command created an intoxicating concoction that forbade me from refusing his demand. With my heart beating faster and lashes lowered, I gazed down at the small buttons and slowly slid one through the opening. When I looked up, the fire from earlier was no longer contained to his fingertips; green flames burnt within his eyes.

"Another one," he ordered.

With my fingers now trembling, I did as he said, looking up to him as it slid free.

"Fucking keep going, Laurel." His deep voice was the growl of an animal about to break free.

I'd never stripped in front of a man. I mean, I'd taken off my clothes but not like this. With each button my skin warmed and nipples went from hard to diamonds. My circulation rerouted as my breasts grew heavy and my drenched core clenched.

Though I was obeying his commands, what I was doing was powerful in a way I'd never anticipated. Witnessing Kader's growing erection beneath his pants, the wanton desire in his eyes, and the deep reverberation of his tone had me electrified. I was doing this to him, affecting him, and the sense of influence was exhilarating.

It was as I reached the final button that he came closer, brushing the large shirt from my shoulders. Fluttering to the floor, the cotton puddled at my feet. His palm floated over my skin, a ghost of a touch, bringing the small hairs on my arms to attention.

"Fucking gorgeous."

My smile bloomed. Kader was doing it again, distracting me, and it was working. There was nothing I wanted to think about at this moment but him, us, now.

"Turn around," he said, the huskiness in his tone saturating the air around us. "I want to see every inch of you."

Doing as he said, I slowly turned. Once I was facing him again, a mere nod of his chin told me he wanted me to do it again. With each spin my insides wound tighter and tighter until I was certain they may snap under the strain.

Finally, I stepped toward him, inhaling the fresh scent of bodywash and the richness of his cologne. With my hand on his shoulder, I reached upward, straining my toes and neck until my lips met his.

A transformer blowing.

Lightning striking.

A cosmic boom.

Kader's strong arms surrounded me as our lips continued their battle. One of his hands moved higher, his fingers fisting my hair, pulling me closer and bruising my lips. My tongue was the first to seek entrance and his followed. Our moans of pleasure and promise echoed about the room, bouncing off the large windows and filling our ears.

Still holding on to one of his broad shoulders, with my other hand I reached lower, finding the waist of his pants. Slipping my fingers beneath the elastic band and under the soft fabric, I grasped his hard cock. The velvety surface of stretched skin was a drastic contrast to the rigidity of his shaft. Surrounding it as best I could, I squeezed tighter, all the while moving my hand up and down.

"Fuck," Kader groaned as the strain on my scalp increased.

A whimper bubbled in my throat as he continued to wind his fingers, pulling my hair harder and keeping my face tilted upward. Our kiss grew heated, a battle for domination. My grasp moved faster, my thumb occasionally sliding over the moist tip.

All at once, Kader reached for my hand, pulling it away as he took a step back.

When our gazes met, I couldn't read his thoughts.

There were too many emotions swirling in the depths of his green eyes.

Pain.

Pleasure.

Desire.

Anger.

The seams of his shirt strained beneath his chest as our heavy breathing filled my ears.

"Did...I do something wrong?"

He didn't answer, stepping past me.

I spun, following his movements with my eyes. Crushing disappointment descended as I anticipated him leaving, going to his own room, and not fulfilling his promise to stay with me.

The room went dark as he hit the switch near the door. With only the illumination from the reflective snow beyond the windows, I watched his darkened silhouette, waiting for the door to open and close. Instead, he turned and came back until he was before me. Although I couldn't see clearly, I was certain his cock was no longer contained.

With one swift move from him, I was falling, my hands before me landing upon the mattress. Holding my ass, his foot tapped my ankles, encouraging my stance to widen.

"Oh," I panted as his fingers found my entrance.

"You are fucking soaked."

"I-I want you."

One hand masterfully taunted my breasts while the other stayed at my core. His mastery was beyond my comprehension as if he knew my body better than I, fulfilling desires I never knew existed.

While words were beyond my ability, Kader continued to speak, his deep tenor ringing in my ears as his warm breath skirted my skin. Repeatedly he questioned, the inquiries followed by declarations of admiration.

"What are you doing to me? You're like a fucking drug and I'm an addict. I can't get enough of you."

A flick of my clit and my body stilled. The taunting had been too much, the pressure building too high. I was ready to implode. "I-I"

Kader's hands stopped what they'd been doing as his fingers again splayed over my hips. My forehead fell to the mattress, my back arched, and my cry filled the air. Primal and needy, the depth and power of his invasion stunned me. For a moment he remained unmoving with his grasp of my hips growing tighter.

"Laurel, you can take me."

It wasn't a question but another command.

"I belong in your pussy."

I nodded.

"Say it."

My eyes closed as I worked to relax my core's defensive reaction. "I can. I want you where you are."

Though his grip continued to intensify, his rhythm began slowly. With each thrust the pleasure built. My fingers clawed at the blankets below me as I struggled to stay earthbound. My lungs fought for air as my breathing grew shallower. I was back at the edge of the ravine and in a few moments, I would fall to the river below. My toes curled as words I didn't comprehend spilled from my lips.

And then he was gone. Before I could ascertain what had

happened, I was flipped to my back, my ass on the edge of the bed and knees lifted. In the dimness of the room I looked up to his gaze.

"Put your arms around my neck, Laurel. I want you to touch me."

Sitting upward and ignoring the growing lump in my throat, I did as he said. My arms reached over his broad shoulders, my fingers grasping behind his neck. My eyes closed and head fell back as we were once again one. Threading my fingers in his hair, I lifted myself farther and brought my lips to his. Splaying his fingers under my ass, he lifted me higher, creating the perfect friction.

It was almost too much stimulation, the fullness and friction, the touch of his skin and my fingers in his hair, and the beating of hearts in unison as we created a chorus of sounds.

As the cliff reappeared, I held tighter to his shoulders. My muscles grew taut as did those beneath the shirt. Kader's roar was the bass to my mezzo-soprano. Together we were the music behind the fireworks finale. It wasn't until the air settled and we were both lying in bed that Kader declared my destiny.

My eyes had grown heavy and his breathing steady. His words were the last I heard before falling into a restless sleep.

Had I heard them or were they a dream?

Was their meaning a dream come true or the end of everything I knew?

"I'm no fucking good for you. You're too good for me. None of it matters. I'm not letting you go. You're mine."

LAUREL

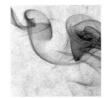

*W*aking to the glow of sunshine streaming through the windows and empty bed beside me wasn't a surprise. What had surprised me was when I'd wakened during the night, Kader had still been with me, beside me, and even reaching out to me. One time, the warmth of his body was curled behind me and his strong arm over me.

Each time his words came back to me.

I'm not letting you go. You're mine.

There was an eerie finality about them.

Now as I stood under the warm spray of the shower, I contemplated their meaning, much as I'd done throughout the night. It wasn't only their meaning but the man who'd spoken them. In my limited experience, Kader was a man of few words, yet the ones he spoke, he meant. He didn't waver and—by his own proclamation—had never lied. The words he spoke, he meant and fully believed.

As I washed my hair and the glass stall filled with a sweet-scented steam, I recalled when Kader told me that we were leaving the basement. I'd argued and still, here we were, no longer in Indianapolis but in Montana. His stance of never negotiating was as much a part of him as curiosity was a part of me.

Russ and I used to discuss the differences in different subjects' reactions to our compound. We hadn't determined how to respond to the discrepancies—we'd assumed we had time. However, in our limited clinical trials, we'd come to the conclusion that no two people would react exactly the same. We needed to broaden our observations and results because simply put, all people were hardwired differently.

The everyday term became our personal joke as participants were attached to sensors with literal wires recording physiological responses to stimuli.

Kader was hardwired to mean what he said and only say what he meant.

Could a passion-filled situation cause him to speak emotionally instead of intellectually?

For most people, I would have answered yes.

Kader wasn't most people.

After I'd readied myself for whatever the day would bring, I donned the fresh button-down shirt I'd found lying on the chaise by the windows and gathered my dirty clothes. Leaving them in the bedroom in a pile, I stepped into the hallway, determined to accomplish two goals. First, I wanted to learn exactly what Kader had meant and second, to find the laundry room.

My bare feet stilled at the top of the stairs, my attention focused on the large window above the front doors. The snow had stopped falling after covering the world in a fresh blanket of white. The mountains in the distance were dark, their peaks topped with snow. With all of that, it was the sky that had me entranced, bright and blue and seemingly going on forever.

Turning back, I took in the number of closed doors and reasoned that it would make sense with this large of a house for the laundry room to be on the second floor. My lip momentarily disappeared behind my teeth as memories of being caught in Kader's bedroom came back to me. And then I recalled that the only areas he'd deemed as off-limits were his bedroom and office.

In less than twenty-four hours, those were two of the rooms I had entered.

Avoiding Kader's room, I stopped at the door closest to it. Turning the knob, I pushed the door inward. It wasn't much unlike the room where we'd slept, the one he'd declared mine. The only noticeable difference was that the windows held a different view. This morning, I'd stood at the window in my room, taking in the raw beauty of the ravine, the plains beyond, the mountains in the distance, and the brightening sun.

Truly it was spectacular.

I went to another door across the hallway and peered inside. Back to the other side, I opened another. They were all similar.

Why would a man who was a self-proclaimed recluse have so many furnished bedrooms?

Back to the landing and beyond Kader's bedroom there was a second hallway, one not as long as the one leading to my room. The first door I opened was a bathroom, nearly as big as the one attached to my suite. It was at the final door where I found what I'd sought.

In the grand scheme of life, it seemed odd to be excited about the sheer discovery of a laundry room, yet I was.

Hurrying back to my bedroom, I gathered my dirty clothes and rushed back to the newly found location.

As I turned the corner, I stopped.

It wasn't that I stopped. I was stopped.

I collided head-on with a very tall, solid-chested, and wide-shouldered roadblock.

"Have you enjoyed your tour?"

Gripping the clothes in my grasp tighter, I pressed my lips together. "Did your house tell on me, again?"

"Yes."

"You said it was only your bedroom and your office—"

Kader reached for the clothes and took them from my arms. "I also said your argument was faulty."

"Give those back."

"What if I said I'm satisfied with keeping you here as you are? I have an entire closet of shirts and my argument to keep only those laundered is better than your argument to launder these." He glanced down at the clothes he was now holding. "Yes, my plan is better. Each day you'll wake to what I allow you to wear."

"Are you crazy? It's freezing cold out there. I'm not spending another day without..." I huffed, slapping my now-empty hands on my thighs. "...underwear or pants or shirts or socks." I pursed my lips. "You wear socks to sleep."

He dropped the clothes at our feet and took a step toward me, his expression morphing into the man I'd first met—granite and hard as stone. "Tell me, Laurel, are you cold?"

I wasn't. That wasn't the point.

Stepping in time with one another, we continued until my heels came into contact with the wall behind me. "Kader, this is a ridiculous conversation. You can't keep me here, wearing your shirts and nothing else. It's kidnapping—captivity. Shit, it's like something from the news or a crazy novel."

His finger traced over my cheek, making my eyes close and breathing deepen. With a simple touch he incited reactions that should not occur outside the bedroom. Pressing myself against the wall, I backed up as far as I could go, attempting to keep my traitorous nipples away from his chest.

Kader's gaze lowered and stalled at the level of my breasts. "I guess you are cold."

My palms came to his chest, pushing him away. "You're being a jerk."

He seized my wrist as his tenor cooled with each word. "Be careful. That's not the way to speak to your kidnapper."

Before I could answer, he released my wrist and turned his attention to the first secured button on the shirt I was wearing. The cadence of his speech slowed. "Maybe this was my plan all along." He slid the button from its place. His large hand moved downward, reaching for the next. "I convinced you that there was danger." Another button. "I killed your lover." Another button. "I took you to him." Another button. "I showed you his body, knowing it would terrify you." The final button. "And I took you—in every sense of the word—because you're too fucking sexy. It wasn't a difficult decision to decide to keep you for myself." He pushed the shirt to my shoulders. "My own personal sex toy. Come on, Laurel, let's play."

Sex toy?

"Stop it." There was a cold, calculating edge to his tone that sent shivers down my spine. Possessive and threatening, the emotion it evoked was no longer desire.

Kader lifted one arm to the side of my face, caging me against the wall as my breathing accelerated, knees locked, and trembling fingers fisted. Looking up at him, my eyelids blinked rapidly and my lips opened, yet no other words came forward. This was insane.

Another nudge of the shirt with his long finger. One more and it would fall.

A brush of my shoulder caused me to stiffen as he teased the material.

Finding my ability to move, I yanked the shirt from his

grasp, gripping the cotton, I wrapped it around my body. "Why would you say that?"

"Maybe it's true."

"You said you wouldn't lie."

"Maybe I lied. Maybe I'm lying now. I think I'll fuck you and then we can decide."

This wasn't happening.

Not after last night.

My arms wrapped defensively around my midsection as fear snaked up my spine. Thoughts and scenes swirled through my mind, timelines and instances. I shook my head. "No, you're lying now. What you said isn't true. I don't know why, but you're doing that thing, that thing where you try to scare me. That's what this is about."

He stood taller, letting go of the wall. "Go downstairs and eat. I'll take care of your clothes."

"I can do my own laundry."

"You aren't paying attention." His words slowed. "Let me make it clear. I don't plan on washing your clothes. I said I'd take care of them. My plan is to destroy them." He shrugged. "Incinerate. Evidence, you know." His voice held the same control and domination as last night, but the emotion was gone, leaving a cold, callous replacement.

My hands balled to fists as they came to my hips. My muscle control was back and so was my ire. Straightening my shoulders and neck, I stared Kader in his now-chilling green eyes. "I don't believe you."

His chiseled jaw jutted forward. "What is the first thing they tell you in self-defense classes?"

It seemed like an odd question. "I-I don't know. Kick them in the balls."

"Did you know that women are instrumental in ten percent of all kidnappings? Often they help lure the victim. More importantly, no balls to kick."

I stared dumbfounded, unsure of what answer he wanted or expected.

Kader went on, "No, Laurel. The first thing they tell you to do is to never leave with a kidnapper. Never get relocated to a second location." He gestured toward the window. "Look where you are. I can do whatever I want. You could fight me. You could scream. You could run. Without shoes or a coat, you'd freeze before noon. Even if I kept you here into the summer, you wouldn't make it to civilization. Well, unless you have mad survival skills I'm unaware you possess. If the bears or lynx don't find you, there's always the rattlesnakes.

"Let's say you make it past those. The second highest animal-related cause of death in this state is insects: wasps, bees, and hornets." He straightened his lips for a few moments. "Now, that is a thought. Once I'm done with you— finished with my toy—I might enjoy watching how long you'd survive.

"Most likely the big game won't cause your death. They will, however, service in your disposal—at first. Then the birds will take over before the insects. It's a rather tidy system Mother Nature has working in the wild. Just like the clothes, by the time those creatures are done, nothing will be left to identify."

I couldn't comprehend his cruel, unveiled threats.

Images of each danger flashed through my mind.

Hypothermia.

Mauling.

A snake's fangs.

The sting of insects.

Lost in the wilderness.

Remains.

Memories of cadavers in biology courses throughout my education added to the horror his words conjured.

Kader reached again for my hair, a stray lock between his fingers.

Flinching, I batted his hand away. "Stop it."

A new thought came to my scrambled mind as I pushed potential causes of my demise away and recalled the surveillance of my kitchen. "I don't know what you think you're doing, why you're being an ass, but you didn't kill Russ. He entered my house with a second person. I saw him with my own eyes. It was in real time." Though tears threatened, I refused to give in. "You were with me. You didn't do it."

"I kill people. It's what I do."

"Fine. That's what you do. I'm not sure what lures a person into your line of work, but I'd suspect that the people you...do that to—"

"Kill," Kader interrupted. "The word you're refusing to say is kill."

I inhaled and exhaled. "The people you *kill* are bad people."

"I was hired to kill you. Do you qualify as bad? Or maybe I was hired to kill Cartwright and decided to keep you in the process. You could consider yourself a bonus for a job well done."

"You didn't kill him." My voice grew higher, shriller. "You're not going to do any of those things to me that you said."

"I have you here in the middle of nowhere, wearing only my shirt."

Despite my obvious distress, his timbre remained cold.

"I fucked you in a dark basement. I took you again last night. I could do it again, right here, maybe your ass this time. I can only imagine how fucking tight that would be." He reached for my hand and pressed it over the top of his blue jeans. "Feel that? I'm getting hard even thinking about it." Releasing my hand, he again teased the edge of the shirt. "Go ahead, Laurel. Tell me again what I won't do."

My head was shaking as I used two hands to push against his solid chest. "Stop this. You're not scaring me." It was a lie. He was. "You can't keep me. I'm not a possession to be played with."

Taking a deep breath, Kader nodded before tilting his head toward the short hallway. "I'm glad you finally realize the truth. Don't fool yourself into a false sense of security. This isn't some fairy tale with a happy ending. We aren't fucking playing house.

"You're an assignment—a job. Nothing more. I can make big money with your research and development. I'm a businessman. I never said I was ethical. You will be leaving here as soon as possible. Behave, do as I say, when I say it, and your departure won't be out to Mother Nature." He took a step back, his gaze scanning from my head to my toes. "Button my shirt. Put your clothes in the washer. There's food downstairs in the kitchen. I expect you to eat. And then we have video surveillance to watch. Knock before entering my office. Today's top priority is your assistance in writing the notice announcing the sale of your research and development. It has to sound knowledgeable."

My head was spinning.

What the hell happened?

With Kader's list of decrees delivered, he took another step back. The spark from last night long extinguished, in its place was a green icy chill. "Just so we're clear, all of the rules are back in place. Stay out of my bedroom, touching me is prohibited, and enter my office only with my permission. Break even one of those and you won't have to wonder if I mean what I say. We're far from civilization. My options for punishment are vast."

The heaviness of his words fell over both of us, a black cloud obliterating any previous connection.

"Kader."

My single-worded plea hung unanswered in the air. He turned his back, displaying his ponytail, broad shoulders, and long, jean-covered legs. Without another word—or even so much as a glance my direction—Kader descended the stairs, leaving me more alone.

Maybe he'd lied.

Maybe he told the truth.

Which Kader was real?

Which one could I believe?

KADER

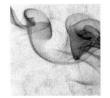

The pressure should have splintered my teeth. Second by second, I applied more and more until my jaw ached and my facial muscles grew taut. It wasn't only the information I'd learned—at least that wasn't the most prevalent cause of my distress. The internal battle within me showed no signs of ending anytime soon. My only hope was to do as I'd said—get Laurel the fuck away from me and end this assignment once and for all.

Regarding my assignment, the avalanche was still falling, one flake leading to another, burying me in information.

What was important?

What could I disregard?

There were a few newly discovered items that Laurel needed to know. The first was that her house was processed by an IMPD forensic team prior to her parents' arrival. That didn't fully answer my questions.

If a forensic team had already been there, dusted for prints, and searched for evidence, why would the detective and uniformed policewoman enter first? They should have known there was nothing present to surprise her parents.

The sweep had been done Thursday morning. That timing fit the forty-eight-hour window but barely.

What prompted the investigation?

Had the police received a call?

Was it a tip about Cartwright?

Had Laurel been set up?

Why didn't they find my cameras?

The answer to my last question was because I was fucking good at what I did. That led to the next question.

How had the person with Cartwright found them so quickly upon entry?

My setup had many different computers, networks, and VPNs. Currently on a different system, I had facial recognition running on both the detective and the officer. After what happened the night I saved Laurel from the university—with the fake policemen—I was beginning to wonder if the two accompanying the Drs. Carlson were truly IMPD.

Or maybe it was the forensic team that wasn't legitimate.

Besides the added pressure to my teeth and jaw, my current headache was exacerbated by the woman on the other screen high above my head. I had the house set for motion detection as well as one on her bedroom. That was how I'd been alerted to her fishing expedition for the laundry room. It was also how I knew that at this moment, she had a load of laundry running and one drying. She'd also gone down to the kitchen to find the food I'd left out for her on the island, had taken it back up to her room, and was currently sitting on the chaise in her room looking out the window. The fucking protein bar and yogurt were on a table beside her—unopened. The only thing she'd consumed were a few drinks from the water bottle.

Yes, I was aware that a protein bar, yogurt, and water did not constitute a breakfast of champions. I'd watched her morphing expression as she entered the otherwise empty kitchen, as well as the one from earlier on the landing when I'd walked away from her, the way her hands trembled as she slowly closed the buttons on my shirt. I'd zoomed in to see the tears descending her cheeks and the red blotches that climbed higher and higher up her neck as she stoically fought her myriad emotions, no doubt wondering what the fuck had happened.

The end justifies the means.

That was what they said—whoever the hell *they* were.

My goal was to save her. That meant she needed to get away from me. I was the last person in the world to be labeled a savior. I was the opposite and it was time she faced that— time I faced it.

It didn't matter. It was done. I couldn't go back, and I wouldn't admit that every fucking word out of my mouth this morning was laced with lies. Laced with—not outright lies. If she'd truly listened, Laurel would realize I'd spoken in general-izations, maybes, and perhaps.

Maybe I lied.

Maybe I'm lying now.

This was for the best. No matter how much it hurt, it would be for the best.

Once during the night, Laurel had stirred, sitting straight up. In her sleep, she'd called out for Cartwright. That didn't bother me. They had a history and what she'd seen could not be unseen.

What happened next was what bothered me. Laurel had been asleep with her subconscious speaking. Even in that state, when I reached out to her, when our hands touched, she sighed, lay back on her pillow, and said my name.

Not my given name—the one I'd been told. The name Laurel knew.

"Kader."

After that, it took me a while to fall back to sleep. My mind was a hurricane of thoughts. I'd fucked up the assign-ment. I had taken her from her life's work. I was the opposite of what she should have in her life. With a thousand strikes against me, while in a state of slumber, she'd found solace in my presence.

And then there was last night. I couldn't come up with an explanation for my behavior or reactions. It would be similar to a dieter devouring a chocolate cake. As the sweet aroma filled the air and the fork descended through the layers of icing and moist cake, there was elation. As the decadence

OBSESSED   147

landed upon the tongue and incited the taste buds, there was satisfaction. And yet, once it was over and the cake was consumed, the overpowering guilt brought on by self-indulgence was crushing. It wasn't only the cake but the loss of willpower, the loss of self-control.

Laurel was my downfall and it had to stop.

After her emotional breakdown at the sight of her parents, something came over me. Back in Indianapolis, I'd had an unfamiliar need to protect her. No...fuck. It started before that. It began the first time I saw her picture. And while at the time that instinct consumed me, urging me to learn more about this woman, it was nothing close to what came over me last night.

I would have killed for Laurel to bring her peace. The yearning to be close to her was like nothing I'd ever known. When she'd told me that she didn't want to be alone, I almost responded with the truth. I had already decided she wouldn't be.

Then after her midnight settling at my presence, when I woke beside her, the sun was just beginning to rise, casting reddened hues through the blinds we'd left open. I lay upon the bed and stared at the beautiful woman beside me, torn between wanting to wake her and fuck her to consciousness, or stay where I was, only to listen to the soft mews she made as she slept.

Watching her in the dawn's early light, my rational mind returned.

In what alternative universe had I been last night?

Dr. Laurel Carlson had a life, family, and friends. Even thinking for a moment that ripping her away from her life would result in her finding contentment in a man like me was laughable. From the moment our eyes met on the screen, she saw me differently than others did. I wasn't certain what that meant, only that for both of us, this charade had to end.

My decision to stop whatever it was that we shared was made as I eased out of her bed. It was time Laurel Carlson saw me for who I really was. I wouldn't show her the monster under the colors—not literally. However, I'd make damn sure she saw me.

Now, as I gaze up at the screen, seeing her uneaten break-fast, her arms crossed defensively over her breasts with a blanket over her legs, and the set expression devoid of emotion, I believed I'd succeeded. She'd never again be relieved or comforted by my presence. She'd never reach out to me for security.

It was better this way.

It was.

Then why did I want to go upstairs and tell her to eat?

Why did I long to see her stand, leave the blanket behind, and join me in this office?

Why was there a metaphoric hole in the middle of my chest that wasn't present before?

A ding came from one of my many computers.

Turning away from Laurel's barely moving screen, I searched for the source of the alarm.

Fuck.

The national headline scrolled over the bottom of one screen.

UNIVERSITY IN INDIANAPOLIS, INDIANA, HALTS RESEARCH PROJECT AS FBI JOINS INVESTIGATION INTO MISSING RESEARCHERS.

"Laurel, your little sulking session needs to wait," I said aloud though I knew she couldn't hear. "You're coming down here, now." I walked to the door. Opening it, I peered down the hallway toward the living room and the stairs beyond. "It's time to move on, Doc, walking or over my shoulder. I'll decide whose choice that is when I get upstairs."

MASON

Over seven years ago within a Chicago skyscraper

Sitting in Sparrow's private office, I sighed as I leaned back, brought my elbow to the arm of the comfortable chair, and rested my chin upon my fist. The elation I'd been holding back at finally beating him at chess was mounting inside of me. My grin grew as I watched my opponent. Sparrow was bent at the waist, leaning forward to study the board as if it was a military strategy—in a way it was.

We'd been playing this particular game going on three days now. Sparrow's lack of concentration was another clue that his winning streak was about to come to an end. My knight had his rook under attack. "Give it up," I teased. "You're not getting out of this."

Sparrow looked up, his dark eyes narrowing. "You've never beat me. It's not happening today."

I looked down at my watch. The time was nearly midnight. "Probably right. It will be tomorrow."

Without making a chess move he sat taller, stretching the muscles in his neck and back. "I knew it would be bloody, but fuck."

He wasn't talking about our game. He was talking about the takeover of the Sparrow organization.

I nodded.

It had been two weeks since Allister Sparrow had been found dead at a construction site. It had been a week since he was laid to rest.

Not all of the casualties occurred within the old guard. This hadn't been a simple revolution. The senior Sparrow's death and that of his right-hand man, Rudy Carlson, had been construed as an opening to take over dominance.

Every two-bit petty criminal in Chicago saw this change of leadership as an opportunity to assert control. Of course, there was the McFadden organization. Along with the Sparrows, the two had been the ultimate authorizers in this city.

Our new capos were scattered on many fronts. One of those fronts was working to bring the low-life, bottom-feeding dwellers in line. Gangs were attacking neighboring gangs. Self-proclaimed drug lords were knocking off runners and working to get a bigger piece of the pie. Until earlier this morning, all four of us, Sparrow, Reid, Patrick, and I had been out on the street—in the shadows. It was a huge risk.

Nothing could happen to Sparrow. If it did, the whole city would implode.

One of our biggest oppositions came from the participants in Allister's sex-and-exploitation ring.

As his first decree, the new king, Sterling Sparrow, shut the ring down.

Period.

Lights out.

Closed for business.

It was a bomb drop—an ATBIP, the father of all bombs.

The destruction wasn't limited to those participants in Chicago. Repercussions were occurring throughout the world. It would take a strong stand to stay diligent. We all knew that.

It hadn't just been the customers who were angered by the sudden change. There was a long line of supply and demand, traffickers who wanted payment for their shipments, as well as the sellers. There were two different levels of sellers, those that delivered the kids to the organization and those whose job it was to sell the kids who were no longer profitable to the ring. Once a kid had been deemed less useful—used up— Allister and his men wouldn't release or even kill them. They couldn't take the chance of discovery that could have come with either option.

Instead, there was a secondary market for permanent sales. The best way to guarantee that the merchandise would not alert anyone to their fate was to sell them off overseas. My expertise in linguistics aided in finding many of the prominent buyers. Of course, the kids weren't sold directly to individuals, but to other organizations.

Every stop on the supply chain was pissed about Sparrow's stand.

The shock waves were rumbling around the world. India was one of the biggest markets with multiple sales routes. It wasn't alone. The oil-rich countries of Saudi Arabia, Yemen, and Kuwait paid handsomely for girls, especially if they were too young to menstruate. South America contained other prominent selling opportunities in countries such as Venezuela.

According to some of the shit we found in Allister's office, for the right price his men would bypass the local sites, keep some of the kids away from the local ring, and sell directly overseas upon acquisition.

We'd hoped there would be names, a system to follow to learn who each individual was and determine that child's destination. Patrick had gathered a lot of data from the National Center for Missing and Exploited Children.

So far, we'd come up empty.

The shitstains in Allister's operation numbered the children. The ledgers we found were sick as fuck, reminding me of what had been done in concentration camps during World War II.

To the Sparrow organization's credit—not that the old guard deserved any—at least they didn't tattoo the numbers on the kids' wrists.

For me, this quest began when I was eleven years old and my sister Missy disappeared. Though we'd made enormous strides, it seemed clear that there was little to no hope of learning her fate.

Had she been one of Sparrow's acquisitions?

All I knew was that one day she was part of us, the next she was gone.

While Missy began my desire to end this atrocity, with each new discovery, my desire grew deeper. Viewing the sheer quantity of numbers and knowing that each one was a life, I often wished I could have been the one to take Allister down, literally.

Sparrow flexed his right hand, the golden crest ring sparkling under the lights of his private office. "I'm going out again tonight."

My head shook back and forth. "You can't. Word's out there. You were seen last night."

He stood and walked to the large desk and back.

That gigantic wooden antique monstrosity stuck out in this office like a sore thumb.

Sparrow didn't care. It was the principle of the matter.

Similar to the ring on his finger, the desk had belonged to Sparrow's father. Sterling's mantra that he wanted repeated on the streets of Chicago was that everything that had been Allister's was now controlled by Sterling Sparrow.

Everything.

There were no exceptions.

"It's my fight," he said.

I stood, meeting him nose to nose. "It's all of ours. We aren't doing this for you. We're one hundred percent behind this operation for the organization. It's your name. Let us take care of the heat."

"The capos—" he began.

"We vetted our men," I interrupted. "But they need to see us and they will. They need to see that we represent the new king. Reid, Patrick, and I represent *you*. Let us do that. If you're out there, we have another back to watch."

"I can watch my own back."

"But you won't. You'll be watching ours."

"Maybe that's what I want to do."

"No, man. Give it another twenty-four hours."

Sparrow shook his head. "I'm heading down to 2 to find out what's happening."

Our control center was on 2. Reid and Patrick were likely there or on 1 with the capos. Either way, we would get reports from the street before we stepped into the Chicago shadows.

I nodded toward the chessboard. "Calling uncle?"

"Fuck no," Sparrow said. "You're not going to win while my mind is on other things."

"Doesn't matter where your mind is, I'm going to win."

"In your dreams, Mason. Hasn't happened yet. Not happening."

Leaving his office on the first floor of Sparrow's apartment, we walked to the internal elevator. Once inside, Sparrow hit the number 2 and I hit the A. It was the level with the other apartments.

His dark gaze gave me a sideways glance.

"I'm going to check on her. Then I'll be down."

"We don't need distractions."

Inhaling, I let the breath out slowly. "She's my sister, not a distraction."

The flattening of his lips silently reiterated his displeasure about my bringing my sister here. Strict rules had been established regarding the privacy and safety of our living arrangements. Visitors weren't part of the equation.

The thing was that my sister was fucking tough. Growing up as we had, she had to be. That didn't mean that I wanted her out in the world while this war was occurring. I'd lost one sister. I wasn't losing another.

The elevator stopped at A.

"Only be a few," I said.

Though Sparrow's expression had darkened and neck drawn taut, he didn't say another word about my reason for being delayed. Instead, he said, "Hurry. We need you."

As the doors to the elevator closed, I entered the common area between the three apartments. It was a large hallway space and looked like a fucking hotel with sofas and shit. The area, stupid and wasted space, was bigger than the apartments where I grew up. Patrick, Reid, and I each had our own apartments with living rooms, bedrooms, and kitchens—apartment shit. If we wanted to hang out, we went into each other's space, or we all went up to Sparrow's. This little gathering space was for show, hidden in a secure tower where no one else would see it.

Opening the door to my apartment, I called her name.

No answer.

My steps quickened as I walked to the spare room where she had been staying.

Flipping the switch, I saw the bed was made and the room unoccupied.

What the fuck?

Where would she go?

I clenched my teeth as concerns bombarded my thoughts.

Damn her, I'd told her it was dangerous outside the apartment and forbid her from leaving. She's always been strong-willed. That was different than being stupid. My order hadn't been negotiable.

Reaching for my phone, I sent a text to Patrick, Reid, and Sparrow.

"MY SISTER ISN'T IN THE APARTMENT. WHAT THE FUCK? CHECK THE CAMERAS. I'M ON MY WAY TO 2."

She didn't have access to the garage or our command center. She could, however, get up to Sparrow's apartment. From there, she could have entered the public elevator. Not that it was really public, but I knew my sister. She could sweet-talk the guard with a flash of her smile and change to her voice. Those skills came in handy when she was surviving on the streets. As soon as I could, I started sending money home to her.

Our younger sister was gone. Our mother could rot in hell —maybe she was. Our fathers—make that sperm donors, plural—were gone before any of us were born. That left me, and I wasn't letting her down.

My heart pounded in my chest as my thoughts filled with the war happening on the streets. The four of us were known. That was why I didn't want her out and about. Sparrow had called her a distraction. She wasn't, but she sure has hell could be used as a liability, the perfect weapon to be used against me.

If some two-bit wannabe found her, I'll fucking rip his beating heart from his chest.

Passing my hand over the sensor of the elevator, I waited. As I did, a door opened behind me.

"Mason." Reid's deep voice prompted me to turn.

My eyes went from his wide stance and dark eyes to the woman standing beside him. Her red hair was mussed, lips puffy, and blouse crooked.

"Mason, Reid got your text," she said. "I'm good. Didn't mean to worry you."

Her words were barely audible as blood rushed through my veins. I was no longer looking at my sister but at the man at her side.

My friend.

My confidant.

The man who'd had my back.

With red blurring my vision, I rushed toward Reid, my hands balled into fists and arms ready to swing. "You fucking dick. What the hell are you doing with my sister?"

LAUREL

Present Day

*W*rapped in a blanket, I waited on my laundry. The first load was in the clothes dryer with the second load washing. Kader's orders for my appearance in his office could wait. I had no intention of leaving this floor again until I could do so fully clothed. That predicament left me alone, staring out the large windows with my thoughts, currently, not a good place to be.

The sunshine glistening upon the fallen snow no longer displayed its splendor. The crystal sapphire sky lost its appeal. The river at the basin of the ravine was now infested with rattle snakes and insects waiting for the spring thaw to increase their activity and sink their fangs into the nearest prey.

Kader's performance hadn't ripped off my rose-colored glasses; it had shattered them, the heel of his boot grinding the shards into the hard floor until they were beyond repair. Peering out of the large windows, now I saw the reality beyond the panes: freezing temperatures, potential hypothermia, and probable dangers at every turn. The view wasn't the only thing he'd spoiled with his performance.

Everything associated with him was tainted.

I tried to rationalize that Kader had lied to scare me. But how does one rationalize lying from a man who claimed not to lie? Why after what he'd said last night had he pushed me away? I hadn't been the one to make the binding statement of staying. It had been he who'd claimed he wouldn't let me go.

I'd been replaying that scene as well as every moment since our first meeting, on repeat in my head. Like snippets of film by a cinematographer, I'd dissected and critiqued each frame. The result was a headache. The conclusion was that I couldn't be certain of anything.

After Kader had walked away, a part of me hoped that when I went downstairs to the kitchen, we could try to discuss how he'd behaved and what he'd said. Perhaps it was my background in psychology that pushed me to seek understanding. That part of me was willing to listen—until I entered the kitchen. Finding a protein bar, yogurt, and water on the counter and Kader nowhere in sight was the final blow to his assault.

He's beaten me without throwing an actual punch.

It wasn't that I expected a champagne brunch. After what we'd shared and how he'd behaved last night, I simply expected *something*. Instead, I was down for the count.

The door behind me rattled. With a gasp I pulled the blanket defensively higher, covering his shirt I was still wearing, as the sound of the opening door amplified like fingernails on a chalkboard. I wasn't certain of his aversion to locks, but like the bathroom in the basement, this bedroom was without one.

Although I'd heard Kader enter, besides lifting the blanket, I refused to turn, to see his hauntingly handsome face and associate that vision with his earlier cruel words.

"I told you to eat."

My gaze stayed fixed on the outside scene.

His steps neared. His voice came closer, deeper, his sentences more concise. "I also told you to come to my office. Apparently, my statement about disobeying went unheeded."

Clenching my teeth, my nostrils flared, yet I didn't move, didn't take my eyes away from the patch of trees in the distance. Conifers, I could hardly disassociate one with another, yet as I counted, I decided there were twenty-seven.

I decided to count them again.

One.

Two.

Three.

Four.

My count ended as Kader blocked the view, standing near

the end of the chaise. His chest and waist were before me as I stubbornly refused to look upward, not wanting to see the icy stare from this morning.

"Your pouting session has gone on too long," he said as the long legs before me bent.

The chaise moved as he sat, settling near my legs. My body stiffened, and yet I still didn't look up, didn't speak, not until his large hand came to rest on the blanket covering my lower leg.

"Don't touch me." My words were a growl coming from between my clenched teeth.

"That's not how that rule works."

I twisted my legs to the floor on the opposite side from where he sat. Standing, I wrapped the blanket tighter around me and began walking. "Fuck you."

The bathroom door was not far away, maybe ten or fifteen feet. I'd almost reached my temporary escape when his long fingers wrapped around my upper arm, yanking me to a stop.

"Stop it, Laurel. You're above petty behavior. We have work to do, and then you can get what you want—away from me."

I spun on my bare heels toward him, pulling myself free from his grasp. "Above?" I asked louder than I wanted. "No, Kader. Dr. Laurel Carlson was above petty behavior. She was renowned, respected, and had a life that kept her too busy to sit for hours staring out a window." I gestured toward the large panes. "Remember, that's not me any longer. I'm a thief, a runaway, and oh yes, a sex toy. So what is a bit of petty behavior over the cataclysmic change in my life? I'm not above pouting. Obviously, as you so eloquently pointed out to me this morning, I've reached an all-time low."

"If this were a contest for the most despicable bio, yours doesn't even come close."

As I looked up, I concentrated on his neck. His Adam's apple bobbed and the cords under his skin grew taut, protruding and pulsating.

"It's not a contest," I said, making myself look higher and meet his green gaze. "You wanted me to see you as a killer. Fine, that's what I see. That's what you do. You didn't kill Russell. I know that. So now you're a killer, a liar, and a kidnapper. I see it. That's what you wanted. You've got it. I hope you're happy."

His head shook. "Not even close."

"Good. That makes two of us."

"I want you downstairs in my office. We have—"

"Not until," I interrupted, "I have clothes to wear." Before he could speak, I added, "...clothes that don't include your shirts."

"I told you, I liked—"

"Go to hell. Get out of my bedroom and from now on the touching rule goes both ways. We can work together to get me my life back, and then you'll be happy and I'll be gone. Other than that, I'm done. I'm done with your DID—dissociative identity disorder."

He lifted his chin. "The great Dr. Carlson has made her

diagnosis. Too bad you're fucking wrong. And just so you know, as for hell, I've been there."

I scoffed. "My diagnosis has merit. You don't know why you named your house after a female. You don't know why you have furnished, decorated extra bedrooms. You keep yourself isolated. One minute you can be caring and comforting, the next you're a total asshole. Have you named your personalities as well as your house?"

"Stop it, Doc. You don't know what the fuck you're saying."

"And then there's the obsession with being touched. Did you know that in most cases of DID there was a traumatic or chronic event such as being abused repeatedly as a child? The young mind can't handle it, so it separates that trauma and compartmentalizes the fear and lack of control to a weaker personality, the one who endured the incident. Then the mind creates a stronger personality to protect the other. In most cases it's two or three different personalities with one in charge. That was part of our research. We wanted to separate the traumatic event, not by compartmentalizing a personality, but with our compound allowing the victim to live without the trauma the memory evoked.

"Was that it, Kader, were you abused as a child?"

The blanket fell to the ground as Kader's hands came to my shoulders, shoving me backward until my back was against the wall. He didn't let go. His fingers dug into the flesh below the cotton of his shirt as flames shot from his green stare. "I said to fucking stop analyzing me."

I should listen to his warnings. I should be terrified of his hold.

I wasn't.

I was energized, believing that I was on the road to learning more.

With this discussion, I'd melted the ice and now the fire was back in his green orbs. What I saw wasn't desire as I'd witnessed last night; nevertheless, it was emotion.

"It is nothing to be ashamed about," I said, ignoring the pain in my shoulders. "You have no control when you're a child."

His grip intensified.

"Is that why you want control now?" I wasn't doing this questioning by the textbook. My parents, as well as every other psychologist or psychiatrist, would probably ream me for my current approach. A therapist should never lead memories. Yet because of his expression, I couldn't stop.

"Laurel..." Kader stood straighter, loosened his grip, and took a step back. "...I heard the dryer. Change clothes and come downstairs."

"My dad," I said, grasping at straws. "...when I was a kid, used to volunteer."

Kader's hand ran over his hair. "Give it up."

"I was just a kid," I said, reaching for his hand, trying to keep him from leaving. "...but we would drive to different neighborhoods around the city, ones not like Wicker Park."

"Your dad took you slumming as a kid? Interesting parenting."

I shrugged. "I think it was a good thing. I saw life differently than many of my friends did. I even made friends I
never would have made. We went to after-school programs
and places like Boys and Girls Clubs." Since he hadn't taken it
back, I held Kader's hand between both of mine. "I didn't
learn in books about things that happened to other people. I
saw it. At the time I didn't understand the gravity of their
plights or..." I shook my head at the stowed memories. "...the
severity. I never imagined some of the situations, and my dad
didn't give me details. He respected the children's privacy and
encouraged them to talk and share. He didn't take me with
him to be traumatized. I was with him because I wanted
to be."

Kader's lips straightened. "I'm sure those kids were
thrilled to have a rich bitch grace them with their presence.
Did you go home and shower afterward?"

Dropping his hand, I swallowed as tears reappeared.
"No..." My shoulders slumped forward as I bent down to
retrieve the blanket. "...that wasn't... You know what? You're
probably right. I never saw myself that way. I saw myself as
their friend, maybe even more. They were always polite
around my dad and seemed happy when we arrived or if we
were there when they arrived, but maybe I was a joke to
them. It would explain why..." I blinked away the tears. "Go
downstairs. I'll get dressed and be down. The sooner we do
what needs to be done, the sooner you can be rid of me."

Kader turned to leave but stopped short of the door. He

didn't turn my way or look back my direction. "I don't think anything like that happened to me."

With that he picked up his pace and disappeared.

What did that mean—he didn't *think* it did? Could he have DID?

LAUREL

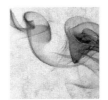

Stopping at the closed door to Kader's office, I knocked. As I waited for the royal decree bidding me entrance, I ran my palm over the denim of my blue jeans. They were covering my panties while the long-sleeved top I wore covered my bra. I looked down as I wiggled my sock-covered toes.

It wasn't as much anticipation pent up inside of me as it was the desire to get this over with.

"Who is it?" Kader's voice came from the other side of the door.

Was that an attempt at humor?

Sorry, dick. I wasn't smiling.

Instead of answering, I knocked again.

"Come in."

As it had the night before, the cold decor of his office hit me. Taking another step, I left the warmth of the hardwood floor and stepped upon the gray surface. Looking up, I noticed the large screens overhead were again dark.

"What did you turn off so I couldn't see?"

"You."

My chest inflated as I took a deep breath. "You were watching me?"

"It wasn't exactly spellbinding viewing. You don't move much when you sulk."

"In the bathroom...dressing?"

Kader shook his head. "No, Laurel. I know what you look like naked. I don't need that image on a recording. It's one I'll never forget."

Definitely DID.

Maybe I should name the different personalities so I could familiarize myself with each one I encountered. Or I could take a more clinical approach and number them. The mystery man set on doing his assignment who I met at the gathering could be number one. The protector who came to my house and wanted to save and later feed me would be number two. The man who talked seductively and delivered me to new sexual heights could be number three. And finally, number four was the threatening asshole from this morning.

Sitting in the chair beside Kader, I tilted my head, taking him in. I wondered on my new scale of one through four who I was seeing. I scanned his handsome features—his protruding forehead, high cheekbones, and chiseled chin now covered with the beard growth since last night. His arms and chest were covered by his long-sleeved shirt, the same one he'd been wearing this morning. The collar circled his thick neck, not allowing his colors to show. Like me, blue jeans covered his legs. On his feet he wore his customary black boots.

As his long fingers moved quickly and efficiently over the keyboard, Kader concentrated on the screens. His green eyes narrowed, producing small lines at their corners. His full lips straightened.

Which personality was he now?

Kader tipped his chin toward the screen.

I didn't look. Instead, I said, "I thought you were going to set me up with my own computer?"

"I've been busy."

"Watching me."

"Learning things," he replied. "First I want you to look at this news article."

Number one, I decided. Not my favorite, but a hell of a lot better than number four.

When I turned away from him toward the screen, the headline jumped out at me.

UNIVERSITY IN INDIANAPOLIS, INDIANA, HALTS RESEARCH PROJECT AS FBI JOINS INVESTIGATION INTO MISSING RESEARCHERS.

. . .

I rolled the chair closer as I read. With each word, my stomach twisted, and my current displeasure with Kader became less important. Pouting because he upset me was trivial compared with the reality that my life's work and reputation were being dismantled on a public forum.

The article didn't go into detail about our compound or our research and development. It concentrated more on me and Russell, discussing our administrative roles at the university. According to this publication, we'd orchestrated a recent gathering to bring attention to our work. Prominent attendees at that gathering were listed, many offering statements about the two of us.

There was one statement by Damien Sinclair of Sinclair Pharmaceuticals. "Drs. Carlson and Cartwright are true pioneers in their line of study. Sinclair Pharmaceuticals is still eager to work in conjunction with both of them and the university. This unfortunate development (the sudden disappearance of Dr. Carlson and Dr. Cartwright) will no doubt negatively impact the university for years to come. It's my hope that if the unspeakable has happened and Drs. Cartwright and Carlson are never located, we at Sinclair Pharmaceuticals can and are willing to assist the university with continuing what has been started. As we speak, negotiations with the university are underway. Without giving too much information, I believe we at Sinclair owe it to the people who Drs. Carlson and Cartwright's work will benefit to continue and fulfill their goal.

"I also hope that Drs. Carlson and Cartwright will return to join us in this endeavor."

I shook my head. With each word my life was slipping farther and farther away.

The article went on to give statements from Dean Oaks, Dean Olsen, Stephanie Moore, and Jennifer Skills, Russell's assistant. They all talked about our dedication and how worried they were about us. When asked if there was anything between Russell and myself beyond work, both deans denied any knowledge. Stephanie and Jennifer withheld their comments.

I stopped reading and turned to Kader. "Jennifer. I forgot about her when you asked who would have known enough to write that first email."

He nodded.

Near the end of the article was the mention of the FBI's involvement. While the bureau offered no official statement verifying or negating its role, there was a statement from the chief communications director of the Indianapolis Metro Police Department confirming that the department was not working alone and went on to urge anyone with any information as to our safety or whereabouts to contact the department immediately.

Once I was done, I leaned back in the chair and let out a long breath. There were too many emotions, thoughts, and questions to sort through. I wanted to move forward.

"You read it," I finally said to Kader, my statement wasn't formed as a question. "What do you think?"

"I wanted your thoughts first."

"It sounds like without saying the things my parents and Stephanie discussed in my house, this article is leaning the same way: Russell and I were involved beyond the scope of our work. Together, we drew attention to our research and development and then absconded with the data."

"Are," Kader corrected.

"Are what?"

"According to this article you two *are* involved beyond your work. That means they believe you both to be alive."

"Okay." I didn't want to think about Russ. "Moving on, I also think it's interesting that they quoted Sinclair. Eric told me that Sinclair asked Dean Oaks to attend the gathering, and then after it was over, the same night he was with Dean Oaks back at the university. Sinclair told both deans that there was a deal in the works. He said Russell had verbally agreed to take an offer from Sinclair Pharmaceuticals and that Russ promised that he'd convince me to do the same."

Kader leaned back and crossed his arms over his chest. "Go on."

I shrugged. "It wasn't true. Russ came to my house after the gathering." When Kader nodded, I asked, "Were you watching? So you already know what was said."

"Not in real time, but yes, I watched. He wanted to fuck you and talk about the offer."

My head shook, thinking back to that night. Although it had happened only a little over a week ago, it seemed like another lifetime. Maybe it was. "Russ said he wanted to talk to me about Sinclair Pharmaceuticals someplace without ears. He meant not at work. He mentioned that Damien Sinclair had made him an offer, and said he'd told Sinclair to stick it up his ass."

Kader's lips twitched. "He also wanted to fuck you."

Ignoring his comment, I continued, "I asked Russ if he had a price. It was what you'd asked me."

"This would have been much easier if you would have given me one."

"And what? You would have paid me with your own money and I would still be me. The person who hired you would know that I wasn't dead."

"Your death was to guarantee ceasing the research. I thought if I brought them the data with a guarantee that you wouldn't continue...I hoped."

"I want to know more about the negotiation between the university and Sinclair. The university has incomplete data. Are they bartering that? What about the bidding on the dark web?"

"Currently, it's stalled at 1.2 billion."

My eyes opened wide. "Shit. What does stalled mean?"

"It means there haven't been any additional bids recently, but the site isn't closed."

"What will happen when you put the up-to-date R&D on the dark web? Whoever has the external hard drive will be upset to lose that kind of money."

"That's what I'm hoping." Kader shifted in his chair. "I

have some more interesting findings. Do you want to watch the videos?"

I shook my head. "CliffsNotes please. I had enough watching my parents."

"All right," Kader said. "Prior to your parents' arrival to your house, earlier that same morning, an IMPD forensics crew went inside. They dusted for prints and searched for signs of foul play. I verified that they were IMPD. It's impossible to know until they file a report, but I don't think they found anything, well, except for Mrs. Beeson's fingerprints. Before she let herself in, I had that place spick-and-span."

"Poor Mrs. Beeson," I sighed. "Wait. If they'd been inside already, why did the detective and officer with my parents enter first? They should have known there was nothing there."

"You're starting to think this through. Very good. I had the same question. And before you freak out, your parents are still in Indianapolis. They're staying downtown. I've breached the hotel's security and have verified their safety. Your father likes Starbucks."

Though my lips turned upward at Kader's observation, my fingers gripped the arms of the chair. "Why am I going to freak out?"

"Your parents were summoned to Indianapolis by Eric Olsen. I found the telephone logs. His first call to them was on Tuesday after he couldn't reach you or Cartwright. The day the lab was closed. By the way, I found an internal memo. The lab wasn't closed because of you or Cartwright. It was closed due to a safety issue, a reported gas leak."

My forehead scrunched. "Didn't you say that you accessed the floor that day?"

"I did. No gas leak. No repairmen." Kader shrugged. "So...everyone was contacted. You and Cartwright didn't respond. Olsen sent Stephanie to your house and the Jennifer you hadn't mentioned to Cartwright's.

"Back to you, Stephanie didn't enter your house. She knocked multiple times on the front and side doors. That afternoon, Dr. Olsen called your parents for the first time. I don't have a recording of the call. It came from his cell, not office or home. He called again on Wednesday, and they arrived Thursday."

"Don't you think that's odd?"

"What?"

"One day of not being able to reach me and he resorts to calling my parents who live out of state."

"It does seem like a jump. What I do know is that the telephone logs show that after Olsen's initial contact, both of your parents called your phone repeatedly. Stephanie also called you. She was the one who picked up your parents at the airport, and then she took them directly to the university. I have footage of them in Olsen's office. You can watch it if you want. He asked them if you'd been in touch. He also asked about your relationship with Dr. Cartwright."

I swallowed, my heart growing heavier as I thought about

my parents being questioned. "I feel so bad for my parents. How did they answer the question about Russ?"

"Your mother said she believed you two to be friends, coworkers. She went on to say she'd met him a time or two and he'd always been nice."

My head shook. "She's covering for me."

Did that mean she believes the lies, believes that I'd run off with Russ?

"He wasn't nice?" Kader asked, his words separated.

"No, he was. I always said the two of us were only friends, but my mom knew it was more."

"How?"

I shrugged as tears prickled my eyes. "She's my mom. She just did."

Kader sat taller, continuing, "Stephanie then drove them to your house. The people with them that we watched weren't IMPD. I hadn't looked closely at the badge or pins on the officer's uniform."

"Were they like the men who came to my house?"

"No, they weren't impostors. I ran facial recognition. They came up as employees of the university, the university police."

My nose scrunched. "How could they enter my house? The campus cops wouldn't be able to get a search warrant for off-campus."

"No, but they probably avoided the issue by gaining your parents' permission. Did your parents or anyone at your work have a key to your house...besides Cartwright?"

"I had one hidden outside. My dad knew where it was."

Letting out a long breath, Kader shrugged. "The campus cops wouldn't hold up in court, but if your dad used that key, there was no trespassing. Given the circumstances, I can understand why your parents wouldn't question their authority. As for the men who took you to your lab, remember, I put trackers in their wallets? They've been off the grid since Thursday."

I was thinking more about my parents than what Kader was saying about those men. I looked up to his green stare. "Kader, where is my phone?"

"I destroyed it."

My nostrils flared as I exhaled. The news of my phone's demise crushed me even more than learning of my own. With tears in my eyes, I said, "I had pictures and files."

"Cell phones are too easy to track, especially with social media apps that alert half the world to your current location."

Logically, I understood. Emotionally, it was another blow in a series of blows.

Kader's hand came toward my knee and just as quickly retreated before making contact. "I saved your pictures and any files. This afternoon, I'll put them on a laptop, one I'll get set up for you. The thing I have to know, with one hundred percent certainty, is that if I set you up with this unknown presence on the internet, you promise you won't search yourself. The FBI is involved now. You could inadvertently set off red flags."

My lower lip disappeared beneath my upper teeth as I considered Kader's warning. "How can you search about me?"

"I'm one hundred percent invisible. I don't leave a trail or a footprint. You will be mostly hidden. It takes more time to do what I've done with this." He waved his hand over his keyboards.

His answer made me think of something else. "Kader, did you wear gloves?"

"Did I wear gloves?"

"When you...cleaned my house."

Lifting his hand again, he turned it over, revealing his palm. "No fingerprints. No worries."

I reached for Kader's hand and holding it in mine, I ran my finger over the underside of his fingers and then over his palm. From the first time he'd touched me, in my bedroom with the transmitter in the bra, I'd thought his fingers were callused. They weren't; they were rough from the removal of his fingerprints. "How did you do that?"

"It's handy for my line of work."

"I get that, but how? New skin regenerates our fingerprints."

Kader's chest moved as he contemplated his answer. Despite how he'd behaved this morning, I didn't expect him to lie. He might deny me the information, but he wouldn't lie.

Finally, he said, "I don't recall exactly."

LAUREL

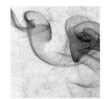

*M*y head ached as we sat down to dinner in the large kitchen. The day had been long, and beyond the windows, night had fallen. Without the lights on within, the windows throughout Kader's house showcased a black velvet sky glittering with more stars than I ever recalled seeing, even at my parents' home in Iowa. I'd almost commented on the splendor, but then Kader's words came back to me from earlier in the day. A clear sky meant the loss of warmth, no clouds to retain it.

How fast could a person freeze to death on a night like tonight?

The lights now illuminating the kitchen bathed it in their golden hue. The large windows were no longer revealing the night sky; instead, they were mirrors featuring two individuals doing their best to eat a meal and stay on the topic of Kader's assignment—me.

Unlike last night, tonight I'd helped with the food preparation. It wasn't as scrumptious as last night's steaks, yet the tilapia and salad were better than the uneaten protein bar and yogurt. I pushed the lettuce around my plate as my thoughts were frenzied with all that we'd learned. I also couldn't get my mind off the proposed statement of sale I'd helped Kader write, constructed in a way to alert a knowing potential bidder to the fact that what Kader had up for sale was the latest and most up-to-date R&D for our compound.

I laid my fork down and let out a breath as I looked up at Kader. "What if it's a sting? The FBI is involved. Don't they have task forces that scour the dark web?"

"They do."

"Aren't you worried?"

"No."

I leaned back against the back of the chair and took in the length of the table. "This is a long table. Why do you have all these seats if you never have company?"

Pressing his lips together, Kader tilted his head as his gaze met mine. "I could tell you the same answer, that I don't know, but I've got this one. The interior designer thought it was a good idea."

"So...the bedrooms...did the designer choose the furnishings for those also?"

He nodded as he lifted his fork to his lips. I shouldn't notice their fullness or think about their possessive strength as they have taken mine. After how he'd treated me and acted this morning, any thoughts of pleasure with Kader should be few and far between.

They weren't.

Perhaps, I preferred those memories to the thoughts that had dominated all day long.

In an attempt to stay on the mundane subject of furnishings, I scanned the table and chairs. "She was right. It's perfect for this area."

Kader shrugged. "Last night was the first time it's been used. It seems fine."

"What? Why wouldn't you use it?"

"Why would I?" He tilted his head toward the tall stools at the breakfast bar attached to the island. "That works too."

A small smile began to bud as my lips curled upward. The first time he'd used his table was for me, for us. "How long have you lived here?"

Kader laid his fork beside his plate and exhaled. "I expect the offers to be coming in as early as tonight for the R&D. I've been able to backdoor some of the early offers on the original post. Sinclair isn't one of the bidders, unless they're doing it with extravagant firewalls and protection. Unfortunately, that is what the higher bidders have. The only way to find out who they are is to contact them."

"Isn't that dangerous?" I asked.

"It's not like a dead drop. We aren't passing notes in a newspaper. There's no physical location or contact. It's all well encrypted, buried deeper than the FBI task force goes."

"How do you know that?"

"I know."

I looked down at my half-eaten dinner and the glass of ice water that was half-full. Reaching for my plate, I began to stand.

"Laurel, sit down and finish eating."

His directions didn't deter me. I lifted the plate and stepped toward the sink.

"Laurel."

Turning back, our eyes met. "Kader, I'm exhausted. My head hurts and I just want to go to bed."

"Your head hurts because you have barely eaten. Sit back down and finish your dinner. You'll sleep better."

"So now you're the doctor?"

Pushing his chair away from the table, Kader sighed as he stood. It wasn't like I could forget this man's height or girth, but sometimes as I observed his actions, it was as if I were seeing the Hulk growing in front of me, unfolding himself as his neck and broad shoulders straightened. Despite his size, there was nothing awkward about him, as if each movement were calculated, precise, and perhaps even graceful.

He'd wanted me to see him as he truly was or as he saw himself—a killer.

I did, but I didn't.

Thinking back, I remembered the first time I saw him, standing in the shadows at the gathering. I also remembered the way he disappeared into the crowd that night as well as the next morning at the coffee shop. It was as if despite his size, Kader's agility and prowess were assets for his occupation.

In two strides he was before me, taking the plate from my grasp. With a pointed look, he turned and returned my plate to my place setting at the table.

Although he hadn't spoken his directive again—for me to return to the table—the expression he sent my way as he resumed his seat made his intentions clear.

"Fine," I said as I returned to the chair and lifted my fork.

Each bite was more difficult than the last. It wasn't the food. The fish was tender and flaky. The salad was crisp and fresh. The vinaigrette dressing was sweet and tangy. We'd even made rolls. They weren't anything special, the kind you pop out of a tube and bake in the oven. It was the day that had taken away my appetite, the discoveries and the new encrypted post floating through the depths of the dark web.

Had I said too much?

To the knowing individual, there was too much information to have been written by anyone besides Russ or myself.

Kader said that he wasn't worried. Of course, he wasn't. He had no digital footprint. I was the one accused of stealing my own research and now, if that post were to be discovered, the accusations would be confirmed.

Will his plan help us or hurt me?

My stomach continued to twist, each thought another knot in a litany of knots.

The temperature of the kitchen increased as my skin grew warm. My throat dried with each bite despite my continued sipping of the cool, lubricating water. With more food eaten than before, I turned to Kader. Instead of eating his dinner, he was staring my direction.

"I can't..." I motioned to the plate. "...eat any more. It was good." When he didn't respond, I shook my head. "I'm not asking your permission to leave the table."

His green eyes narrowed. "You're pale."

Personality number two was back, the one who protected and cared. Its presence was becoming visible, not only in his words but also in his changing tone and expression.

Kader reached toward me, his hand on the table and arm extended yet not touching. "It was like your circulation drained from your cheeks as I watched."

When I started to stand, Kader extended his reach, the sleeve of his shirt pulling upward, revealing the color just above his wrist. "Laurel, tell me you're all right."

Although I wanted to stare at the colorful ink, I feared that if I did, he'd cover it. Instead, I pretended to look at my plate as I fought the urge to run the tips of my fingers over the tattoos. Similar to the texture of his hands, his ink appeared coarse. Then again, I wasn't certain it was possible to interpret feel with only visual clues.

"Laurel."

Prying my gaze upward, I met his. "Am I all right? No, I'm not all right. I'm not sure I will ever be all right again."

"That isn't what—"

Standing and lifting the plate for the second time, I took

it to the sink and laid it in the depth. When I turned, Kader was near, not close enough to touch yet barely out of range.

"What do you want from me?" I asked, again meeting his gaze.

"Everything and nothing."

I shook my head. "I don't know what that means."

Kader ran his hand over his tethered-back hair. Taking a step back, he turned a complete circle as his bicep under his shirt flexed, his Adam's apple bobbed, and the cords in his neck pulsated. When he made it back to me and our gazes once again connected, he sighed. "You asked me earlier about my need to be in control."

Leaning back against the counter, I nodded.

"A man who does what I do...control is essential."

"Okay."

"You've asked a million questions."

"I want to know more about you," I replied.

"Why?"

"Why? Because I'm here with you. When you're not being number four, I'm attracted to you like nothing I've known, nothing for a long time."

His brow furrowed. "Four?"

"Never mind." I cocked my head to the side. "I don't really understand you or why I'm so..." I shrugged with a half grin. "I just want to know you better. I guess it's also because you know more about me than I know about you. I'm curious."

"Quid pro quo?"

"No, Kader. It's not just because you know about me. I *want* to know more about you."

"I told you, it's not a pretty story with a nice happy ever after."

I let out a long breath. "I think I get it. My story isn't either. It was. At one time it had potential."

"Laurel, you're nothing like me."

"You're probably right. It's just that whether I'm here with you or buried in a shallow grave, according to you, my life ended a day ago."

He nodded. "I could say you get used to it. In some ways you do."

"I don't understand. Have you done this before, claimed someone is dead when the person wasn't?" My tone went higher. "The same as you're helping me do."

If he had, maybe he knew what would happen.

Kader shook his head. "No, this is new for me. You're new for me."

"Oh," I replied disappointedly. "Then how do you know if I'll get used to it?"

"Personal experience."

LAUREL

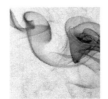

*S*leep came in restless snippets throughout the long night. One would think after my first day of being reported dead—even if only to the person who hired Kader— I'd have been asleep as soon as my head hit the pillow. That wasn't the case as I struggled to find a comfortable position in the large, otherwise empty bed and wrestled with questions that had no answers.

Kader didn't elaborate on the statement he'd made about personal experience, and for some unknown reason, I didn't push. My exhaustion compiled with the growing gravity of my situation quelled my usual curiosity. Besides, I didn't think he'd explain.

Maybe I was getting to know him.

If I were to ever figure this man out, I would need to take the clues he offered.

After coming upstairs, I soaked in a warm bath and then, wearing one of Kader's long t-shirts, I climbed into bed. I didn't analyze why I chose his shirt. Number four had frightened me, accomplishing his goal. And yet the shirt didn't represent number four. The lingering aroma of cologne combined with the knowledge that at one time the soft material had covered his rock-hard body and colorful ink brought thoughts of number three, the man who brought me pleasure. If I could learn to isolate his personalities, I could admit that I found comfort in numbers one through three.

Slumber came and went.

While asleep, my dreams were plentiful and disjointed. Scenes and characters from a different time in my life floated through my thoughts as if the players weren't humans but ghosts paying me a visit, only to disappear into the breeze.

Upon waking to the dark room, one of the many times throughout the night, I reasoned to myself that mentioning my father and childhood to Kader, combined with the name of his house, triggered the return of forgotten recollections.

My mind scrambled to put the pieces into place before they were out of reach, but like grasping at smoke, unable to hold it in your hand, my dreams were fading.

Perhaps it was my current predicament that had me reminiscing. There was nothing certain about my future and yet my past was set. The disjointed dreams caused my mind to go back to a time long ago.

The dream sparked the memory of the first time I'd joined my father during his volunteer work. Instead of being a participant, as I recalled in my thoughts, I was now an observer. No longer a young girl, I watched the scenes as a woman my current age viewing a younger version of myself and my father.

That first visit had been out of necessity. I couldn't recall the details, but something had happened with one of my mother's patients and she was needed at the hospital. Ally was at a friend's house. If my father hadn't taken me along with him, I would have been left home alone. Although I proclaimed that I could handle it, my father decided otherwise.

For as long as I could recall, it had been my father's practice to visit different locations, counseling youth. Later, I'd learned that the people from the various YMCAs, Boys and Girls Clubs, and after-school programs would call my father whenever something significant occurred or if there was someone they felt would benefit from his assistance.

As we drove the fringes of the city, the landscape of the different Chicago neighborhoods was lost on me. The diverse population of Wicker Park was my norm. I didn't understand that as we traveled to various locations, potential dangers lurked beyond the walls of the centers.

Now, reminiscing as an adult, I marvel at the innocence I possessed and credit my parents for raising us to see the person beneath the surface.

Maybe that is why I have difficulty seeing the man Kader claims to be.

Curled on my side as my gaze went beyond the large

windows to the night sky, I couldn't help but wonder if I'd ever see my father again. Those were thoughts I tried to avoid as I blinked away the tears teetering on my lower lids.

Had I told my dad how meaningful those visits were to me?

Perhaps Kader was right and the other children saw me as an outsider. That wasn't how I felt or how the others made me feel.

Why hadn't I done more in Indianapolis to help others like my father had?

I'd always been too busy with work and our research. No, I'd seen my way of helping differently. It was my belief in our compound. Creating it had been my way of contributing.

The reality hit me.

The compound may never go to market. My dreams of helping others were dying along with my reputation. Sighing, I closed my eyes, allowing my mind to drift back to the memories my dreams had revived.

That first visit with my dad came back to me.

With my dad leading me, we approached the big brick-and-limestone building. I recalled the blue sky and orange and yellow leaves swirling in mini cyclones that danced across the parking lot. With my hand in his, Daddy and I entered a big gymnasium. Waiting inside at a tall desk was a woman with a pretty smile and bright fingernails.

Those may be odd qualities for a girl of about eleven years old to recall, but I did.

Her name was Miss Betsy. After we'd visited a few times, she'd come around the desk and greet me with a hug. A smile came to my lips, recalling how she always smelled of vanilla, like the kind my mom added to chocolate chip cookies.

Maybe it was Miss Betsy's initial response that made me feel welcome.

On that first visit, my dad apologized to her for bringing me along. Coming around the desk, Miss Betsy's friendly smile never wavered as she told my dad that I was welcome anytime.

Dad and I both glanced into the expanse of gym. There were multiple basketball rims hanging from the tall ceiling. The wood floor was lined, dividing the greater court into smaller courts. The height of the baskets on each smaller court seemed to be dictated by the height of the players. Both boys and girls were playing, bouncing and shooting orange balls.

"Betsy," my dad said, "you have enough children to watch."

"Don't be silly. There's no such thing as too many children, Dr. Carlson. Besides, we have help today." Crouching down, she looked me in the eye. "Honey, are you a basketball player?"

Shyly, I shook my head as my gaze scanned the children of all ages.

Some were tall, others short, some heavy while others were thin. Dark hair and light hair. Long hair and short hair. There were some with pale complexions like mine and others in all shades of brown. No one was the same and together they were moving, playing, and having fun.

"Dr. Carlson," Miss Betsy said in a low whisper, "Willie is

waiting in 101. I told him I called you." Her volume rose. "Now, you just leave Miss Laurel with me. I promise she's no trouble." She smiled my way. "We'll have fun, won't we?"

I nodded.

After my dad gave me a hug and made me promise to be good, I turned to Miss Betsy and pointed to a raised stage area across the gymnasium. "What's that?"

"Oh, that's our craft center. Today, Miss Jean is helping, and oh..." Her voice grew high. "...she loves sparkles and glitter. Do you like crafts?" The way Miss Betsy spoke boosted my enthusiasm.

Nodding quickly, I told her that I did.

Taking Miss Betsy's hand, we walked along the perimeter of the gymnasium. The air around us filled with the squeals of tennis shoes on the hardwood floor, as well as whistles, grunts, complaints, and laughter.

In this unfamiliar neighborhood, within the gym, it was much like my own school.

"Miss Jean," Miss Betsy said as we arrived onto the stage, "we have a new friend."

Miss Jean, a bigger woman who waddled when she walked, flashed me a welcoming grin. "Well, hello, sweetie. What's your name?"

"Laurel," I replied, aware the other children had stopped their work on crafts to look at me.

"Welcome, Laurel." Miss Jean turned to the tables surrounded by chairs holding both boys and girls. On their surfaces were colorful pieces of construction paper, glue, scissors, glitter and sparkles. "Let's all say hello to our new friend Laurel."

"Hi, Laurel," came softly and repeatedly.

A pretty girl with red hair lifted her hand.

"Yes, Lorna?" Miss Jean asked.

"Miss Jean, Missy and me got room over here if Laurel wants to sit with us."

Miss Jean pointed a finger toward the girl and after pursing her lips, she said, "Missy and..." She didn't finish the sentence.

Lorna smiled, her big front teeth reminding me of mine. "Missy and *I*..." She paused. "...we *have* room," Lorna said proudly.

"That's very nice of you, Lorna." Miss Jean looked down at me. "It's up to you, Laurel. You may sit wherever you'd like."

Thrilled to have received an invitation from a girl about my age, I nodded energetically toward Lorna and Missy as my smile grew. Lorna had big green eyes, freckles on her cheeks and nose, and curly red hair that reminded me of Annie from the musical. Missy, on the other hand, had dark hair like me but her eyes were big and brown and her skin was a light shade of brown, almost gold.

"Where do you live? Why are you here? Is Dr. Carlson really your dad? Do you have a sister? How about a brother?" The questions continued throughout the afternoon as we worked together on our creations.

Taking their lead, we created bright and colorful butterflies covered in all shades of glitter.

My new friends weren't the only ones to ask questions. I asked my share too, learning that Lorna and Missy were sisters and that they had an older brother.

The memories stirred around my thoughts as I tossed and turned, fading in and out of sleep.

I didn't want to think of those three little girls growing up. It was easier to recall a simpler time. As Kader would say, the story of all three didn't have a happy ending. Missy disappeared a few months after we met. I was now declared dead.

That only left one—I hoped—the girl with red hair, freckles, and big front teeth.

The last time I'd seen Lorna was before leaving for my freshman year of college. Petite and athletic, she'd grown into her smile. Though she had one more year in high school, college wasn't in her future.

A random tear slid down my cheek onto the pillow.

I couldn't fathom the rabbit hole my memories had taken me down.

These were thoughts I hadn't had in years.

Though I hadn't seen Lorna since that time long ago, she'd been the one who reached out to me, informing me that her brother had died. It was sad to think that she'd had two siblings and she'd lost both.

Was that an unusual statistic for the South Chicago neighborhood?

Where were the other children in that gym today?

My thoughts returned to Ally, my sister.

Did she think I was dead?

Kader said I can't search myself on the laptop he'd set up for me. I hadn't done anything today—yesterday—other than load the two flash drives.

My memories made me wonder if I could search my sister or maybe my childhood friend.

I'd ask him in the morning.

KADER

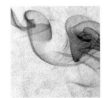

*L*aurel's comments had me thinking as I clicked and pulled up the old footage. It was the scene she'd talked about, well, had started to tell me. Yes, I may now be a bit obsessed about Cartwright's motivation for showing up at Laurel's house after the gathering.

Leaning back in my chair, I stretched my arms above my head and pushed up my sleeves. Lifting my chin, I took a quick glance at the screen above, the one where I could check on Laurel in real time. It was nearly two in the morning and I'd yet to go to bed, much less to sleep. There were too many facets of this case I couldn't grasp. It wasn't like me to fail. The fucking answers had to be right in front of me, and I was too blinded by the woman sleeping in my house—in my shirt —to see them.

She'd been tossing and turning, but it looked like she'd finally fallen asleep.

It shouldn't please me that Laurel wore one of my shirts to bed. It should be the opposite. I should be upset. After all, I'd done my best to show her the real me.

Then why after her bath had she donned my shirt?

Knowing she'd been in the bathroom for a while had me thinking about my cameras. I'd told her the truth. I didn't have one in the bathroom, but when she came out, her exposed skin pink, I was considering adding one.

Laurel Carlson had me distracted and asking more questions than I could find answers.

No matter her motivation for wearing my shirt, I couldn't deny that she looked hot as hell as she climbed onto the mattress, her round ass barely covered by white panties peeking out as the shirt pulled upward and she crawled forward.

Granted, it was only a few scoots of her hands and knees, but it had my mind imagining more. Her on her hands and knees...

"Fucking get your shit together, Mason."

My neck straightened at my audible use of the name I'd been told was mine. The one that held no past and I gave no future.

This was out of hand.

Laurel Carlson shouldn't be on her knees. Fuck, I should be.

My chest expanded and contracted as my breathing deepened.

Happy.

Sad.

Upset.

Horny.

Angry.

They were emotions that up until Laurel's blue eyes stared at me through the fucking screen, I'd successfully compartmentalized away. I'd let them die along with the rest of me. I had no need for them, no motivation to cultivate feelings that no longer existed. Before her, I'd been the job, an assignment. I'd been satisfied.

And now, somehow and without my consent, Laurel had raised emotions from the dead, bringing them to life inside me.

To life or back to life?

I didn't know.

Shaking my head, I concentrated on the scene from last week, bringing my eyes back to the screen before me. It was Laurel's home the night of the gathering. I began the feed as Laurel threw a canister of pepper spray onto her kitchen table and opened the outside door.

Was my obsession with Laurel affecting the way I saw this unfold?

Was there more to see that was right in front of me?

Hitting fast forward, the feed sped up until I slowed the footage. Laurel was standing on her stairs, her long black dress dotted from the rain. Cartwright was near. I'd watched this particular footage before and knew this was where she and Cartwright discussed a possible price for the R&D. With a click to the volume, their voices came from my computer.

"Laurel, I wanted to talk to you about Sinclair Pharmaceuticals someplace without ears."

"So...not at work."

"We can talk here, but with our heads on a pillow would be another option."

Yeah, motherfucker, nice try.

"There's nothing to talk about," Laurel said. "The decision isn't ours. It's up to Eric if he accepts their money."

So get the fuck out.

"Is it?" Russ asked. "Eric told me that Dean Oaks was the one who invited Damien."

"Yes, he told me the same thing."

"We've worked too damn hard for them to come in, take the credit." Cartwright said. "Damien had another offer, one to hire us, moving the research to Sinclair."

"I'm not for sale."

Hey, don't take it personally, I thought with a scoff. *She'd told me the same thing earlier that night.*

"Do you have numbers?" Laurel asked. "Did he make a specific offer?"

"Hell no," Cartwright replied. "I told Damien to stick his offer up his ass. We weren't interested."

"Would you...?" Her plump lip disappeared under her teeth.

Seeing it there made me want to bite it, tug it free.

Fuck, my commentary wasn't helping me learn clues. Concentrate.

I hit pause and rewound a few seconds.

"I mean..." Laurel said, "...is there a price that would make you sell."

"To Sinclair?"

"To anyone."

It was probably my imagination, but as I watched it again, I believed Laurel was feeling Cartwright out, trying to learn if he'd been made an offer like the one I'd made her. My gut said it was more than that. He was feeling her out too.

Just not the way he fucking wanted.

I hit play again, wondering what he knew.

"Is there a price you'd sell?" Cartwright asked.

My eyes narrowed.

Did you have a price?

Who was your contact?

Who double-crossed you?

"I didn't think there was," Laurel replied. "As you said, we've worked too hard and for too long. The potential for this drug is far-reaching. I want to be around to see it come to fruition."

Fucking do-gooder. Laurel's good intentions blinded her to what was happening around her.

Cartwright nodded. "Then we're on the same page."

I doubt it.

"We'll tell Eric on Monday that our vote is for no," Cartwright said.

"Damien essentially offered me a job in front of Eric," Laurel said. "I think we should make it clear to Eric and Damien that neither of us have intentions of jumping ship." Her grip of the banister shifted. "I mean, I'm sure Eric's worried. He knows the university can't possibly offer us the kind of money Sinclair would offer."

"I agree. We'll tell him where we stand and let him handle Dr. Oaks." Cartwright reached for her hand.

Don't touch her, douchebag. I don't trust you. Well, you're dead. It's a good thing I don't believe the saying that dead men tell no tales. Fucker, you have a story, and I'm going to find out what it was.

"I'll see you Monday," Cartwright said.

"You don't have to go."

Yes, he does. Let him go.

"I do because if I stay here, I won't stay on that couch."

My teeth clenched as he wavered, not leaving, not moving.

She's not kissing you goodbye. Leave.

It wasn't like I hadn't watched it numerous times. I knew the way it ended.

Kicking my boots against the shiny surface, the wheels on my chair spun as I rolled to another keyboard. Much like other cities, the city streets of Indianapolis as well as the state highways were constantly monitored by traffic cams. Local news crews used the cams for traffic reports. Weather crews used them to display road conditions. The city and state police had access to them to determine circumstances of accidents and incidents. Most of the time, the footage was retained on a cloud for thirty to sixty days before disappearing.

Nothing truly disappeared. The older recordings were simply more difficult to access.

As my fingers raced across the keyboard, I knew I was still within the accessible time period. It was only a matter of finding the right cameras and time stamps.

Within a few minutes, I found the right system of feeds, carefully labeled by intersection or highway exit. "Well, thank you for not even trying to make this difficult."

On another screen, I pulled up the map of Indianapolis proper and studied the streets. The quickest route, especially late at night, from Laurel's house to Cartwright's apartment on the north side would be Forty-sixth Street to North Meridian until he reached Carmel.

The neighborhood streets were tougher. Not all were monitored, only major intersections.

Forty-sixth and Meridian was an option. I pulled up that feed entering the time Cartwright left Laurel's house. It didn't take long. "There you are," I said aloud to the grainy image. Cartwright's black truck was easy to spot.

My back straightened. "What the fuck?" Cartwright didn't head north on Meridian after visiting Laurel. He went south. "Where the fuck are you going?"

Pushing off, my chair rolled back to the screen with the footage of Laurel's house. Clicking that off, I pulled up Cartwright's apartment.

Why had I never verified that he'd gone home?

A quick glance upward at the sleeping woman wearing my shirt was my answer.

I hadn't given a shit about Cartwright.

Laurel was my only concern.

Pulling up the coverage of Cartwright's apartment, I rewound to the night in question. Once there, I sped up the video. It didn't take watching in real time to show me that the fucker never made it to his place, not until the sun was rising. And then it was a quick shower and a change of clothes before he was out the door again.

"You're on your way to that coffee shop. Where had you been?"

Leaning back against the back of the chair, I contemplated the options. I could pull up every damn intersection on Meridian, or I could...

I needed to stop thinking about Laurel and listen to my gut.

I hadn't placed cameras in everyone's home. I'd only set up auxiliary surveillance at the locations and of people relevant to Laurel.

Where would a drunk man go—one who is involved in something he shouldn't be—after a failed booty call?

The answer was obvious.

Cartwright went to another woman's place.

Whose?

LAUREL

*A*fter my morning shower and dressing again in clothes that covered, well, everything, I opened the door to my bedroom, thoughts of yesterday morning's encounter running through my mind. In our current situation it was nearly impossible to avoid Kader, and honestly, I didn't want to. I simply wanted to avoid number four.

The hallway all the way to the landing was clear, bathed in morning sunlight. Keeping my gaze focused on the large window over the door, I took a deep breath, steeled my shoulders, and exhaled. Repeating the process, I pushed myself forward, step by step, following the sunlit path.

My unease was easily attributed to number four, but it probably also had something to do with my restless sleep and onslaught of childhood memories. They say that before you die you see your life flash before your eyes. Maybe that was what happened last night. My current death was not acute. It was chronic. I had time to see my life slowly, frame by frame. Last night I'd been a child.

Would tonight bring me my teenage years?

I didn't want to think about it. In reality, during the night, I wanted morning to come. Now that it was here, I had visions of hiding under the covers and letting the day pass by.

As I reached the bottom of the staircase, I stood and listened. There was nothing. Even though it was after eight in the morning, the house was quiet. Wandering into the kitchen, I found nothing. No coffee or breakfast, not even a protein bar and yogurt.

Perhaps my status as guest had expired. It was time to make myself at home.

It didn't take long to find coffee mugs or bring the coffee maker to life. Adding a bit of cream, I secured the warm mug in my grip and began making my way toward Kader's office.

Stopping in the living room before the giant fireplace, I reconsidered. Maybe he was still upstairs. I'd left him in the kitchen last night after dinner.

What if he were still asleep?

Pushing forward I stopped outside the closed office door. As I lifted my fist, ready to rap my knuckles against the door, I gasped. The familiar voice coming from within caused my hands to tremble. The light brown liquid sloshed in the mug.

Without knocking, I turned the knob and pushed the door inward.

"R-Russ?" I asked, my voice shaky as I gripped the mug tighter.

Kader looked up from the screen, his green gaze meeting mine, holding it. He didn't look away as he did something on the keyboard silencing the soundtrack to whatever he'd been watching.

I looked up at the illuminated large screen, seeing the hallway where I'd just entered.

Back to Kader, I searched for answers.

"I heard Russ's voice."

Kader nodded as he stood. His hair was no longer secured, he was still wearing the same shirt as yesterday and more than likely, the same blue jeans. His facial hair was going on two days without trim, the scruff now softer.

My lip slipped below my teeth as he stepped toward me and his exposed forearms came into view. Purples, teals, and greens created a twisted kaleidoscope of colors. I resisted my urge to step forward, take his hand in mine, and move the sleeves of his shirt higher over his biceps. For a split second, I imagined doing more, lifting the hem over his head.

"Laurel, I told you to knock."

Blinking my eyes, my gaze moved back to his. "I-I..." I looked back at the open door and nodded. "I was going to. I-I didn't expect..."

Kader didn't let me finish as he reached for my mug and took it from my grasp. Placing it on a nearby surface, he turned, seizing my shoulders and pulling me to him. My cheek came into contact with the soft shirt covering the hardness of his chest, as the beat of his heart rumbled in my ear.

"What is it?" I asked, craning my neck upward.

Kader nodded toward the mug he'd set down. "That's a good idea. I was engrossed." He nodded toward the big screen. "I didn't see you come downstairs or realize the time."

I took a step back. "Did you sleep?"

"Grab your coffee."

After I'd secured my mug, Kader reached for my other hand, his long fingers encasing mine as he tugged me toward the hallway. "Let's go to the kitchen."

With each step, my mind filled with possibilities.

What wasn't he telling me?

What had him engrossed?

I set my coffee on the breakfast bar as Kader placed another mug within the coffee maker. As the machine roared back to life, he turned my direction, his arms crossed over his chest.

I wasn't certain if he didn't realize that his ink was exposed or if he no longer cared. I hoped the latter yet feared that mentioning anything about the colorful mosaic before me would prompt him to lower his sleeves.

"Did you sleep?" I asked again, willing myself to keep my eyes set on his.

His Adam's apple bobbed. "No, I never got around to it."

"You have to sleep."

Uncrossing his arms, Kader leaned back, gripping the edge

of the counter at his sides. "Tell me about Cartwright," Kader said.

Lifting myself to one of the tall stools, I wrapped my fingers around the warm mug and looked down into the soft brown liquid. "It was his voice...?" Through veiled lashes my eyes looked up from the coffee in my grasp. "...Answer me."

"Yes." Kader replied, bringing his coffee to the breakfast bar and sitting around the corner from me.

The bright sky filled the room with natural light. In the sunlit room, shadows formed under Kader's eyes. His cheekbones appeared more prominent. Keeping his gaze on me, the muscles in his face tightened as his jaw clenched.

"Cartwright," he said again, bringing the mug to his lips.

"I don't know what you want," I said. "He was a brilliant man." Using the past tense caused my skin to bristle. "He was kind and could be funny." A small smile came to my lips. "He had a dry sense of humor. Our—whatever we had—worked because we could talk about things with one another that we couldn't discuss with others."

"Such as..."

"Our work. That should be obvious. It was our bond."

"You said your mother knew there was more between you two than work."

It hadn't been phrased as a question, but I nodded anyway. "How much more?"

"What do you want?" I wasn't certain where this conversation was supposed to go. "You said yourself he wanted to fuck me. Obviously, you know we were intimate." My neck straightened. "I think there are too many things happening for this to be about jealousy."

"I'm not jealous," he said matter-of-factly. "He's dead, remember?"

"Yes, I remember. Then what is this about?"

"Were you exclusive?"

"No." I shook my head. "Why do you care?"

Ignoring my question, he asked, "And you were both good with that?"

No longer able to sit, I stepped down from the stool and paced toward the counter. "I-I mean, yes." I stopped near the stove, needing—no, wanting—to change the subject. "I could cook something for breakfast," I offered. "Do you want anything?"

"I want to find out who hired me and how Cartwright and Ms. Moore were involved."

I'd made it to the refrigerator and opened the doors before his answer stopped me. Spinning on my sock-covered heels, I narrowed my gaze. "What does Stephanie have to do with it?"

Kader's eyes closed as he bowed his head forward. Upon opening them, he released the mug in his grip and lowered his sleeves.

"You know," I said, "you don't have to do that for my benefit."

Pivoting, I removed a container of fruit from the refrigerator and turning back, placed it on the island.

"Laurel."

"You can argue with me all you want, but I think the colors are magical. I wish you'd let me see them closer." When he didn't protest, I went on. "Bright and intricate. How long did your sleeves take to do?" Warmth filled my cheeks as I felt pink climb up my neck as I confessed what I'd never said aloud. "I've always wanted to get one."

"Where?"

"I don't know. That was part of why I haven't."

"What do you want?"

"You'll think it's stupid."

Kader stood and walked toward me. "Doc, you're anything and everything." His head shook, locks of his hair curving near his chin. "Stupid is not one of them."

"A colorful butterfly." I shrugged. "See. Stupid. And common."

He ran his finger over my cheek.

The coarseness of his touch caused my smile to grow.

"If there was a butterfly on your flawless, soft, warm skin..." He grinned. "...it would be like no other. Not stupid and not common."

Did this personality have a number?

I couldn't remember. At the moment, I also wasn't remembering our no-touching rule. Instead, I reached for his hand and turning it over in mine, I gazed at the pads of his fingers and ran my fingertip over them. "If you ever let me see what's under that shirt, I believe I'll see it the same way."

"Doc, it's not—"

"It's unique." *Like you.* I didn't say the last part. Releasing his hand, I changed the subject. "Now tell me what you want to tell me, and I'll cook some scrambled eggs and toast for us." I peered his way. "Do you like eggs?"

"Eggs are fine. See, that's the thing. I don't *want* to tell you."

As I gathered the ingredients, my thoughts went to Stephanie. She'd been my assistant for over two years. Basically overqualified for her position, she was a tremendous asset to our department. It wasn't unusual for her to ask questions that led to discoveries.

Kader was sitting back at the counter as I turned on the burner's flame and sprayed the frying pan with cooking spray. "You know," I said as I whipped the eggs and water in a separate bowl, "she could probably get a job with Sinclair if they negotiate the deal with the university."

"She?"

"Stephanie. You brought her up."

He nodded. "You do realize there are currently two separate illegal attempts to sell your research and development and possibly one legal one."

After I poured the mixture into the pan, I turned. "I'm dead. Russ is...*really* gone. That article, what Damien Sinclair said...your employer won't be happy. And what if someone paid for Russ to die?" The inflection of my voice made it a question. "It's either the same person or someone else." My heart was beating faster than a moment before. "Could Stephanie be in danger? What about Eric or even Sinclair?"

Kader let out a long breath. "Everyone associated with your research will die. I guarantee."

The long plastic spoon I'd been using to stir the cooking eggs came to a stop. With my eyes wide, I twisted my body toward Kader. "Why would you say that? Will you...?"

"No, not me. However, they all will because, Laurel, everyone dies. I didn't say they'd be killed. They will die. It might be today or in fifty years. My point is that the survival rate of any one of those people isn't your concern or mine. Besides, you have a lot of loyalty to people who didn't share that quality."

I was still reeling from Kader's declaration of everyone's impending death. He was right, a little morbid but correct. I'd forgotten about the toast. Pushing the lever, I separated the eggs onto two plates and delivered them to our seats. As the toaster popped and I buttered each slice, his words replayed.

Sitting, I asked, "Who?"

"Who?"

"Who didn't share my loyalty?"

"You and Cartwright weren't exclusive?"

"I told you that. On-again, off-again. We had an understanding."

"Did you know that your understanding included someone else with whom he could pillow talk?"

I shook my head. "No, not about the compound. That's what made us..." The fork I'd lifted went back to the plate as hurt and disappointment flooded my circulation, constricting my lungs until I gasped for air.

KADER

*L*aurel's big blue eyes stared at me, the hurt from my discoveries spilling from her expression. Instinctively, I reached out, covering her hand with mine.

Intellectually, I understood my inconsistent actions made no sense.

Yesterday, I'd done my best to turn Laurel against me, to make her see me for who I am. And at the same time, I didn't want her to turn away. I couldn't recall experiencing jealousy. Coveting something wasn't my style. Money was no object. If I wanted something, I bought it. And yet watching her interact with Cartwright brought about emotions I could only describe as possessive. I hated the idea of her with Cartwright.

It wasn't that I had claims to this woman, hadn't tried to

turn her away multiple times, and even continued to tell myself to get rid of her. While that was all factual, still with each passing minute, each glance of her sapphire-blue eyes or flash of beautiful smile, I wanted what my mind told me I couldn't have—what I didn't deserve.

I was perfectly all right with the knowledge that Cartwright had taken advantage of their non-exclusive clause. I wasn't fine with the way the news hit Laurel.

Looking down at where we were touching, Laurel pulled her hand away as her shoulders straightened. With her dark hair pulled back into a low ponytail, I could see the way her neck strained as she swallowed. "Stephanie?" she finally asked.

I nodded.

"How long has it been happening?"

"I don't know. I could only go back as long as I've been on this case."

Her head tilted. "How long has that been?"

"I accepted it nearly a month ago. The first week was reconnaissance—going to Indianapolis, learning about you, your compound, the players in your life. Oh, and making that pit livable."

The last part brought back her smile if for only a moment. "If that was livable, I can't imagine how it started."

"You don't want to. I didn't get cameras set up at various locations until maybe two weeks before the gathering. The secure email had already been sent."

The wheels were turning as Laurel was thinking back. "So

how many times..." She shook her head. "No, I don't want to know."

"On my surveillance, Stephanie never went to his apartment. I would have noticed that. The night after the gathering, after he left your house, he went to hers." When Laurel didn't respond, I added. "He was there until morning, leaving after he received the call from Olsen." I swallowed, unsure if I should give her the last bit of information.

Laurel's eyes opened wider. "I called her early that morning."

I didn't need to tell her. She was placing the pieces.

Nodding, I pressed my lips together.

"He was there...with her? They were together?" Her voice cracked with emotion.

"I didn't have cameras inside her place, just watching the outside." I shrugged. "Maybe he slept on the couch."

"And then we met at the coffee shop..." She lifted her fork and took a bite. "You know what? It doesn't matter. We weren't exclusive. I don't want to talk about him or them." Quickly, she finished the scrambled eggs and fruit she had on her plate before standing. "Should I feel bad that she doesn't know the truth? That she thinks he and I ran off?"

"Do you?" I asked.

"Not really." Laurel placed the plate in the sink. Spinning, she slapped her hand over her thigh as her head shook. "Right in front of me."

I carried my emptied plate to the sink. Once my hands were free, I reached for Laurel's waist. My fingers spread as I pulled her to me. Her small hands landed on the sleeves covering my forearms.

"We're touching," she said, as if I was unaware.

Instead of responding, I brought her hips to mine. "He was a fool. Now he's a dead fool. It makes me wish I had been the one to kill him."

Laurel's lips curled as she leaned back and peered upward. "I knew you didn't do it."

I shrugged. "I still haven't lied to you."

"You meant all those things you said yesterday morning?"

"Not one fucking word. Each phrase began with *maybe* or *perhaps*."

Her head began to bob. "You're right. At the time, I...it doesn't matter. I didn't believe you."

"I hate that this discovery has upset you," I said. "I debated if I should tell you about the two of them."

"No, Kader, you need to tell me everything. I mean, if they did *pillow talk*..." She sighed before steeling her neck and shoulders. "...Stephanie could have written that first email. The more I think about it, the more it makes sense. Maybe she was using Russ to profit from our compound."

"Or they were working together," I offered.

"I know it's stupid that I want to believe he wasn't involved." Her head tilted. "This may sound like a jealous lover and maybe it is, but now that I think about it, there were a few different times when..." Her words trailed away as if following her faraway expression.

"What?"

Her slender shoulder shrugged. "During the day...Russell would leave the fifth floor to go...different places, like the facility where our limited clinical trials were occurring. Yet sometimes he was difficult to reach. I don't know. He'd leave and Stephanie would be out on errands, or she'd be out and he'd disappear. I never thought about it before."

"Were they gone long enough to go to either one of their places?"

Her nose scrunched. "I don't know. I don't think so." Her lips pursed in concentration. "It wouldn't have given them much time to...maybe."

I wanted to smile, to ponder longer on the fact that Laurel was essentially saying Cartwright was quick on the draw. I wanted to. I didn't.

"I'll check their credit cards and bank records," I offered. "Maybe they were meeting at a hotel or restaurant. If there's evidence that they were meeting—anywhere—we might be on to something, something more than one late-night booty call."

"That first email?" Laurel said, her inflection sounding like a question. "I'd like to read it again. You said it was sent out from the university, not an individual."

"I said it was sent through the university servers. It wasn't connected to any viable account. Whoever sent it knew what they were doing and how to access the hidden part of the internet."

Laurel looked down at her hands still holding my forearms. "Kader." She looked up through her damn lashes. "May I...please...will you let me see your tattoos?"

There was something in her voice, a desire that only I could fulfill, an opportunity to take her mind off of Cartwright. And yet I couldn't. I wouldn't show her what she wanted to see. Yesterday, I'd tried to make her see that I was a monster. Now, I wanted to hide the indisputable proof.

"Laurel, I'm going to go upstairs and shower. Your laptop is in the dining room. It's signed out of the internet. I'll sign you in when I'm done. Don't go in my office or in my—"

Disappointment washed over her, darkening her expression as she lifted her hands, stopping my sentence. "It would be better if you didn't continue to repeat yourself. I know your rules. I won't risk being discovered. I also respect your privacy..." She shrugged. "...even if you don't always respect mine."

I took a step back. Without another word, Laurel turned toward the sink. Turning on the water, she began to rinse our breakfast dishes.

I should have moved.

I should have walked away.

I didn't.

My feet remained rooted to the floor as my eyes stayed glued on her, unable to look away. My gaze scanned from her long, shiny ponytail to her petite frame with sexy curves. Disappointment emanated from her every pore.

Was it about Cartwright or my latest denial?

All I knew was that standing there watching Laurel was a different kind of painful.

I was experienced with pain.

This was different—deeper—not physical yet inside me.

I couldn't figure out my obsession with this woman or hers with me. I wanted it, and yet I didn't. I was drawn to the way she looked at me—saw me, drawn to how it was different than with anyone else.

What would happen if I truly let her see?

My neck stiffened.

Maybe it would be the real end.

That would be better for both of us.

Closing my eyes, I pushed my sleeves up to my elbows. Looking down, I saw the colorful ink, the designs that twisted over my skin as nothing more than an attempt to beautify what was gruesome. Over the years the scars and colors had become one. It would only take a glance for Laurel to shudder in horror.

Though I wanted to do this, to end her curiosity, I found moving difficult. It was as if my steps were fighting a current —moving toward her yet simultaneously being swept away by the metaphoric water. My heart thumped against my breastbone, and my mouth grew dry as I came to a stop behind her. We weren't touching, yet the warmth of her body radiated from her.

"Kader?" she asked, unmoving.

Did I want to see her expression of disgust?

No.

It would be better if I stayed behind her.

Holding my breath, I moved my hands to each side of the sink, caging her between my repugnant scars.

I waited.

The kitchen remained still.

There was no gasp, no voicing of revulsion. Her body didn't flinch or stiffen at the sight.

Without a word, Laurel reached for the faucet and turned off the water. Slowly, her face bowed one direction and then the other. All at once, she spun within my entrapment. Looking up at me, her blue eyes were again filled with tears; however, the sadness from earlier was gone. Her cheeks were raised and she was smiling.

"They're..." She looked down. "...truly beautiful and intricate." Her eyes met mine again. "May I touch them?"

I couldn't answer, not verbally; however, a quick nod granted her permission. My consent was spurred by the knowledge that once she did, this would be the last time we'd touch. After this she'd rightfully run.

Gently, Laurel brushed her fingertips over my mutilated skin. I saw her touch more than felt it through the damaged nerve endings. Taking one of my hands, she turned it over, examining the underside of my arm. Again, our eyes met. "These must have taken many sessions."

I'd never allowed anyone to see my ink—other than the artist—much less touch my skin. My neck stiffened as the hairs of my neck bristled. "Don't pretend, Laurel. Now you're seeing it. The monster I am."

Her head shook. "I don't see a monster."

"Then you're not looking hard enough."

Letting go of my hand, Laurel raised both of hers to my chest. Rising on her toes, she didn't stop until her lips were a breath from mine. The temptation was too strong. I leaned forward or was it her?

Our connection was fire.

The flames made processing difficult.

The pieces didn't fit.

Laurel should want to get away, to hide in a safe place. Instead, she reached higher, palming my cheeks and pulling me toward her. The spark our kiss ignited incinerated my dread. Like the rebirth of a forest after a devastating wildfire, a bud of hope threatened to bloom within me as our lips battled and our tongues joined the attack.

No longer caging Laurel, my arms snaked around her soft frame, my fingers moving lower and splaying over her round ass. With little effort, I lifted her to me, her legs surrounding my torso.

The kitchen filled with sounds.

Laurel's moans were the trip wire, her tongue and lips the igniter. My detonation was imminent as her body wiggled in my grasp, her core rubbing over my hardening dick, and her tits smashing against my chest.

No, this wasn't right.

Taking a step to the side, I released her, sitting her on the edge of the counter.

As I stepped back, her beautiful, surprised expression and

pink, puffy lips came into view. My neck straightened. "I-I..." It was a rare loss of words. "Why aren't you repulsed?"

"Why would I be?"

"Because I'm grotesque."

Laurel again reached for one of my arms. Looking upward to my eyes and then back down, she teased the sleeve, moving it higher. "All the way up?" she asked.

"And more."

"I'd like to see."

I shook my head. "You can't be seeing what's right here."

"I'm seeing you." Her palms were again at my cheeks, our noses nearly touching, as her blue orbs stared into mine. "Kader, I'm looking. I'm seeing. And what I see is a man who has hidden himself for too long, for reasons I can't comprehend, behind an extravagant work of art." Her lips brushed mine. "Thank you. I won't push you, but someday, I'd like to see it all, all of you, like you did me."

"Not the same thing."

Her gaze went back to the art on my forearms. "You're right."

As I started to pull away, she tightened her grasp. "Laurel."

Taking my arm, she pulled it behind her and lifted hers to my shoulders. "It's not the same thing. Not because of your tattoos or my lack thereof. It's different because right now I'm overwhelmed by your gift."

"What gift?"

"Sharing your secret with me."

Fuck.

Taking a step back, I ran my hand over my hair, realizing that during the night I'd removed the tie. A monster with a mane should incite dread.

Why wasn't that happening?

"I don't understand you," I admitted.

Laurel's smile beamed my direction as her knees spread and she pulled me into the space between. "I'm not as complicated as you."

"I have no idea what to do with you," I said.

She reached back and removed the tie from her hair, allowing it to flow over his slender shoulders. Her tone turned sultry. Her tongue darted to her swollen lips and her head tilted suggestively just before she asked, "What do you want to do?"

"I want to take you upstairs and fuck some sense into you."

Laurel's smile grew. Pink radiated from her neck, filling her cheeks as she leaned back. Looking up with a sexy-as-fuck spark in her eyes, she undid the top button of her jeans. "If that sense is supposed to make me see you differently than I do at this moment, we'd better get started because it may take a long time."

Fuck.

Laurel's shriek and squeal filled the air as I stepped back, scooped her legs into my arms, and tossed her soft curves over my shoulder.

Her small fists pounded against my back. "You can't do this," she protested as I began to climb the stairs.

Throwing open the door to my bedroom, I tossed her onto the bed. Her body bounced as her unrestrained hair fanned on the cover below, all the while her eyes staying fixed on mine.

"I can't believe you did that."

An unfamiliar smile came to my lips as a laugh bubbled from my chest. "I've been wanting to do that since the first time I saw you."

"Anything else that you want to do?" she teased, her tits pushing against her shirt as her back arched and breathing deepened.

I took a step back. "My turn to look."

"You've already seen."

Crossing my arms over my chest, I widened my stance and squared my shoulders. With a shake of my head, I conveyed my message.

Sitting up, with her lip tucked under her front teeth, Laurel lifted her shirt over her head revealing the white bra that at one time had a sensor inserted. As she reached for the clasp, I stopped her. "No, blue jeans next."

"You're bossy."

"You're gorgeous. I want to see if your panties are—"

Fucking white.

When the only remaining clothes were her white bra and panties, I nodded and offered her my hand. As she stood, I commanded, "Let me see."

Laurel spun slowly as her hair fell in waves over her slender shoulders, and goose bumps brought the small hairs to life on her arms. The cups of her bra tented with her hard-ening nipples.

"You're stunning."

Again she reached for the clasp. "No, Laurel, leave the rest for me."

MASON

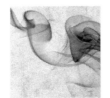

Over seven years ago within a Chicago skyscraper

"Stop! Mason, stop." My sister's cries weren't registering as my fist collided with Reid's cheek.

While powerful, it was the only punch I'd land. Reid spun, secured my elbows behind my back, and bent me forward at the waist. "He'll throw her out." His voice was a low growl in my ear. "Is that what you want?"

I struggled against his hold. "Fucking let go of me."

"Mason." Lorna's face appeared before me as she crouched lower. "Reid hasn't done anything I didn't want."

My eyes closed as my nostrils flared and jaw clenched.

This was my fucking sister. "Let. Go. Of. Me." The words came through gritted teeth.

Apprehensively, Reid's grip of my elbows loosened.

Standing, I shook out my arms and straightened my shoulders. "You," I said, pointing to Lorna, "go in our apartment. Don't come out."

Instead of obeying, my sister reached for Reid's arm. "Mason, I'm not a kid."

"I fucking know that."

"Then don't treat me like one. While you weren't looking, I grew up. We're not in some one-room excuse for an apartment. Our mother isn't out turning tricks, forgetting she had kids to feed. You don't need to take care of me."

The dark memories of our childhood brought back a vision of Missy. Rarely was she mentioned though she was always present. The memory was too painful for both of us. I'd failed her. I didn't want to fail Lorna.

"You're here," I said. "I'm taking care of you."

"She's here," Reid interjected, "because you thought it would be best. She was and is capable of taking care of herself."

"Is that what you think is best?" I asked, louder than I should. "Do you want her back out there instead of here and safe?"

"No. I want her here—with me, not you."

I took a step back. Spinning, I ran my hand over my hair; the short strands bristled against my palm. If Lorna wouldn't listen to me, I'd make damn sure Reid did. Stepping closer to him, I stopped an inch before our chests touched. My gaze sent daggers into his brown eyes. "You and me, we're not done. We're going to talk."

"It's not up to you," Lorna said while at the same time, Reid spoke.

"Mason, I wanted to tell you. There's been too much happening with Allister and Sparrow. The timing didn't seem right—"

"What the actual fuck?" I interrupted as my eyes went from one to the other and back. "This isn't new? How long?"

Lorna shrugged. "This..." She motioned between the two of them. "...not long..." She looked up at Reid, a smile coming to her lips as pink filled her cheeks. "...although, I think I've wanted it for a long time."

What the fuck was she saying?

Thinking was beyond my comprehension. This didn't make sense.

Lorna stepped forward and reached for my hand. The creamy porcelain hue of her skin and the bright redness of her hair were stark reminders that we shared a worthless mother, but not a father. Visually, our only common denominator was the green eyes staring at me, the same color as mine.

"Are you going to tell me to fuck off?" I asked. "You're done with me and don't need me anymore."

"No, I'm going to remind you that I'm twenty-six years old."

"I fucking know your age."

"You've done so much for me. It was hard when you left,

but..." Her gaze scanned the stupid gathering space. "...it was meant to be. This, Mace, is the life you were meant to live. The four of you will rule this city. You will help more people like Missy."

The hair on the back of my neck bristled at the sound of our sister's name.

"I'll never be able to thank you enough for all you've done," she continued. "You even took care of me from overseas. Now, it's time to let me live."

"With him?" I asked, my neck straightening.

"Do you have a better prospect?" Reid asked, his chest puffed and jaw clenched while the dark skin of his left cheek showed signs of swelling. "I'm not good enough?"

I scanned him up and down. "Fuck no." His question hit me, reminding me how my statement may have sounded. This had nothing to do with the way he looked. In reality, no man alive was good enough for my sister. I didn't give a shit about the color of their skin or anything else.

Reid Murray was one of my best friends and had been for nearly a decade. He was six feet six of solid muscle and probably one of the smartest men I knew. That was saying a lot with our group. For a rich kid and three losers, we packed a punch physically as well as intellectually.

"Fuck, Reid," I said, "this is about my sister. Not about you."

We all turned as the elevator doors behind me opened.

Shit.

"Tell me what the fuck is going on," Sparrow bellowed, his

displeasure radiating in ripples as he stalked closer to our group, leaving Patrick a few steps behind in his wake.

When no one replied, Sparrow stopped and scanned from Reid to Lorna and finally to me.

"Our city is under siege and you two are fighting over her?"

Lorna took a step forward, her neck straightening. "I'll pack my things and be gone before the four of you return in the morning."

My little sister had more courage than more than half the city of Chicago to stand up to Sterling Sparrow. While that impressed me, I feared her strength may hurt my case for her remaining here.

"You're staying."

My gaze went to Reid and his to mine. Neither of us had been the one to make the deep-toned proclamation. Everyone including Sparrow turned toward Patrick.

"Come on," Patrick said. "We have a city to control. Lorna is your family, Mason. Sparrow, you say all the time that we watch out for our own. That includes Lorna. No one in this room will be responsible for her being on the street where there's the possibility of anything happening to her."

"Get her a plane ticket," Sparrow said. "She can be out of the country by tomorrow. You heard her. She's ready to leave. We can assure her safety in Europe."

Patrick shook his head. "The ultimate decision may be yours, boss. Right now, you're not thinking about family. Your mind's on the fight for control of Chicago as it should be.

Give this..." He lifted his hand toward us. "... time. We all have time."

Lorna had stepped back and was now wedged between me and Reid.

Patrick spoke toward the three of us. "Mason, your family is our family." He smirked as he turned to Reid. "In light of recent developments that sounds a bit gross, but go with me on this. Forget your last names. If we're in this fight, we're all Sparrows."

My skin prickled, thinking of Sparrow's father. That wasn't what Patrick meant and I knew it.

"The three of you will work out your issues with time," Patrick continued. "Currently, we have more important things to deal with. McFadden's men are, as we speak, gathering at an abandoned flophouse in East Garfield Park. Shit's happening. We have one man on the inside. Either we'll get the intel or we'll lose a man. Then there's the shipment at the shipyard. I can't get ahold of the capo we sent to investigate. That is where our heads need to be. This here—can wait."

All eyes turned toward Sparrow. With a grunt, he barked, "Down to 2, now." His dark eyes zeroed in on Lorna. "Stay put. You're already too much of a distraction."

"I'll take the ticket if that's what you want," she said, her chin high while her usually strong voice cracked.

I reached for her hand. "Lorna."

"No," Sparrow said. "You're not going anywhere until things are settled. Just stay out of the way." He scanned the group. "Now, if you have balls, get in the elevator. If you don't, go to bed." Reaching the elevator, he stepped inside. Turning to us, he continued speaking to Lorna, "I mean it. Stay put. Don't try to leave, the elevators won't work."

Patrick was the first to enter the elevator after Sparrow.

I nodded at Lorna, silently pleading with her to listen to Sparrow as I squeezed her hand. "I know you're grown up," I finally said. "It's just..." Mush wasn't my thing. I was more about action.

"Me too, Mace."

Releasing her hand, I followed the other two men into the elevator.

From where we stood, Lorna and Reid's conversation was unintelligible as they whispered to one another. His grasp of my sister's hand lingered until she reached for the door to my apartment and disappeared inside. As soon as Reid stepped into the elevator, the doors closed.

With all of us staring straight ahead, the elevator descended one more floor. Within a few seconds one of us scanned the sensor on the concrete wall, and we all entered our new command center, the new central for the Sparrow organization. The overhead screens were transmitting feeds from around the city.

There wouldn't be another word about my sister, at least tonight. All of our thoughts needed to be focused on securing Sparrow control. That was our mission. We didn't plan to fail.

LAUREL

Present day

Stilled beneath the blankets of Kader's bed, the man holding me to him—my back to his front, his soft, even breaths skirting across my skin, and his arms wrapped possessively around me—dominated my thoughts. A small wiggle and the resulting recognizable aches reminded me of our recent union, of what he had done, what we'd done. I was no innocent bystander in our encounters. I wanted him in a way I'd never before known. There was something new and yet familiar with him.

Perhaps it was my justification for giving myself so soon to someone I didn't know. In reality there was no justification, and yet the desire existed.

Kader liked control, and for the first time in any relationship—if that was what this was—I'd discovered that I enjoyed him having it. It wasn't that he took it: I willingly relinquished it. His deep, commanding tone and ease in orchestrating our journey benefited me as much as him. If orgasms were the scoreboard, I believed I'd benefitted more. The result was the most titillating ecstasy I'd experienced. Now in his arms, my tender nipples and satiated core were but the physical reminders of what we'd shared.

There was more—so much more.

While I'd slept restlessly through the night, at least I'd slept. Kader had admitted to not sleeping. Even knowing that there were things I should learn—things downstairs—none of them were as pressing as allowing him his much-needed rest. Maybe it was similar to how he protected me. Lying in his arms and letting him sleep was my attempt to take care of him, if for only a short time.

The soft cotton of his shirt was behind me though the sleeves were still raised.

I would wait for future opportunities to see more of his art. My request had been made. Kader's need for control was not limited to our sexual encounters. It was an ingrained part of who he was. My pushing him for more than he was ready to share wouldn't accomplish my goal. While that reality might have bothered me in other situations and with other people, it didn't with him, not while in his embrace, his bed, and his house.

I was smart enough to understand that I was in over my head with what was happening outside of our self-constructed bubble. Kader comprehended the world that included the dark web, billion-dollar offers, illegal transactions, and murders for hire. As with sex, as long as I remained an active participant, I'd willingly defer to his prowess.

Taking advantage of the midmorning sun seeping around the blinds, the ones that Kader had closed before joining me in bed, I could again view the arms holding me. Mindful of not waking him, I used my sense of vision more than touch to further examine what Kader had finally shared.

My initial reaction to his sharing had been genuine.

I was curious.

His unexpected gesture was a gift I welcomed.

Despite Kader's assessment to the contrary, his tattoos were truly stunning.

I'd been right about the depth of his ink. Under the touch of my fingertips, the surfaces were bumpy. That word wasn't the best descriptor, yet it was accurate—uneven with intricate peaks and valleys. Some areas were raised and smooth while others seemed rough and irregular. The ink was a colorful mosaic. Like a true mosaic created with tiles, his tattoos had texture. Perhaps Braille was a better description.

Did they have a story to tell?

My mind battled with the content of that story.

Would I be able to read it in the design or was the ink used to hide the tragedy beneath?

Kader had told me more than once, his wasn't a story with a happy ending.

I wasn't well versed in the art of tattoos. Perhaps the application of the ink into the skin resulted in the roughened texture. I wanted that to be the answer, that Kader had willingly received the ink, accepting the consequence of the inconsistent surface. If that were the case, Kader had maintained his control, receiving what he sought—the beautiful uneven results.

Though I was well educated in a variety of sciences and often trusted my intuition, on this rare and unique occasion, I couldn't accept my mind's conclusion. My heart bled with the belief that Kader's story was far darker.

Maybe Kader hadn't chosen the peaks and valleys; he'd survived them. His colors were his assertion of control at a time when that power had been taken from him.

What had he endured?

My logical mind went to possible factors capable of that magnitude of physical damage. Fire seemed a logical answer, yet if Kader's tattoos covered the entirety of his body, it was unlikely a human body could survive the physical torment and pain associated with that degree of burns.

I didn't want to think about it, not with him or anyone.

And then there was his hauntingly handsome face, his rough yet unscarred hands, and his undamaged penis. Well, I hadn't seen the latter, but I had experience that it worked as one was meant to work.

How had those parts of him survived?

Had they survived or were they restored?

Even with all my education and experience, I had limited understanding of physical scars. My specialty was psychological. My heart and mind together concluded that Kader had both and both he tried to hide.

I held my breath as his body behind me stirred. While I half expected him to wake and perhaps again push me away, he didn't. Instead, Kader mumbled under his breath as his hold of my body tightened, pulling me closer against him.

Once he settled again, I sighed contentedly.

My relief was for more than our current situation. It was the acknowledgment that I'd finally been shown a glimpse into this complicated man. Due to his comments on how I should see him as a monster, I believed Kader had wanted or expected me to shriek in horror at the sight of his skin. Perhaps he'd finally acquiesced in another attempt to push me away, the same as he'd tried to do yesterday with his cruel words. And yet my honest reaction was the opposite.

With each peek at the man beneath the mask, my obsession with Kader grew. I longed to know more, to understand, and perhaps to care.

I wavered a bit on my earlier conclusion. In light of recent discussions, my diagnosis of dissociative identity disorder could still be accurate. However, if he truly had DID, it wasn't the dominant number four who was in charge. If that were the case, Kader wouldn't have admitted misleading me yesterday.

Number four wouldn't have allowed that.

That meant that if DID did apply to him, one of his gentler, possessive, and protective identities was in charge.

That was an interesting observation given his chosen profession.

Nevertheless, I liked the idea.

Numbers one through three were definitely preferred over number four.

The idea that one of those first three personalities was ultimately in control brought a smile to my face.

My mind continued to wander as more questions arose.

I'd told Kader that often DID arises from an acute or chronic traumatic occurrence.

Was whatever had happened to his skin that occurrence?

LAUREL

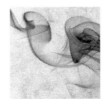

*P*erhaps it was the warmth of Kader's hold or the soothing sound of his even breathing, but at some point during the morning, I'd been lulled back to sleep. I awoke as the bathroom door opened, releasing a cloud of steam saturated with the fresh clean scent of Kader's masculine bodywash.

Blinking my eyes, the man in the doorway came into view. His now-familiar silhouette emerged from the steam as he lowered another long-sleeved shirt over his torso. The distance, lack of lighting, and lingering condensation obscured my view of what had been briefly uncovered. As Kader neared, I noticed the blue jeans covering his legs as well as the socks over his feet.

Without a word, the mattress dipped as Kader lowered his massive frame to the edge. The air around us filled with the fresh aroma of clean. His wet, uncombed, and unrestrained hair sprinkled droplets of water dotting the shoulders of his dark blue shirt.

None of that mattered as Kader turned his sights on me.

I stayed silent, restraining my grin as I awaited the personality I was about to encounter.

With our gazes locked, he ran the pad of a coarse fingertip over my cheek to my neck. One side of Kader's lips curled upward as his green stare left mine and lowered to the blankets currently covering my body. Continuing its track downward, his long finger teased the top edge of the covers. "Do you know how badly I wanted to fuck you again when I woke to your sexy, soft ass taunting my dick?"

No longer hidden, my smile bloomed as I simultaneously secured the blankets in place. "Apparently, not badly enough to do it."

"Fucking won't get you your life back or keep you safe."

It was a nice way to keep my mind occupied. I didn't say that.

"We have too much to learn," he went on. "If I'd have given in to my desires, I saw an endless cycle for the rest of the day—fuck, sleep, fuck, sleep..."

"If that's supposed to be a deterrent, you need to do better," I said, leaning upward and brushing my lips over his.

Kader cupped my cheeks.

Craving his touch, I reached up, covering his hands with mine. As I did, the blanket fell to my lap.

"I may be the one taking you," he began, his fresh mint breath exhaling as his gaze scanned to my exposed breasts and then back to my eyes. "But, Dr. Carlson, you are the one fucking with me."

I let out a breath. "And because of that you want to get rid of me."

Kader released my cheeks and stood. His fingers raked through his wet hair as his bicep bulged beneath the material of his shirt. "I...I..." Shaking his head, Kader exhaled.

Expectancy filled the air. Waiting for him to continue with what he was about to say, I pulled the covers back in place.

Finally, he spoke, "Doc, I'll leave you alone to get dressed. Let's start this day again, not that I'm complaining about where it went. We have work to do. Lunch and then we get busy."

My lip momentarily disappeared as I reminded myself not to push. "Okay."

He turned.

Although I expected him to do as he said and leave, Kader stopped at the desk and sat in the chair. Lifting one leg of his jeans, he slipped his foot into his large black boot. My lip disappeared as I watched him don the second boot. Each movement was graceful and precise, granting me another small glimpse of colors. Not long enough to decipher, I now confirmed that his lower legs too contained colors.

My satisfied core clenched as my circulation settled between my legs. Watching a man put on boots shouldn't be sexy and spellbinding, yet it was.

As Kader stood again, I lost my restraint and gave in to

my curiosity. "You can tell me no. I just...I felt like you were about to say something a minute ago."

"It's nothing."

"Sometimes, nothing is something."

Kader turned toward me and shrugged. "I don't sleep much."

"I figured that out."

"When I do, I sleep."

I nodded.

"I woke to your soft ass because I was someplace else."

"I don't understand."

"I was dreaming."

Oh.

"About what?" I asked.

"No fucking idea. I haven't dreamt in...well, ever that I remember."

I sat up enthusiastically and patted the bed. "Kader, that's exciting. Come talk about it. Maybe you will remember more."

He tilted his head as his chiseled jaw clenched.

I hoped he was considering my offer. My anticipation grew as step by step he returned to the bed. "What do you remember?" I asked.

Reaching for the covers, Kader threw them back, revealing my naked body. Before I could protest, he took my hand and tugged until I was standing.

My shriek filled the bedroom, its shrill sound mixing with the echo of the slap from his hand landing squarely on my ass.

"What the hell?" I asked, hopping backward, my one hand now shielding the stung flesh.

"I told you to stop analyzing me."

"I-I... That doesn't matter. You can't do—"

Again, Kader had my hand, pulling me toward him until his massive clothed body curled over me. With my chin in his other hand, his lips took mine, silencing my protest. The immense unfairness of the situation added to its hotness—tall versus petite, clothed versus nude. My eyes closed as our kiss continued, momentarily erasing the fact that this man was the cause of the tender skin on my backside.

When he finally stood taller and my eyes opened, Kader matter-of-factly replied, "I can. I did. I will again." A grin returned. "Now, spin around. I want to see if your ass is red."

I shook my head as my hands again went to my backside. "No."

"No?"

I cocked my head to the side. "Spank, fuck, sleep...repeat. That's not a cycle I want."

Kader didn't answer, but the gleam in his green-eyed stare accelerated my pulse, making me question his thoughts on the subject.

"Come downstairs as soon as you get dressed." His eyebrows danced. "Or you're welcome to one of my shirts. You know where the closet is."

Defiantly, I pursed my lips and crossed my arms over my breasts.

"Fine," Kader said with a quick scan from my head to my toes, "as you are is also acceptable."

After he walked away, I backed my way into the bathroom. Twisting and turning at the vanity was useless. The smaller than normal mirror over the sink wasn't large enough to see if he'd left a mark on my ass. Nevertheless, under my touch, the flesh felt raised and tender.

What had happened didn't bother me as much as the stupid smile in the reflection. As much as I hated to admit it, I'd take any of the before-mentioned cycles over going downstairs and learning more about the destruction of my life.

LAUREL

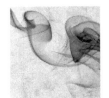

*L*unch was consumed in the kitchen with both of us wearing clothes. That seemed like an unnecessary fact to mention; however, after Kader's comments upstairs, I wanted to be clear.

When I entered the kitchen, Kader's expression changed. His chin lowered and I almost believe his lower lip moved. It wasn't much; nevertheless, the micro change gave me pause to smile.

"You didn't take my offer of my shirt," Kader said as he placed two plates on the breakfast bar.

"Observant," I said with a grin. "I thought this was better for our schedule."

The side of his lips moved minutely upward. Each show of emotion, no matter how small felt like a kind of victory. With the current status of my life, I would claim any win I could.

After Kader sat, he turned my way. "Speaking of schedules, I liked the sound of that second cycle you mentioned." The afternoon sun reflected off the golden flakes in his green eyes, giving him a sexy yet menacing expression.

As Kader mentioned that second cycle—spank, fuck, sleep, repeat—I climbed onto the tall stool. His words and the hard wooden chair brought back the sting to my backside, accompanied by a rush of warmth between my legs. Squeezing my thighs together, I looked down, hoping my bra would restrain my hardening nipples.

Instead of responding to his comment, I changed the subject, taking in our lunch of chicken salad on a bed of lettuce and sliced tomatoes with a glass of iced tea.

"I've never known a man who could cook."

"Only those of us who need to eat."

"Yes, but where are the pizza deliveries or boxed macaroni and cheese."

He sat taller; his expression scrunched as if he'd tasted something sour.

I pointed at the plates. "You have much better taste than most."

"This is hardly cooking. Store-bought chicken salad. Store-bought tea. The fresh vegetables are from a local shop that imports from California. The tomatoes are fresh, not some tasteless hothouse variety."

"How often does Jack bring you food?"

"Usually every two weeks. He's going to question why my normal rations aren't lasting as long."

"And you don't think telling him that it's because you kidnapped a sex toy and have her hidden away in your house is a good idea?"

Kader's cheeks rose. "I can come up with a better story."

"I don't know. You know what they say about truth being stranger than fiction."

"Laurel..." Kader set his fork down. "...it may seem like your life has reached an all-time low. I could be the one to make you think that way, but remember, if that's true it means there's only one way to go."

"This morning, I wasn't complaining about my new role."

"It didn't sound like complaints," he said, lifting his fork.

For a moment, we ate in silence. While I was content to let my thoughts linger on everything that had happened this morning—his gift allowing me to see his arms and the amazing sex that occurred after—I knew it was time to face more facts.

"You could help me review surveillance footage," Kader offered. "I'm trying to track Cartwright's whereabouts over the last month in conjunction with Ms. Moore's."

"You said your footage doesn't go back that far."

"It doesn't. That's why I'll use credit card receipts as well as hacking into other surveillance options. Last night, I hacked into the Indianapolis traffic cams. The university has a thorough system that monitors streets, sidewalks, as well as parking garages, and inside the buildings."

Letting out a long breath, I turned to Kader. "I'll do that if it will help. I'd like to spend some time working on the data from Russ's and my flash drives. I think in some small way, it will give me peace of mind if I know the data is safe, even if it's bait to be sold."

"That reminds me, I'll check on bids."

"Okay." I didn't know what else to say.

"The little I've read about what you accomplished and the information you gave me for the posting..." He shook his head. "...I'm impressed."

A flush of warmth covered my skin. "I used to think it would revolutionize the industry and help victims who have difficulty coping with the memories. I had high hopes."

"It's interesting that no one had gone this route or had these theories before you, and now you and Sinclair Pharmaceuticals are on the same path."

"We're ahead of them. We were. And as for being the first, that's not exactly true."

"What do you mean?"

"When I was in graduate school," I began, "there was a similar study by an independent company who offered, for lack of a better description, internships to graduate students at my university. I was never told the contractor's name." My nose scrunched. "They used a series of letters and numbers on the contract. The thing was that later after the study was suspended, the moniker they'd used no longer existed."

"The company disappeared?"

I shrugged. "I couldn't find anything."

"Yet you were a part of it? You were involved?" Kader asked, seeming genuinely interested.

"I was a small part. Their study had gotten to the first clinical trials with a small sample size. It's about how far we've gotten. It would have been helpful to see the data from that first study, but it was never published."

He shook his head. "You said it was suspended?"

"It was weird. One day we were all working. My job was mostly crunching numbers and verifying conclusions with endless hours spent documenting refereed-source citations, nothing glamorous. Anyway, the facility was just shut down. No warning."

"Was it in Indiana at the university?"

"No. I don't know where we were. We were never told, only that it was classified."

"And the university sanctioned this?"

I shrugged. "They did."

"Did you apply what you learned there to your own research?"

"Not consciously, but I believe possibly. Maybe working on that other project for even a brief time bolstered my curiosity that such a compound could exist."

Kader reached for my empty plate as he stood. "Your laptop is in the dining room. You can bring it to the office."

"I think I'll stay in there. The view is beautiful and I work best in quiet."

"If you need the internet, let me know."

Before leaving the kitchen, I walked to Kader. With only a shy grin, I reached for his hands and pushed up one sleeve and then the other. Though he didn't speak, his body stiffened under my touch.

"Laurel."

"You're going to the office. I won't even be there. This is your house; you should be comfortable."

"What if I told you that this..." He lifted his arms. "...doesn't make me comfortable. It's the opposite."

"If you told me that, I'd ask why?"

"Then, fuck, I won't tell you." He reached for the sleeve.

My hand covered his. "I'm not analyzing."

"Bullshit."

A smile came to my lips. "I'm telling you that your allowing me to see more of who you are makes me more comfortable."

With that, I left him in the kitchen and found my way to his dining room. The table in the kitchen sat eight. This one had chairs for twelve.

Situating myself at one end, I opened a notebook Kader had provided as I brought the laptop to life. I'd uploaded the data yesterday. Today I wanted to begin to go through it, take notes, and cite any findings I could recall.

Four-plus hours later, I looked down at the pages of hand-written notes. Russ liked to refer to my handwriting as chicken scratch. He used to say that if I wrote out all of our findings, they would remain classified in plain sight.

The bittersweet memory was even more tainted than it had been from his death.

It was silly for me to be upset that he was involved with

someone else. We weren't exclusive. That didn't stop the ache in my chest that came from the discovery that it was Stephanie.

Was I a joke?

The recent memory of her shopping with me for my clothes for the gathering came back. Stephanie was my assistant, but over the few years I'd also considered her my friend. Another thought came to mind: her periodic self-deprecating comments. Even as recently as at the gathering, she'd mentioned leaving the neurotransmitters to me while she took care of fashion and wine holding.

Was she jealous of what we'd accomplished, and that Russ and I were the faces Dr. Olsen wanted to put with the research and development?

"Laurel?"

Kader's voice startled me back to reality.

"Yes. Have you found something?"

MASON

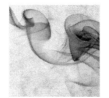

Over seven years ago on the streets of Chicago

*C*urrently, Patrick and Reid were monitoring the McFadden gathering in East Garfield Park, accessing what information they could from the man we had planted inside. Pushback from the McFadden organization was something we'd expected. Rubio McFadden saw Allister Sparrow's death as an opportunity to take control of the entire city of Chicago. Truth be told, if McFadden had been the one found with his skull crushed from an accidental fall off a fifty-foot-high beam at a construction site, the Sparrows —Allister or Sterling—would test the same opportunity.

That's why we planned Allister's demise for years, why

we'd created our headquarters—our command center—and why we'd vetted new blood while unbeknownst to them, vetting old blood. Everything was checked and double-checked. The only unknown variable was the information in Allister's home office. Now that we had that, we had names.

Those names weren't limited to the customers, smugglers, and dealers involved in the human trafficking of children. We also had the names of those who were paid handsomely to turn the other cheek: law enforcement, government officials, and judges on all levels of the court. Essentially, we could bring every one of those scumbags—those willing to profit from the suffering of others—to their knees. However, in doing so, we would also bring the Sparrow organization into the limelight.

This was a marathon, not a sprint.

The exploitation would end.

Sparrow would survive.

The four of us had worked long and hard.

The victims we found would be offered help.

The people in the Sparrow organization who balked about the *closed-for-business* sign were being dealt with. Anyone else who made waves had been or would be reminded of the incriminating evidence we possessed. These individuals had choices: reevaluate their position, go quietly, or be gone.

All options had been utilized over the last weeks.

A few days after Allister's funeral, Sparrow met with McFadden. The meeting wasn't arranged so that McFadden could offer his condolences—he'd done that with splendid fanfare at the funeral. The meeting was set by McFadden with the intention that he'd make Sparrow an offer: the new Sparrow organization could retain the same infrastructure his father's organization had possessed, and if Sparrow was hell-bent on ending his family's part in the trafficking, then Sterling was to hand over the Sparrow portion of the dealings to McFadden. McFadden claimed the new arrangement would keep the customers and suppliers happy while allowing Sterling to wash his hands of any involvement.

Sparrow politely listened to the old man's offer and replied with a counteroffer. The Sparrow organization would retain the previous infrastructure with new oversight including new capos already in place. Sparrow's dealings with trafficking and exploitation would end, and he'd make it his mission to bring down all trafficking of children in the greater Chicago area.

It sounded like a threat.

It was meant to be one.

To say that McFadden was surprised or maybe even shocked by the younger Sparrow's prowess and understanding of this underground world would be an understatement.

Words meant nothing without action.

That was why we were now fighting this war on multiple fronts.

We weren't only battling with all ends of the supply chain Allister had used but also with McFadden's organization, bottom-feeders trying to assert themselves, and a handful of defiant old Sparrows. The latter was lessening. One dead king and a dead consigliere had a way of silencing others.

The only effective way to take down an enemy, even family, was to cut off its head.

Allister Sparrow and Rudy Carlson had been the head.

Our new Sparrow organization had four heads.

We weren't going anywhere.

Currently, Sparrow and I were in the back seat of a reinforced SUV on our way to an abandoned dry shipyard. A shipment of five females had arrived this evening. As Patrick had said, the capo who had been sent to deal with the situation had gone radio silent.

That meant he'd either gotten scared and bolted, or the more likely scenario was that we'd find his body dissolving in a drum of acid.

According to the coded manifest, the females ranged in age from nine to twelve years old. The smuggler wanted payment tonight and threatened that if he didn't receive it, he'd find other buyers.

"This could be a trap," I said, my gut twisting with the possibility.

"I know," Sparrow said. "They'll see us coming. But we're ready. They won't see the ten other men we have there."

I shook my head. "Stay in the car, Sparrow. Your face is currently seconding as a target for half the city. They take you down, all that we've done and what we will do will be lost. Fuck, the three of us know what to do and how to do it, but those others..." I tilted my chin toward the capo driving. "...they're risking their lives and securing control for you, for your name."

"And you think I should pussy out and hide in the sky?"

"It's not fucking pussying out," I growled under my breath, keeping our conversation away from the ears in the front seat. "It's being responsible. It's keeping the king safe. That's our job, not just the three of us—the hundreds of others out on the street. Don't risk it by walking into a trap. They know your weakness."

Sparrow's dark glare came through narrowing eyes. "Walk fucking carefully, Mason. I'm already pissed."

"I'm saying what others won't."

"There's a reason they don't. They want to live to see tomorrow."

"That's what we want *you* to do—see tomorrow. This..." I motioned forward. "...the kids, that's your weakness. Your father would have said fuck it and let them be sold off to someone else if he even smelled a trap."

"I'm not my father."

My jaw strained as I forced myself to stay quiet. There was another way to win this argument.

The reality was that Sparrow and I battled; it had been that way since the day we first met. I was one of the few people who could and would reason with him. I could talk. I couldn't make him listen or heed my advice.

The tension within the vehicle built as the SUV's tires bounced over uneven pavement. We weren't going to a busy hub with cranes unloading cargo containers twenty-four-seven under bright lights. This dry dock off the Calumet River hadn't been active in over a decade. The scattered cargo containers were more shelters for the homeless than usable.

Everything about this pickup screamed setup.

"How many recorded pickups did we find occurring in this abandoned hellhole?" I asked.

"None," Sparrow admitted. "The supplier, he's legit. He's been used many times and should have gotten our message that the ring has been closed for business. After tonight, he'll understand that when I say we're done, we're done."

The vast emptiness of the lot steadied my nerves a bit.

The car we were in came to a stop a few hundred feet from a seemingly abandoned brick building. The windows were broken, but the bars covering the openings were still intact. More than likely, at one time it had held the foremen's offices.

I scanned higher, looking for shooters. Still within the car, I narrowed my gaze. Having the ability—which I had—to fire a kill shot from over two thousand meters meant someone else could do the same.

"It's too fucking dark," I said. "I don't see anyone. Where are our Sparrows?"

Sparrow was looking at the screen of his phone. "They're here. I'm picking up their signals."

"I don't see them."

"You're not supposed to."

I shook my head. "If I can't see them, then I might not be seeing others."

"Fuck," Sparrow said louder than before. "Look."

He shoved his phone my direction.

The picture on the screen turned my stomach. Five girls were huddled together on a filthy concrete floor, their hair stringy and visible stages of bruising on their faces and arms. Thankfully, they were clothed. Yet the clothes they wore could be better described as rags. Each one looked malnourished.

"We're paying," Sparrow said.

"The cash is in the bag in the back," I said. "I agree with you. If the seller doesn't get the money from you, he won't stop until he finds another buyer."

"Probably someone from McFadden," Sparrow said. "The seller wants them unloaded tonight."

"Tell him we'll take the merchandise and to bring them out," I said.

The network transmitting the messages was highly encrypted, causing a delay from time sent to received. Sparrow typed out his message.

"I'll give him the money," I went on. "After the exchange, get another Sparrow to transport the girls to the clinic. Dr. Dixon will check them out."

The clinic was makeshift and poorly staffed. Our doctor was dedicated and capable. It was that once this was done, it would be complete. We saw no reason to put more resources into it.

"This is my operation," Sparrow said. "I'll hand off the cash and make it clear we're done."

I reached for the handle of the door. "It is your operation, boss." I opened the door. "And it's going to stay that way." As I stood, I turned slowly, searching the darkness.

From the depths of the brick building came the muted echo of a child's cry. My neck straightened as I tugged downward on the Kevlar beneath my suit. I hated wearing it, especially as the temperatures rose in the Chicago summer. However, my time in a war that others recognized—unlike the one occurring now—taught me about safety and precautions.

Closing the door, I said a silent prayer that Sparrow would listen to me.

As I opened the back of the SUV, he turned my way. "His message is to come inside. I'm going with you."

I swung the strap of the duffel bag over my shoulder and removed my gun from the holster beneath my suit jacket. "Give me five. If I'm not out, send in every fucking Sparrow in the area."

I didn't wait for a response as I closed the back hatch.

It was the girl's cries that led me toward the old metal door.

With my gun drawn, I pushed the door inward and peered around the darkness. My only clue was the sound of crying. The old brick walls and rotting interior caused the sound to echo, making the direction from which it was coming difficult to assess. Removing the penlight from my pocket, I projected a beam of light.

One step, maybe two.

I strained to listen.

Twisting to my left, the crying grew louder.

Another step.

My ears filled with explosion before my mind had time to register.

Fire erupted, shrapnel and bricks falling as the building's structure gave way. The flames burst out, consuming every flammable thing in their path. The crackling was the backdrop as more explosions echoed in the smoke-filled air.

Screaming and shouts.

Sparrow appeared through the flames.

Get out.

The thought came but words wouldn't form.

The world moved as he dragged me through the debris. In the distance, more voices tried to break through the chaos. Their words were lost to the echo of the explosion.

As the smoke-filled night sky came into view, like the lion before a movie, Sparrow's voice roared. "Fuck. Get him to the hospital now." He continued to yell, but like everything else, his meaning was lost to the flames.

Lights and pain.

Doctors and police.

Where were the girls?

It was my last thought.

Mason Pierce's last thought.

KADER

Present day

I followed Laurel toward the office, my gaze going
to the roundness of her ass in her blue jeans while
my thoughts went to this morning and the way that same ass
fit perfectly in my grasp, the way her body responded, and the
soft noises she made. No woman has affected me the way she
does, and I don't understand it. I know it has to do with the
way she looks right at me, her blue eyes on me as she comes
apart.

It's new and electrifying.

I can't get enough of it.

This must be the way it feels to be addicted. I'm fucking
addicted to Laurel Carlson. I should be satisfied with what we

did this morning. I had been...until I wanted more. It was as if the more I got of her, the more I wanted.

After opening the door, Laurel stilled at the entry to the office. As she did, she turned to me, her blue eyes clouded and lips downturned.

"What is it?"

"Every time I'm in here, I learn something I don't want to know."

Probably not a good time to suggest sex.

"Do you think it's better not to know?"

Her head shook. "I'm at least glad to not learn these things alone."

My goal wasn't to compound her sadness about Cartwright and Moore. It was to shed light on what had been happening around her. With a sigh, she settled in the chair beside mine.

"Why does that screen..." She tilted her head upward. "...always have the hallway outside the office door? You live alone. You said no one comes here."

"I set the cameras to motion. There aren't any located in this room. The last motion they detected was in the hallway."

Laurel nodded. "So you're saying, they were displaying the dining room."

"They were."

"Are you worried I'm going to make a break for it? Because after your little speech yesterday, I don't think that needs to be a concern. Besides, where would I go even if I could?"

"I'm not worried. I like seeing you, knowing you're safe. If you would leave, my first guess would be that you'd go to your parents' or your sister's."

Laurel sat taller. "Did Ally go to Indianapolis?"

"No. She's called your mom many times and your mom has called her. Your parents checked out of the hotel today and have a..." I looked down at the time in the corner of the screen. "...correction. Assuming their flight is on time, they recently left the Indianapolis airport for Des Moines."

"I feel better about them being home. I don't know who to trust at the university."

I sat taller, my exposed lower arms momentarily side-tracking my focus. I'd pulled the sleeves down after Laurel left the kitchen. On my way to get her, I remembered to raise them. To my surprise, since retrieving her, she hadn't mentioned them or even taken a closer look.

It seemed impossible that she was already accustomed to them, and yet that was how it appeared. Granted, her mind was probably a million places besides my tattoos.

It was time that we got down to the business at hand.

Clicking the mouse, I pulled up an Indianapolis map. "As you probably know, there are numerous hotels and restaurants not far from the university. First, I accessed Cartwright's finances. Did you know that eight months ago he was issued a Centurion card?"

Laurel's nose scrunched. "Isn't that one of those invitation-only American Express cards?"

"It is. While there's no published requirement, it's understood that the holder of such a card is expected to spend between $100,000 to $450,000 a year."

"No. You're mistaken. Russ didn't make that much money." Her neck straightened. "Did he?" Her sentences came quicker. "Are you going to tell me that on top of everything else, the university was paying him more—?"

I laid my hand over her knee. "No, Dr. Carlson, I checked. You and Dr. Cartwright were both tenured professors appointed the same year. Your salaries were identical."

"Were," she said with a sigh. "Well, then there was no way—"

"Since securing the Centurion card, Cartwright has accumulated purchases of nearly $200,000."

"What? In eight months?"

"His balance is zero."

"Who is paying his bill and what was he buying?"

"The payments," I began, "didn't flow through his bank accounts. The card was paid in full each month from a corporation located in Delaware. The corporation is a shell company. That's as far as I've currently dug."

"What is the name of the shell company?"

"It really doesn't matter. That's all it does. Shell companies aren't illegal, but they require certain information. I'm still digging."

Laurel leaned forward, her eyes narrowing as she looked at the screen. "Can you show me what he purchased?"

I clicked again, bringing up the activity for the last billing cycle. "The biggest expense was a recurring reservation, a corner suite at the JW Marriott. Over five hundred dollars a night plus taxes adds up. He had it reserved for every day."

"The JW isn't far from..."

"Three keys were issued," I said. "The room and card were canceled the day after Cartwright was killed."

Laurel sat back in the chair. Her sensuous neck strained and her jaw was set. "But no one knows he was killed. They think he's missing."

"Laurel, someone killed him. That person knows he's dead."

"So whoever is behind the shell corp...?"

"I'm not sure," I admitted.

She let out a sigh. "Are there cameras?"

"Yes, within the corridors. I sped through the video rather quickly. Besides hotel staff, the room was frequented by Cartwright, Ms. Moore, and another woman."

"Two women?" she asked. "Do you know who?"

"Yes, I found her listed as staff at the university. Her name is Pamela Browncoski."

"She's Dr. Oaks's assistant." Laurel looked my way, her blue eyes wide as slowly they narrowed and her nose wrinkled. "Together? All three?"

"Only once were they all together, the afternoon before the gathering. Lunch was delivered. My gut tells me it wasn't a ménage à trois. Other than that, it would usually be two people, in any combination."

"Russ met alone with Pam? She's close to retirement. I mean, at least Stephanie is younger."

My head shook. "Again, I don't think this was completely a sexual adventure. That doesn't mean that Cartwright and Moore—I doubt he went to her place for a late-night meeting. And the availability of the suite would have made that arrangement easier for sneaking out of the lab and getting a midday fuck."

"I don't want to think about it."

"There was one other visitor who I found on the hotel's security."

"Who?"

"It was Saturday afternoon, after you met with Cartwright and Olsen at the coffee shop..."

Laurel leaned forward, moving to the edge of the chair.

I clicked on the still picture I'd saved from the feed.

"Damien Sinclair." She turned to me. "Who was there with him?"

"The ready-to-retire assistant, Ms. Browncoski."

Laurel stood and walked around the chair. With each step, her gaze grew glassier and farther away. If I were to guess, she wasn't seeing the office or even the reds and purples in the sky beyond the windows. With each turn, as her expression came into view, she had her lower lip trapped beneath her upper front teeth. By the flexing of the muscles in her cheeks, she wasn't just biting, but nibbling.

"Talk to me, Laurel." *Before you chew a hole in your lip.* I kept the last part to myself.

"And say what?" Laurel stopped pacing. "That the three of them were working together to sabotage our work? I don't want to say that." She slapped the sides of her thighs. "The night those fake police arrived. You said you heard my discussion with Russ."

"I did."

"On tape or in person?"

"I was there."

Her shoulders went slack. "How did I not know?"

"Laurel," I said, lifting my hand, "come here."

Moisture filled her eyes. "How have I been so stupid and blind?"

"Over here," I said again.

Step by small step, she advanced until she was standing in front of me. I reached for her hand. "You are not now nor have you ever been stupid."

Laurel swallowed. Pulling her hand away, she gestured to the screen still containing the purchase activity from the Centurion card. "Then call it something else." Her voice was growing louder with each sentence. "Naïve. Totally oblivious."

Standing, I reached for her shoulders. "I have the correct word and you haven't used it."

"What then?" she asked, her blue eyes staring up at me.

"I knew it the moment I started working this case. It was part of what drew me to it—to you. I do what I do. I've been doing it for a while. Like I told you, it's not always people who I kill. I kill ideas, plans, and deals. I'm no Robin Hood. I don't do what I do because it will make the world a better place. I do it because I have the skills and it pays fucking great. When

I received the request, I couldn't help but wonder why a contract would be taken out on you."

Her shoulders shrugged under my grasp.

"The more I studied and watched, the less I trusted Cartwright. I told you that before. Moore slipped under my radar. I screwed up by being too focused on you."

"You still haven't said that I'm stupid and naïve."

"Because you're not," I replied. "Laurel, why are you here, with me, in no-fucking-place Montana?"

She scanned the office. Beyond the windows the sun was growing closer to the horizon, casting colorful hues on the sparse clouds above. "I'm here because my life as a renowned researcher is over, and I saw the opportunity to change my career to sex toy and figured what the hell. So I took it."

I scoffed as a small smile came to my lips. "You're fucking amazing."

"I'm glad you think so. When you have a minute, could you write a recommendation for my future employment?"

"Not in a hundred years."

"Kader?"

"You're here," I said, "because you trusted me."

She peered upward, her blue eyes searching me. "No, I didn't, not past tense. I did and despite your attempts to deter me, I still do."

"And that's fucking insane. You willingly left your home, city, and state with a self-proclaimed assassin for hire."

Stepping away, she walked to the windows, leaving me with a view of her back.

Who turns their back on the person hired to kill them?

Drawn to her, I followed Laurel to the window and while standing behind her, I wrapped my arms around her waist. With a sigh, she leaned back against me, her head resting on my chest.

"Doc, you aren't and have never been stupid. Your downfall has been trust. You give it too easily."

We stood for a few minutes as the colors began to fade and nighttime replaced the crimson with darkness.

Finally, she spoke, "That night, when you were in my house, fake police were there, and Russ was there. Before you made your presence known, Russ said something about changing his mind. He mentioned Dr. Oaks being greedy. He said something about Eric and that Sinclair had threatened Eric." Laurel spun in my arms. "Is that conversation on there?" she asked, tipping her head toward the screens.

"I can find it."

"Maybe Russ was given a deal and just maybe..." She swallowed as she reached for my arms, laying her hands over my ink.

It took all my self-control to not flinch. The only thing that stopped me was that she wasn't looking down at the mutilated skin beneath her palms.

Her neck straightened as she stared upward at me. "...maybe Russ regretted it. As he said, he changed his mind. He said he came to save me or help me. I can't remember."

Damn, I hated her eternal optimism in that man.

"Laurel, there's a reason that investigators and law enforcement say to follow the money."

"Right, I know. Russ saw dollar signs. He agreed and that deal got him that card. Then he got cold feet. That's why he wanted us to make the backup, the external hard drive." She nodded. "Yes, he was trying to get out of it—whatever deal he was in. He..."

This information was supposed to put the final nail in his coffin—not that he'd ever need one. It wasn't supposed to renew her faith in the cheating bastard.

"I'll pull it up," I said, hoping that seeing him the way he was that night and the memory of him leaving her alone would forever quell her support.

"Okay."

SERGEANT FIRST CLASS PIERCE

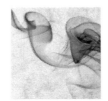

Nearly seven years ago in an undisclosed location

There were no words to describe the excruciating pain. I'd survived wars, wars I'd had the will to survive. This war was different. Internally, I prayed for it to end, to lose this battle. It didn't surprise me that those prayers went unanswered or that eternal damnation was mine. It was the course I'd charted. Reaching the destination shouldn't have come as a surprise.

Parts of my life came back, bits and pieces taunting me with a life that was gone. Small fragments of time littered in the wasteland of my mind, appearing in my sleep, not enough to find joy, only enough to mock my existence.

Not all sleep came naturally.

Weeks and months were lost to drug-induced comas.

The voices told me it was better, a way for me to heal.

"Sergeant First Class Pierce."

That was the name they used.

Scenes from childhood came and went, scrounging for food, searching in dumpsters behind restaurants and grocery stores—anything to feed my sisters. Maybe those memories came to me because I hadn't eaten in months. I'd been fed through a tube as reconstructive surgery repaired broken bones and charred flesh.

At first I had no recollection of how I'd become a mummy unable to move.

And then all at once, I remembered the explosion.

Some of the voices shared information. The Kevlar vest I'd worn had saved me.

I wanted to tell the voices I wasn't saved.

While in contact with the accelerant and fire source, the vest had burned. That wasn't what saved me. It was the vest's ability to protect my organs from the shock wave associated with the blast as well as the shrapnel from the explosion.

Time moved on in cycles filled with bouts of extreme pain —dead skin must be removed—followed by weeks of unconsciousness, allowing the body to heal. When the pain would come, in my mind's eye, I'd see the flames, hear the girls screaming, and recall Sparrow's panic.

And yet not once did he visit or anyone contact me.

In broken thoughts, I wondered about Lorna, about Reid and Patrick.

What did they know?

The voices around me faded in and out like the wind in the open desert.

The air was hot.

The bandages itched.

At one point, the voices secured my wrists to the side of the bed. The mission was to stop me from ripping off the bandages and reopening the wounds while I slept. The result was that I was a prisoner to their treatment.

"Sergeant First Class Pierce. The decision was made that too much had been invested in your skills to allow you to die in that explosion."

"I did my time. I'm fighting a new war."

Had I said the words aloud?

I must have, in a rare bout of consciousness, because the voices answered.

"It's the old war that now owns you. Your body was too badly damaged. Officially, you did not survive. A body was provided and Mason Pierce has been laid to rest."

Through the small slits between the bandages, I could only see parts of the officer speaking.

"I have family. My sister needs to know the truth."

"Sergeant First Class, we are speaking the truth. The army never issued you a family. Your presence will be unidentifiable. Your mission will be to do as your country requests. We're helping you. You'll help us."

I didn't want this help.

The side rails rattled as I strained against the straps to get free.

Sleep returned.

My screams echoed within the small concrete room when the fire returned. Tethered to the bed, I was helpless to the flames. The voices tried to soothe me. I rebuked their assistance. This wasn't a life I wanted. For the first time, I was ready to surrender.

If this was hell, I would never make it out. It was better to stop fighting.

There had been a time when I had hope for a future. Intermittently, I recalled a girl from my youth, one much better than me. I'd kept track of her through the years. The last time I'd checked she was in graduate school. I always knew she was smart. She deserved more than a man like me. Nevertheless, that boyhood crush refused to die.

And then there was Lorna.

What happened to her?

Sometimes, I would recall images from the night I died. There were ones of her and Reid. I wasn't certain if it had happened or if I was hoping. I reasoned that a man in hell— where I was—had no right to make requests, yet if I could, I wanted her safe. If that was with him, so be it.

I'd said no man was good enough for my sister. That was still true.

Reid Murray came damn close.

While the voices continued, I stopped listening. Endless

hours of debriefing, telling me what I knew, what I was, what I believed. I turned away, allowing the voices to be consumed by the fire.

"It could help. The medication is still being tested, but his recurring nightmares won't allow him to be of any use to us. We can't put a trained soldier into an explosive situation who is afraid of fire."

"It could also imperil his skills. We don't have the side effects fully researched."

The debate occurred around me—over me. My input wasn't necessary. The decisions weren't mine.

"If it takes away his skills, he'll be of no less use to us than he is now."

"We'll start slowly, injecting daily, taking him in and out of consciousness and when we can, we'll question him, test his knowledge of strategical issues as well as language. His linguistics skills were superb. Even now, sometimes he screams out in other languages."

"According to his records, his ability to learn has always been one of his assets."

"So we'll reteach him if we have to."

LAUREL

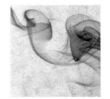

Present day

*D*ays passed in our bubble. The snow outside melted, uncovering a world of greens and browns. When we weren't working on Kader's assignment—me—we ate, slept, and made love. He didn't refer to it that way, yet I did in my thoughts and even dreams. While uncovering more and more evidence of deceptions that I'd blindly allowed to take over my life, I craved the intimacy Kader and I shared. In a short time, he'd become my anchor.

My life was similar to a kite, flying fervently in the spring wind. And through it all, this handsomely beautiful, sometimes confusing, mountain of a man held the string.

Without him, I was certain I'd float away.

One afternoon after we'd eaten lunch, I went with Kader

into the office to check his sales listing. The bids hadn't come as quickly as he'd hoped, but within the last forty-eight hours they'd steadily increased.

"I'm worried about the other listing," he said, "the first one. There haven't been any recent bids. I think I should make a higher bid."

My eyes grew wide. "Higher than 1.2 billion? I can't let you spend that kind of money." I sat straighter. "Do you have that kind of money?"

"Not sitting around the house, if you're planning on killing me in my sleep."

I shrugged. "For 1.3 you'd be a goner. For 1.2 I think I prefer your company."

I couldn't help glancing at his lower arms. Since the day in the kitchen, he'd kept them exposed. Other than a few glimpses—from a distance—of his legs or torso, I hadn't been shown more of his color. That was okay. Each day I saw more of the man. While sometimes he'd turn all business and other times get broody, there were more sightings of emotions— smiles and smirks. I even accepted his anger. It wasn't directed at me, but usually at himself. There were times when he'd learn something and blame himself for not sighting it earlier or perhaps grow agitated when a camera ceased to transmit.

Any emotion was a breakthrough.

We all had good days and bad. To expect to have more of one and less of the other was irrational. My moods too had pendulum swings.

Happiness would come as Kader would smile or cook. It was obviously something he enjoyed.

Overwhelming sadness settled over me as I followed the happenings at the university.

Dean Oaks and a university review board voted to shut down our research. In an effort to recoup their losses, attorneys were negotiating with Sinclair Pharmaceuticals. The filed documents showed no sign that they had any knowledge of the illegal sales. Dr. Olsen was scheduled to meet with Dr. Oaks regarding his future.

The FBI had visited my parents and my sister as well as other university employees such as Dr. Olsen and Stephanie. It was now official. They'd issued a worldwide missing-persons bulletin on both me and Russ. Our pictures would occasionally flash over Kader's screens.

I couldn't bear to think about my parents and sister.

Most members of our staff were being reassigned. The patients in our clinical trials were given the option to continue their treatment with Sinclair or leave the study.

I pointed to an unusual symbol at the top of Kader's screen. "What's that? I haven't seen it before."

"It's a message."

"Are you going to look at it?"

"Not with you here."

"Why?"

"It might be about you or it might be another job offer. Either could have accompanying files you don't need to see."

"Kader, how much were you paid to kill me?"

His green stare came my way. "Not enough."

I smirked. "What does that mean?"

"I took you as an assignment because I was drawn to you and the circumstances of the project, not for the money."

"How much?" I asked again.

"750K."

"Have you received the money?"

"Yes, it was deposited the day after I reported you dead."

I sighed, leaning back. "Have you asked yourself who would have that money and spend it on my death?" It was an odd question to state aloud.

"I've determined that whoever it was believed you were the weak link."

"You mean that I was the one who wouldn't sell. What about Eric? He's still there. He wasn't part of that group."

Kader leaned back and crossed his arms over his wide chest. "I've thought about him. I've thought about the conversation where Cartwright told you to lie about the Sinclair offers and that Sinclair threatened Olsen because Sinclair thought he was standing in the way of getting the compound."

"And?" I asked.

"I don't believe him. What he said doesn't fit."

I stood and walked around the office. "It doesn't. Eric is still there, even if Oaks wants him to retire. Oaks wasn't involved in the meetings, yet Pam was. So perhaps he was by proxy." I had a thought. "Isn't that the way it's done?"

"What?"

"Like crime bosses don't get their hands dirty. Russ said Oaks was greedy. Maybe he's the real brains behind this?"

"I'm looking into him," Kader said.

"And then there's Sinclair. Damien isn't hiding his company's desire for the university's information, no matter how incomplete it is."

Turning, I saw that Kader wasn't listening. Instead, he had leaned forward and was reading from a screen I'd never before seen. I waited as he typed back a message.

"Curiosity got the better of you," I said with a smirk. "What was it?"

The screen went black as Kader stood and came toward me. "We've been cooped up in this house for too long. I sent Jack on a food and supplies run. I think we should get out of the house and see the land."

"Are you going to leave me to freeze?"

The rough pad of his finger skirted over my cheek and down to my neck, leaving a trail of goose bumps in its wake. "I much prefer you warm and breathing heavily."

"So I finally get to see this magical playground?"

Kader's head shook as his lips flattened.

My cheeks rose as they filled with warmth. "Okay, but I don't have boots."

"You won't need them. We're not going to walk."

Wearing one of Kader's large sweatshirts over my clothes, I followed him out onto the front porch. The sensation was indescribable. It wasn't that Kader's home wasn't large and lovely. It was that stepping outside, I was besieged with stimulation—the fresh breeze, the sounds of birds, and the warmth of the sunshine.

I spun in place, allowing my hair to be tossed about. "I didn't realize how much I missed fresh air."

Kader nodded as he took my hand and led me down a crushed-stone path.

He'd said he'd show me the other buildings on his property with time. As we passed one after another, my curiosity grew. "What's in all of these buildings?"

"Nothing as important as where we're going."

We came to a stop near a large pole barn. There was a regular door and three large garage doors. Next to the regular door was a sensor, like on Kader's house. He leaned forward, allowing the sensor to scan his eye.

Unlike his house, this one only beeped as the door opened inward. The small room within was filled with tools and workbenches, reminding me of a mechanic's garage.

"What's in—" My words disappeared as I turned.

What had three garage doors on one side had one large door on the other. Inside was a blue and white airplane. The wingspan extended from one end of the room to the other, and yet the fuselage appeared small. On the very front was a propeller.

I shook my head. "No, I think I'll go back to the house."

"She won't let you in," Kader said with a smirk as he tugged on my hand.

"I'm not a big fan of flying, and when I do, I like planes that hold more than two people."

"Technically, this one holds three. There's a jump seat in the back."

My feet didn't move as my skin coated with perspiration and my knees stiffened. "I don't think so."

"Give it a chance."

"Can you really fly this?" I asked.

"No, Laurel, this is plan number four for your demise. I'm taking the kamikaze approach and going down with you."

"You're not funny."

Kader tilted his head as a small grin appeared. "Give me a break. I'm new at this."

"Piloting?"

"No, Doc. I've been piloting longer than I remember. It's the talking that's new." He pulled again on my hand. "It won't take long to get her out. The sky's clear and it's a good day to show you around."

If Kader didn't look so damn excited to show me his land, I would have protested more. Nevertheless, I tried one more route. "Won't Jack or someone see me?"

"No one can see who's in the plane. He'll assume it's me. It's not unusual for me to take her out on a day like today."

Once the plane was pulled out by a small cart-like vehicle onto the cement, Kader opened the doors. They opened upward—wing doors—such as I'd seen on some Teslas. Before I knew it, I was seat-belted into the copilot's seat with strict orders not to touch anything.

"No worries," I said, tucking my hands into my lap. "Do you have little bags, you know, in case I throw up?"

"You'll be fine. Statistically, you have a better chance of crashing in a commercial aircraft."

"That's because there are more people on a commercial flight and more commercial flights per day. Your data is skewed."

Kader placed earphones over my ears before donning a pair.

"Can you hear me?" he asked through the earphones.

"I can. You didn't answer about the bag."

His deep baritone chuckle filled my ears. He pointed upward. "Hold on to that strap if you want. Just don't touch the door or anything on the instrument panel."

The panel before us was like a fancy car on steroids with screens, gauges, lights, and levers.

"You know, you tell me not to touch a lot."

"And you don't listen."

Memories of not listening came to mind. While Kader continued to wear a shirt, soft pants, and socks in bed, his decree for me not to touch him had been widely breached without protest.

"Oh!" I squealed into the microphone as the whirl of the propeller vibrated the plane and filled our ears, even through the earphones.

Between flipping switches and adjusting a lever, Kader reached over to me and splayed his large fingers over my knee. "How are you doing, Doc?"

"I don't know."

He grinned as we began to move. After a bumpy ride down a dirt-packed runway, the wheels lifted off the ground.

"We-we're flying."

"No wonder people want your research. You're fucking brilliant."

I could have hit his leg or made a production out of pouting, but I didn't. I was too busy taking in the gorgeous scenery below as well as the mountains in the distance. Patches of green and brown created a quilt below. As we passed over a different grouping of buildings, Kader pointed out Jack's house as well as other housing for seasonal ranch hands. He also showed me what seemed like miles of corrals.

"I could make it to his house," I said into the microphone.

"Don't even think about it."

I really wasn't.

I didn't like to think about the real world. With each passing day I found the probability of my regaining my life lessening.

I sat as far forward as the seat belt would allow, taking in the glory of the land below. As we flew, Kader told me more about the ranch hands that will soon be about his property, shoring fences and checking for damage from the winter snows and spring thaws. He talked about the horses and why he bought the property.

For a time while in the air, I listened to his words, recalling something he'd said before we boarded the plane. He'd said that talking was new to him. I wasn't certain how that was possible, but I believed him. Since the first night I woke in the basement, there'd been a change, making him communicate more.

As we were heading back—his words not mine, because I had no idea where we were—in the distance, I spotted a trail of dark smoke.

"What's that?"

Kader's neck stiffened. "Looks like a burn. It might be controlled, but I'll make a call when we land."

"Is that on your property?"

"No, but fire has a way of disrespecting boundaries."

LAUREL

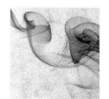

*L*ater the night of our plane adventure, after dinner, we each took a drink into the living room.

Mine was a glass of red wine while Kader's tumbler contained two fingers of bourbon, neat. I'd seen him drink a glass of wine or two, but the stronger liquor was new. I wasn't certain who he called about the burn in the distance. Nevertheless, he'd seemed a bit on edge since we'd returned. I couldn't put my finger on it.

I wasn't in a hurry for the relaxed feeling to end. If I asked him about his mood or the bourbon, he'd accuse me of analyzing. Instead, I stared up at the giant fireplace. "Do you ever build a fire in the fireplace?"

"No."

"Oh, I had fires at my place all the time. I love fires especially on a night like tonight. You know when the warmer day gives way to a cooler night." I smiled. "Today was fun." When he didn't respond, I went on. "I was scared about flying, but your plane was amazing. It was nice to get out."

He nodded. "And come home to some new fresh food."

"So you were just hiding me?"

"Not just," he said.

I turned back to the stone fireplace, taking note of the wood piled within. "So is this gas?" The wood didn't look real. "Where's the switch?"

With a sigh, Kader reached into the fireplace. Something clicked, sounding as if he'd opened a flue. Slapping his hands against one another, he shrugged. "I'm honestly not sure it works. I guess we'll see."

Anticipation grew. We both stood back, our eyes on the stack of unburnable wood as he pressed a button on the side of the stone hearth.

Swoosh.

Blue at first, a bubble of gas gave way to orange and red flames filling the interior of the giant fireplace. I saw it all but only for a split second. My glass of wine and his tumbler of bourbon fell to the floor as we did too.

"N-no!" Kader's one-word roar echoed throughout the house as his large body covered mine. Within his embrace, we rolled as one to the giant rug near the sofas.

I looked up, pushing his large shoulder. "Kader, what happened?"

He didn't answer as his breathing came faster. His eyes were closed and yet his grip of me tightened.

"We're all right," I said as calmly as I could.

I could barely move within his vise of a hold.

Stretching my neck, I attempted to peer beyond his massive body out at the room around us. To one side were the spilled glasses. The puddles of wine and bourbon seeped between the slats of the wood floor.

Everything else was normal.

The crackle of the fire filled the air and the windows were dark.

Nothing was unusual.

I couldn't fathom what had just happened.

Kader's entire body trembled while his heart raced against my chest.

"Kader," I repeated his name.

Slowly, he lifted his torso until he was sitting at my side. His eyes stayed focused on me until they closed and his hands came to the side of his head.

I reached up. "What's happening?"

Kader's eyes began to blink as he lowered his hands. His head tilted as the green orbs opened wide. "You're Laurel. Laurel Carlson." The inflection in his voice was as if he were seeing me for the first time or for the first time in a while. "You're Dr. Carlson's daughter."

I nodded. "Yes, Kader, you know that."

His large hand came to my cheek and his expression darkened with remorse. "God, I was a dick. I fucking should have written. I knew it was a shitty move. I didn't want you to wait. You've always been too good for me. I knew that the first day I saw you."

Confusion came in waves as my body stiffened.

"What are you talking about?"

He sat taller and pulled me to sitting, his gaze continuing to scan me as if he were reassuring himself I was safe or maybe that I was real. He ran his hands over my hair and down my arms. "Fuck, it's really you."

I reached up to his cheek until his gaze met mine. "Kader, tell me what's happening."

He sat taller, his tone clipped. "Don't use that name."

Had I been right about DID?

Was this a psychotic episode isolating one personality?

"You know who I am."

Blood swished in my ears and my stomach knotted. This couldn't be happening. It didn't make sense. Though my mouth had grown drier with each passing second, I forced my tongue to vocalize my question. "What name should I use?"

He cupped my cheeks with his large hands and pulled me toward him. His scented breath skirted my skin as his lips captured mine with a new sense of urgency, passionate and needy. Bourbon and wine created an intoxicating concoction as our tongues sought one another.

"You're so fucking beautiful. You always have been." His praises came as he continued his adoration. The warmth of his hands splayed under my shirt as he unlatched my bra. "I want to see you."

The new flood of emotion lowered his timbre as his deep tone reverberated off the wooden interior. Fire framed his handsome face as he slowly and painstakingly undressed me until I was lying bare on the rug with his green eyes scanning me slowly. Like flames from the fire, his gaze sent heat over my skin and tightened my core.

Pushing my knees upward, Kader covered me with his body as he unbuttoned his jeans, releasing his cock. As I waited in wanton anticipation, his deep voice directed my next move.

"Laurel, use my real name."

I shook my head as tears flooded my eyes. "You haven't told me."

"You know. I fucking need you to know."

I did.

I didn't believe it.

This wasn't dissociative identity disorder.

Though my mind argued that it couldn't be real, my heart knew it was the truth.

"You've been mine since we were kids," he said as anguish clouded his handsome face. "I'd forgotten. It all had gone away—everything. Now I understand why you've been fucking with my mind." He lowered his torso over me. "You did this. Tell me you remember."

I swallowed.

Oh God. It was real.

How else would he know about the letter writing and about being his?

My eyes closed as childhood memories bombarded my thoughts. I'd loved him too. We'd kissed and made plans.

We'd petted and made promises we never kept. I'd wanted to give myself to him before we separated. He wouldn't do it. He said we'd wait until he could make it special.

"It can't be you," I said, my voice cracking. "You died."

My tears blurred his stoic features.

"I did. I was dead. It's you."

I started to say his name, but his finger came to my lips.

"Laurel, you're the only one. The person I'd become had given up hope."

My lips opened as my back arched and we became one.

A small whimper escaped as I reached for his broad shoulder and buried my face in the cotton. My one word was muffled, yet we both heard it.

"Mason."

LAUREL

I woke with a gasp, my mind suddenly awake with my body twisted in the sheets of Mason's bed. Even in my thoughts, it was difficult to rationalize that Kader and Mason were one and the same. I sat upward, peering about the room. The sky beyond the window told me it was still nighttime though the clock's numbers let me know a new day had begun. My eyes adjusted as the soft glow of moonlight bathed the room in an eerie silver hue, not bright enough to chase away the shadows lurking in the corners. And yet I knew I was alone.

The bed beside me was empty, and as I ran my palm over the sheet, the coolness told me that I'd been alone for a while. Mason had been with me when I fell asleep; now he was gone.

To where?

My mind resumed reeling with the revelations of the night.

Kader.

Mason.

With the exception of his eyes, the man looked nothing like the boy I remembered. Nevertheless, I knew in my heart it was him.

While he'd talked, I tried not to push or to lead. And with every word he spoke, it was painful to watch the man he'd thought had died—who we all thought had died—come to terms with the man he was today.

Unwinding the sheets, I climbed out of bed.

Instead of dressing in my clothes, I went into Mason's closet and found one of his button-down shirts. The lingering scent of rich birch cologne brought back memories of the man with one name.

Would I be able to fuse the two?

Would he?

In a way, it was as if a dam had been placed inside Mason's mind and last night it broke, unleashing a flood of overpowering images and memories. As a scientist and expert in memories, I feared what he'd find. As the girl who'd fallen in love with a boy from South Chicago, I was also scared of how his two worlds would come together, if they could unite.

There was a true battle waging inside his mind, one that wasn't visible to the outside world. It was one with two participants on a singular battlefield. The epiphany of his true identity had been sudden and overwhelming, leaving Mason to press through beliefs, preconceptions, and walls Kader had established. It could take him years to come to terms with what was real and what had been planted.

In reality, both identities were real.

That was a lot to comprehend.

While Mason talked last night about our childhood, I cautioned him against learning too much too fast. He had a life to recall and doing it too quickly could be detrimental. Now with his absence from the bedroom, I was afraid of what he may be doing, using his invisibility online to search for information about himself.

Descending the stairs into the dark entry, my fingers worked to fasten the buttons on his shirt. Once on the ground floor, I began rolling the sleeves. My bare feet barely made a sound as I walked past and through the darkened rooms, following the literal light at the end of the dark tunnel—the light coming from Mason's office.

I slowed as I came closer.

Never had I seen the door left open.

My heartbeat rang in my ears as I listened for activity, the sound of a keyboard or the click of a mouse. At the doorway, I stopped and searched the gray industrial room. "Mason?" I turned toward the hallway, swallowed, and tried again, "Kader?"

No answer.

The chairs before the computers sat empty. From my vantage point, the entire room was visible, and yet he wasn't present.

Where did he go?

Looking up, one of the screens displayed the hallway where I'd just been. Another showed what I recognized as the kitchen though it was difficult to see anything other than the moonlight streaming through the windows. For a moment, I stared, wondering if that was where he'd gone. And then on the screen, the light from the moon's rays lessened.

Clouds.

That made sense.

The motion detection was picking up the changing light.

Stepping around the long desk, my curiosity piqued.

What had he been researching?

How much did he recall?

Reaching toward the desk, I lowered myself, sitting on the edge of his large chair. As I did, my movement stirred the mouse, bringing one of the smaller screens to life. My pulse increased as I recognized what was on display. It was the screen with the message he'd received this afternoon.

My gaze searched again around the screens to the doorway as I contemplated my next move. With the doorway still clear, I rubbed my clammy, trembling palms over his shirttails covering my thighs.

Where was he?

I knew better than to look further, and yet I couldn't stop.

The header read: image attached.

He'd warned me about viewing files on his computer.

Would this be another gruesome image, one I couldn't unsee?

Moving the mouse, I clicked the attachment as an image took over the screen.

My lip disappeared behind my front teeth and my head tilted as I tried to make out the grainy attachment. I leaned closer, doing my best to decipher what was before me. The black and white image was overly pixilated as if it had been enlarged too many times. And then such as with an optical illusion photo, I saw behind the film, reminding me of what it was like to look into a steam-covered mirror. The subjects were present, yet masked by smoke, steam, or fog.

My eyes squinted as I made out a large hooded figure with a woman in his arms. I sat back, knowing the location. It was the elevator at the university. My circulation redirected, racing to my limbs, leaving me uneasy as more and more of the picture made sense.

I clicked the upper box, decreasing the size of the image and read the short message.

If I wasn't already sitting, I had the feeling I may faint.

This troubling information has been brought to light. Advise that measures will be taken if you do not reply and comply. Keep in mind that you have been paid for services rendered.

Identify this man as yourself. If he is not, we have reason to believe Dr. Carlson's death was contrived. The ambiguity of her missing status must end. This man must be identified and dealt with.

No loose ends. That was our deal.

Produce Dr. Carlson's body or notify us of its location.

Verify receipt of message and reply with acceptable timetable.
Our only alternative is to make this photo public. If it is you, your career will be over.

Reply sent this afternoon:
Evidence will be produced within forty-eight hours.

"Following rules isn't your thing, is it?"

Startled, I jumped as the sound of his voice echoed within the office. Looking up, I took him in, the way he was standing, unmoving within the door's frame. His arm was raised to the doorjamb, similar to the way Kader had done back in the basement.

"U-uh, Mason," I stammered.

"I told you not to come in here without me."

"I-I was looking for you."

He let go of the doorjamb and took a step inside the office. "Did you think you'd find me on the computer? Come now, Doc, you're smarter than that."

The combination of what I'd just read and the chilly timbre of his voice set my nerves on edge. The hairs on the back of my neck stood to attention. With each second his green eyes bore my direction, their gaze grew cooler and cooler until their icy chill continued the uneasy sensation, snaking its way down my spine, lifting the small hairs on my arms and legs, and curling my toes.

He took another step my direction, stopping as he scanned my attire—his shirt. The cool green of his eyes darkened as the muscles in his cheeks pulled tight. "Does this attire mean that you've embraced your new profession?"

"I thought..."

"If I open my shirt, will I find you wet and ready for me?"

"Stop it."

"Nipples hard?"

"Why are you doing this?"

His head shook. "Just making sure you're fulfilling your job requirements."

My heart beat in double time as my stomach twisted.

This wasn't Mason.

He wasn't even Kader, not the one whose company I enjoyed.

The man before me was personality number four.

Standing, I took a step back. Attempting to reach the man from earlier tonight, the one who protected me from the fireplace, I softened my tone. "Mason, it's me, Laurel."

"I know your name, Doc. Remember, I know everything about you."

My hands trembled as I pointed to the screen. "Tell me what that means."

His neck straightened, the cords pulling taut, yet his words were eerily calm. "Always so curious. You have heard what they say about curiosity and the cat." His lips formed a sinister grin. "Of course, you have. You're a fucking genius."

I shuffled my feet backward until my backside collided

with another of his tables. The contents rattled, bringing my attention to an array of handguns, ones I hadn't seen before.

Mason was in front of me, reaching for my hand. "Don't think about it. They're not loaded."

Think about it?

My head shook. "I-I wouldn't ever think of..." The content of his reply to the message came back to me. "You replied to that email before...before the plane. You seemed excited to show me your land. And you had already sent that message. I don't understand."

His large fingers toyed with the buttons on the shirt I wore as his head tilted. "What don't you understand?" He unbuttoned the highest button. "I couldn't let Jack find you." He reached for the next button.

I pushed his hand away. "Tell me what that message means."

"It's quite simple. The entity that paid me for your death wants proof."

"Proof. It said they want my body."

His lips curled upward as he scanned me from head to toe. "Can't blame them. I want it too."

"Stop this. You're trying to frighten me."

His long finger trailed over my cheek, to my neck, and lower to the valley between my breasts before moving upward and lifting my chin. "Dr. Carlson, you've fucked with my mind, making me think and act..." He stood taller, his shoulders straightening as his broad chest filled with air.

It was then I noticed his sleeves. They were no longer exposing his kaleidoscope of colors.

"Mason." I reached for his arm. "We'll figure this out together. I'll help you."

"I've told you what I think of you analyzing me. Besides, Doc, you read the message. You're smart enough to decipher the meaning: time's up. And just to be clear, remember what I said: my story doesn't get a happy ending. Despite what you may think or may try to convince me to believe with your bag of psychological tricks, Mason Pierce died in that explosion nearly seven years ago. Kader was hired for a job and he doesn't fail."

Mason and Laurel's story concludes in *BOUND*. You're not going to want to miss a moment of *TANGLED WEB* as the mysteries and secrets continue to be unraveled.
Preorder *BOUND* now by tapping on the title.

If you're enjoying *TANGLED WEB*, don't miss *WEB OF SIN*, the trilogy is complete. Turn to the next page for a peek at *SECRETS*, book #1, *WEB OF SIN*.

A PEEK AT SECRETS, BOOK #1 WEB OF SIN

Araneae

PROLOGUE

*M*y mother's fingers blanched as She gripped the steering wheel tighter with each turn. The traffic on the interstate seemed to barely move, yet we continued to swerve in, out, and around other cars. From my angle I couldn't read the speedometer, though I knew we were bordering on reckless driving. I jumped, holding my breath as we pulled in front of the monstrous semi, the blare of a truck's horn filling our ears. Tons of metal and sixteen wheels screeched as brakes locked behind us, yet my mother's erratic driving continued.

"Listen very carefully," she said, her words muffled by the quagmire of whatever She was about to say, the weight pulling them down as she fluttered her gaze between the road ahead and the rearview mirror.

"Mom, you're scaring me."

I reached for the handle of the car door and held on as if the seat belt couldn't keep me safe while she continued to weave from lane to lane.

"Your father," she began, "made mistakes, deadly mistakes."

My head shook side to side. "No, Dad was a good man. Why would you say that?"

My father, the man I called Dad for as long as I could remember, was the epitome of everything good: honest and hardworking, a faithful husband, and an omnipresent father.

He *was*.

He died less than a week ago.

"Listen, child. Don't interrupt me." She reached into her purse with one hand while the other gripped tighter to the wheel. Removing an envelope from the depths of the bag, she handed it my direction. "Take this. Inside are your plane tickets. God knows if I could afford to send you away farther than Colorado, I would."

My fingers began to tremble as I looked down at the envelope in my grasp. "You're sending me away?" The words were barely audible as my throat tightened and heaviness weighed down upon my chest. "Mom—"

Her chin lifted in the way it did when her mind was set. I had a million visions of the times I'd seen her stand up for what she believed. At only five feet three, she was a pit bull in a toy poodle body. That didn't mean her bark was worse than her bite. No, my mother always followed through. In all things she was a great example of survival and fortitude.

"When I say your father," she went on, "I don't mean my husband—may the Lord rest his soul. Byron was a good man who gave his...everything...for you, for *us*. He and I have always been honest with you. We wanted you to know that we loved you as our own. God knows that I wanted to give birth. I tried to get pregnant for years. When you were presented to us, we knew you were a gift from heaven." Her bloodshot eyes —those from crying through the past week since the death of my dad—briefly turned my direction and then back to the highway. "Renee, never doubt that you're our angel. However, the reality is somewhere darker. The devil has been searching for you. And my greatest fear has always been that he'd find you."

The devil?

My skin peppered with goose bumps as I imagined the biblical creature: male-like with red skin, pointed teeth, and a pitchfork. Surely that wasn't what she meant?

Her next words brought me back to reality.

"I used to wake in a cold sweat, fearing the day had arrived. It's no longer a nightmare. You've been found."

"Found? I don't understand."

"Your biological father made a deal against the devil. He thought if he did what was right, he could... well, he could *survive*. The woman who gave birth to you was my best friend —a long time ago. We hadn't been in contact for years. She hoped that would secure your safety and keep you hidden. That deal...it didn't work the way he hoped. Saving themselves was a long shot. Their hope was to save you. That's how you became our child."

It was more information than I'd ever been told. I have always known I was adopted but nothing more. There was a promise of *one day*. I used to hope for that time to come. With the lead weight in the pit of my stomach, I knew that now that *one day* had arrived, and I wasn't ready. I wanted more time.

The only woman I knew as my mother shook her head just before wiping a tear from her cheek. "I prayed you'd be older before we had this talk, that you would be able to comprehend the gravity of this information. But as I said, things have changed."

The writing on the envelope blurred as tears filled my sixteen-year-old eyes. The man I knew as my dad was gone, and now the woman who had raised me was sending me away. "Where are you sending me?"

"Colorado. There's a boarding school in the mountains, St. Mary of the Forest. It's private and elite. They'll protect you."

I couldn't comprehend. "For how long? What about you? What about my friends? When will I be able to come home?"

"You'll stay until you're eighteen and graduated. And then it will be up to you. There's no coming back here...ever. This city isn't home, not anymore. I'm leaving Chicago, too, as soon as I get you out." Her neck stiffened as she swallowed her tears. "We both have to be brave. I thought at first

Byron's accident was just that—an accident. But then this morning...I knew. Our time is up. They'll kill me if they find me, just as they did Byron. And Renee..." She looked my way, her gray eyes swirling with emotion. While I'd expect sadness, it was fear that dominated. "...my fate would be easy compared to yours."

She cleared her throat, pretending that tears weren't cascading down her pale cheeks.

"Honey, these people are dangerous. They don't mess around, and they don't play fair. We don't know how, but they found you, and your dad paid the price. I will forever believe that he died to protect you. That's why we have this small window of time. I want you to know that if necessary, I'll do the same. The thing is, my death won't stop them. And no matter what, I won't hand you over."

"Hand me over?"

We swerved again, barreling down an exit until Mom slammed on her brakes, leaving us in bumper-to-bumper traffic. Her gaze again went to the rearview mirror.

"Are we being followed?" I asked.

Instead of answering, she continued her instructions. "In that envelope is information for your new identity, a trust fund, and where you'll be living. Your dad and I had this backup plan waiting. We hoped we'd never have to use it, but he insisted on being prepared." Her gaze went upward. "Thank you, Byron. You're still watching over us from heaven."

Slowly, I peeled back the envelope's flap and pulled out

two Colorado driver's licenses. They both contained my picture—that was the only recognizable part. The name, address, and even birth dates were different. "Kennedy Hawkins," I said, the fictitious name thick on my tongue.

"Why are there two?"

"Look at the dates. Use the one that makes you eighteen years old for this flight. It's to ensure the airline will allow you to fly unaccompanied. Once you're in Colorado, destroy the one with the added two years. The school needs your real age for your grade in school."

I stared down at one and then the other. The name was the same. I repeated it again, "Kennedy Hawkins."

"Learn it. Live it. Become Kennedy."

A never-before-thought-of question came to my mind. "Did I have a different name before I came to you?"

My mother's eyes widened as her pallid complexion changed from white to gray. "It's better if you don't know."

I sat taller in the seat, mimicking the strength she'd shown me all of my life. "You're sending me away. You're saying we may never see one another again. This is my only chance. I think I deserve to be told everything."

"Not everything." She blinked rapidly. "About your name, your dad and I decided to alter your birth name, not change it completely. You were very young, and we hoped having a derivation of what you'd heard would help make the transition easier. Of course, we gave you our last name."

"My real name isn't Renee? What is it?"

"Araneae."

The syllables played on repeat in my head, bringing back memories I couldn't catch. "I've heard that before, but not as a name."

She nodded. "I always thought it was ironic how you loved insects. Your name means spider. Your birth mother thought it gave you strength, a hard outer shell, and the ability to spin silk, beautiful and strong."

"Araneae," I repeated aloud.

Her stern stare turned my way. "Forget that name. Forget Araneae and Renee. We were wrong to allow you any connection. Embrace Kennedy."

My heart beat rapidly in my chest as I examined all of the paperwork. My parents, the ones I knew, were thorough in their plan B. I had a birth certificate, a Social Security card, a passport matching the more accurate age, and the driver's license that I'd seen earlier, all with my most recent school picture. According to the documentation, my parents' names were Phillip and Debbie Hawkins. The perfect boring family. Boring or exciting, family was something I would never have again.

"And what happened to Phillip and Debbie?" I asked as if any of this made sense.

"They died in an automobile accident. Their life insurance funded your trust fund. You are an only child."

The car crept forward in the line of traffic near the departure terminal of O'Hare Airport. A million questions swirled through my head, and yet I struggled to voice even one. I reached out to my mother's arm. "I don't want to leave you."

"I'll always be with you, always."

"How will we talk?"

She lifted her fist to her chest. "In here. Listen to your heart."

Pulling to the curb and placing the car in park, she leaned my direction and wrapped me in her arms. The familiar scent of lotions and perfumes comforted me as much as her hug. "Know you're loved. Never forget that, Kennedy."

I swallowed back the tears brought on by her calling me by the unfamiliar name.

She reached for her wrist and unclasped the bracelet she always wore. "I want you to have this."

I shook my head. "Mom, I never remember seeing you without it."

"It's very important. I've protected it as I have you. Now, I'm giving it to you." She forced a smile. "Maybe it will remind you of me."

"Mom, I'd never forget you." I looked down to the gold bracelet in the palm of my hand as my mom picked it up, the small charms dangling as she secured it around my wrist.

"Now, it's time for you to go."

"I don't know what to do."

"You do. Go to the counter for the airlines. Hand them your ticket and the correct identification. Stay strong."

"What about those people?" I asked. "Who are they? Will you be safe?"

"I'll worry about me once I'm sure that you're safe."

"I don't even know who they are."

Her gaze moved from me to the world beyond the windshield. For what seemed like hours, she stared as the slight glint of sunshine reflected on the frost-covered January ground. Snow spit through the air, blowing in waves. Finally, she spoke, "Never repeat the name."

"What name?"

"Swear it," she said, her voice trembling with emotion.

It was almost too much. I nodded.

"No. I need to hear you promise me. This name can never be spoken aloud."

"I swear," I said.

"Sparrow, Allister Sparrow. He's currently in charge, but one day it will be his son, Sterling."

I wished for a pen to write the names down; however, from the way they sent a chill down my spine, I was most certain that I'd never forget.

~

WEB OF SIN is completely available: *SECRETS, LIES*, and *PROMISES*.

WHAT TO DO NOW

LEND IT: Did you enjoy TWISTED? Do you have a friend who'd enjoy TWISTED? TWISTED may be lent one time. Sharing is caring!

RECOMMEND IT: Do you have multiple friends who'd enjoy my dark romance with twists and turns and an all new sexy and infuriating anti-hero? Tell them about it! Call, text, post, tweet...your recommendation is the nicest gift you can give to an author!

REVIEW IT: Tell the world. Please go to the retailer where you purchased this book, as well as Goodreads, and write a review. Please share your thoughts about TWISTED on:

*Amazon, TWISTED Customer Reviews

*Barnes & Noble, TWISTED, Customer Reviews

*iBooks, TWISTED Customer Reviews

* BookBub, TWISTED Customer Reviews

*Goodreads.com/Aleatha Romig

BOOKS BY NEW YORK TIMES BESTSELLING AUTHOR ALEATHA ROMIG

TANGLED WEB:

TWISTED

Coming May 21, 2019

OBSESSED

Coming 2019

BOUND

Coming 2019

WEB OF SIN:

SECRETS

Oct. 30, 2018

LIES

Dec. 4, 2018

PROMISES

Jan. 8, 2019

THE INFIDELITY SERIES:

BETRAYAL

Book #1

Released October 2015

CUNNING

Book #2

Released January 2016

DECEPTION

Book #3

Released May 2016

ENTRAPMENT

Book #4

Released September 2016

FIDELITY

Book #5

Released January 2017

THE CONSEQUENCES SERIES:

CONSEQUENCES

(Book #1)

Released August 2011

TRUTH

(Book #2)

Released October 2012

CONVICTED

(Book #3)

Released October 2013

REVEALED

(Book #4)

Previously titled: Behind His Eyes Convicted: The Missing Years

Re-released June 2014

BEYOND THE CONSEQUENCES

(Book #5)

Released January 2015

RIPPLES

Released Oct 2017

CONSEQUENCES COMPANION READS:

BEHIND HIS EYES-CONSEQUENCES

Released January 2014

BEHIND HIS EYES-TRUTH

Released March 2014

STAND ALONE MAFIA THRILLER:

PRICE OF HONOR

Available Now

THE LIGHT DUET:

Published through Thomas and Mercer Amazon exclusive

INTO THE LIGHT

Released 2016

AWAY FROM THE DARK

Released 2016

TALES FROM THE DARK SIDE SERIES:

INSIDIOUS

(All books in this series are stand-alone erotic thrillers)

Released October 2014

DUPLICITY

(Completely unrelated to book #1)

Release TBA

ALEATHA'S LIGHTER ONES:

PLUS ONE

Stand-alone fun, sexy romance

Released May 2017

A SECRET ONE

Fun, sexy novella

Released April 2018

ANOTHER ONE

Stand-alone fun, sexy romance

Releasing May 2018

ONE NIGHT

Stand-alone, sexy contemporary romance

September 2017

THE VAULT:

UNEXPECTED

Released August 27, 2018

UNCONVENTIONAL

Released individually

January 1, 2018

ABOUT THE AUTHOR

Aleatha Romig is a New York Times, Wall Street Journal, and USA Today bestselling author who lives in Indiana, USA. She has raised three children with her high school sweetheart and husband of over thirty years. Before she became a full-time author, she worked days as a dental hygienist and spent her nights writing. Now, when she's not imagining mind-blowing twists and turns, she likes to spend her time with her family and friends. Her other pastimes include reading and creating heroes/anti-heroes who haunt your dreams!

Aleatha impresses with her versatility in writing. She released her first novel, CONSEQUENCES, in August of 2011. CONSEQUENCES, a dark romance, became a bestselling series with five novels and two companions released from 2011 through 2015. The compelling and epic story of Anthony and Claire Rawlings has graced more than half a million e-readers. Her first stand-alone smart, sexy thriller INSIDIOUS was next. Then Aleatha released the five-novel INFIDELITY series, a romantic suspense saga, that took the reading world by storm, the final book landing on three of the top bestseller lists. She ventured into traditional publishing with Thomas and Mercer. Her books INTO THE LIGHT and AWAY FROM THE DARK were published through this mystery/thriller publisher in 2016. In the spring of 2017, Aleatha again ventured into a different genre with her first fun and sexy stand-alone romantic comedy with the USA Today bestseller PLUS ONE. She continued with ONE NIGHT and ANOTHER ONE. If you like fun, sexy, novellas that make your heart pound, try her UNCONVENTIONAL and UNEXPECTED. In 2018 Aleatha returned to her dark romance roots with WEB OF SIN.

Aleatha is a "Published Author's Network" member of the Romance Writers of America and PEN America. She is represented by Kevan Lyon of Marsal Lyon Literary Agency.

facebook.com/aleatharomig

twitter.com/aleatharomig

instagram.com/aleatharomig

Made in the USA
Lexington, KY
02 July 2019